Soldier, there is a war between the mind
And sky, between thought and day and night.
—WALLACE STEVENS

babylon

babylon

WAR PORN

Dedicated to the interpreters

WAR PORN

ROY SCRANTON

SOHO

"Notes Toward a Supreme Fiction" from THE COLLECTED POEMS OF WALLACE STEVENS by Wallace Stevens, copyright © 1954 by Wallace Stevens and copyright renewed 1982 by Holly Stevens. Used by permission of Alfred A. Knopf, an imprint of the Knopf Doubleday Publishing Group, a division of Penguin Random House LLC. All rights reserved.

"The Dragon" by Abd al-Wahhab al-Bayyati, translated by Farouk Abdel Wahab, Najat Rahman, and Carolina Hotchandani, from IRAQI POETRY TODAY © 2003 by Modern Poetry in Translation. Reprinted with permission. All rights reserved.

"Panegyric for Abu l-Fadl Muhammed Ibn al-Amid" and "Panegyric to Kafur on joining his court" by Abu at-Tayyib Ahmad ibn al-Husayn al-Mutanabbi al-Kindi, translated by A.J. Arberry, from POEMS OF AL-MUTANABBI © 1967 by Cambridge University Press. Reprinted with the permission of Cambridge University Press. All rights reserved.

This book is a work of fiction. References to real people, events, establishments, organizations, or locales are intended only to provide a sense of authenticity, and are used ficticiously. All other characters, and all incidents and dialogue, are drawn from the author's imagination and are not to be construed as real.

Published by
Soho Press, Inc.
853 Broadway
New York, NY 10003

Library of Congress Cataloging-in-Publication Data

Scranton, Roy, 1976–
War porn / Roy Scranton.
ISBN 978-1-61695-715-5
eISBN 978-1-61695-716-2
1. Iraq War, 2003–2011—Psychological aspects—Fiction.
2. Combat—Psychological aspects—Fiction. I. Title
PS3619.C743 W37 2016   813'.6—dc23   2016011288

Interior design by Janine Agro, Soho Press, Inc.

Printed in the United States of America

10 9 8 7 6 5 4 3 2 1

rage forth, bold hero & man of war, you have no

flood documenting her lament, no legal recourse in re:
administrative decisions on the matter of

                                        torture TV rage the

rockets red not singly but in global consensus: vanquished
by my spear, the highest levels of the Department
beginning a world with no tomorrow

such is the word of man. We lurch to a halt. "Humvees!"
Abu says—electroshocks about a half mile off, down the
end of a wide, empty

bombs bursting   dawn country   victorious unless

Draw your wound. Defend the gun.

The will to prevail. God's blessings upon you—the importance Arabs place on honor cherished and protected above
all else, sometimes circumventing even the need for survival.
Even the need. Even constructive criticism can threaten or

damage an Arab's honor; it will be taken as a personal insult. The Arab must, above all, protect himself and his honor from critical onslaught. Therefore, when an American is confronted with criticism, you require a yes or no, such as

FIGHT EVIL

peace merciful, most compassionate, the government agreed: made of values to kill God in remote deserts

FULL STORY

Allah does not desire soldiers committed to patrol the day of calling out, sniper police under no savior for you from Allah devised a way to get them masters in Washington for the least of those who arrested them in the first place: suicide bombings killed hundreds, GWOT authors of the latest detainee to be released for fear that any and all the world sees America
          themselves
the heart of the TV and

sizable Kurdish, Assyrian, Palestine. The Kurds farm in the north and these groups' inability to reconcile their differences prevent them from forming a unified front against the Arab population forced
          blood
                    yet he believes in the possibility of goodness and the triumph of ideas, believes in the father of democracy and the leader of nations, like he believes in the natural pairing of compassion and discipline, love and

images become

electroshocks

which will, with the muj behind us and trigger happy

have come today therefore pointless to question the political shrapnel not only nails and patients believing that
        assailants, victims of IED attacks can exsanguinate not
trusting the next level could even
those
        have therefore learned during the first few months
of the war, it took not knowing who or what is past in what
feels like her lament, no recourse, how things are done: luck-
ily, the Red Cross jumped right to some real-time global
consensus—"That was not the sound of a world with no
tomorrow."

does there not pass over man a space of time
when his life is a blank?

strange hells
(columbus day, 2004)

Lifting the flowers, letting them drop. Asters and chrysanthemums, zinnias and goldenrod—extravagant for a barbecue maybe, but fuck it. A little reckless beauty my mark on rockface. Remember you're the one who got your shit together and you're the one who changes tires. You're the one who rode out here with him and now you're the one who's waiting. I was all-state soccer once, MVP. I can read stress lines in bones dug from mass graves. We know what comes next: we fly home, I teach and go back to school, I have his baby. That's the plan. But here I am killing time and going a little crazy. Why are we still here?

Dahlia fussed with the flowers, their separate stems, the whole bouquet. That friend Wendy was bringing—Aaron—had just come back, she'd said. What would it feel like, do something like that? Break a world in two and walk away?

Would it change you?

Had it?

She looked at Matt out through the window, sitting there in his lawn chair drinking beer, his face in the fading sun so kind, his wounded eyes, his belly. He doesn't see her, lost in thought like he is so often. And just who is this man of mine? Who's this guy desiccating in the scrub grass, who brought me to the desert like a Mormon wife, who's come this far for what, who's doing what, and what is he, this man, what kind of man?

The questions a cool black stone. She washed her hands, took the parsley from the colander to the counter and daubed it dry, then picked up her Wüsthof santoku and cut.

Kerosene's sweet tang, barbecue shimmering, watching the sun sinking slow behind the edge of the redrock. Matt checked his watch, wondering how long till he could justifiably open another beer, then heard the screen creak and turned, watching her cross the yard: summer skirt brushing her legs, the lean muscles in her arms tense with the weight of the food, the firm curve of her breasts under her blue tank top. Here was beauty—a form compact and efficient, round at the edges yet taut, small and smooth and sleek. Then he looked in her face, her pale lips frowning slightly, the tiny wrinkling at the corners of her eyes, her clenched jaw.

The scherzo came to an end. Toom, toom, the march began and Dahlia squinted at the boombox: "What the heck you listening to?"

"Chopin," Matt said.

"Oh Lord," she said, putting the tray of steaks, salmon, and tofu on the picnic table, stepping to him and laying her palm on his chest. "You alright?"

"Yeah, I'm fine," he said. "Just thinking."

"Well, knock it off. We're supposed to be having a party."

He shambled up and jabbed at the machine, cutting the

piano into silence. "Here," he said, handing her the wallet, "pick something." As she flipped through the discs, he asked: "Who called earlier?"

"Wendy," she said. "What about Jolie Holland?"

"What'd she want?"

"She wanted to know if she could bring a friend. *Catalpa* or the new one?"

"We don't have enough steaks."

"He can have my steak. I'll have the salmon we just bought."

Matt grunted. "So what is he, another one of Wendy's lost boys?"

"A friend of hers from college. Aaron. He just got home from Iraq."

"No way. Was he in the shit?"

She put in a new CD. "Don't be all . . . She said he's a little sensitive."

"Maybe he's got pictures," Matt said, snapping his fingers and pointing them, thumbs up, across his hips.

"That's what I'm talking about. Seriously. And if you're done moping, help me bring out food."

He swallowed the last of his beer and the music started up with a jingle and Rachel yelled "Hey" from the gate all at once, causing Dahlia to spin and wave and bang her ear on the bottom of Matt's bottle with a plonk and "Yowch!" The bottle whacked back into Matt's teeth, sending him stumbling and gripping his mouth. Dahlia turned as Rachel came through crying "Oh" and a bright-eyed black Lab in a red kerchief bounded into the yard, followed by Mel in her leather jacket with Tupperware in both hands and Johnnie

Walker dangling from her fingers. "You kids okay?" she asked, bumping the gate closed with her hip, taking in the scene: Dahlia holding the side of her head, Matt covering his mouth, Rachel sweeping toward them blinking, hair in her eyes, with Xena cavorting along, whirling and barking, thinking it's all some game.

Then Dahlia laughed and they all started talking at once, Matt petting Xena, Mel cramming the whiskey in the ice chest and pulling out two Fat Tires for her and Rache, who was already complimenting them on their music, she just *loved* this album, it had such a *real* sound, you know, like her voice was just uncanny, wasn't it great and did they know it was all just four-tracks?

Matt said, "Gotta check the grill," and Mel followed, telling him all about their fridge crapping out. She explained to him the difference between the compressor, the compressor relay, and the overload, and how she hoped it would just turn out to be a bad circuit, but if they had an airflow problem around the condenser it'd mean tearing the whole goddamned thing apart and replacing it. Matt nodded and rubbed his sore lip. Condenser? Compressor? He asked about their plans for Halloween.

"We're gonna spend the weekend with some friends down in Flag," Mel said, "one of them big pagan-hippie things for Samhain. Like a naked dancing bonfire kind of deal. Rache loves that shit."

"You sacrifice a goat?"

"Naw, man, vegetarian. Sacrifice a huge block of tofu."

"Gotcha. Seitan worship."

"Audible groan. You guys got plans?"

"You know, what if we just stayed home and handed out candy this year? Somebody has to, right? I feel too old to dress up, anyway. They say twenty-seven's the new thirty-five."

"Don't stop believin', bro. I think you'd make a great Bush. Hey Rache," Mel shouted over to the picnic table, "wouldn't Matt make a great Bush?"

"A what?" Rachel peered back, confused.

"Bush. Wouldn't he make a great Bush?"

"You mean like a vagina?"

"No, like the president and shit."

"He's very photogenic."

Mel shot her a thumbs-up and turned back to Matt: "See? Photogenic."

"So Bush, huh? Not Kerry? You switch teams?"

"Aw, man, fuck that shit. Don't even get me started. Fucking Democans and Republicrats. This is what democracy looks like, huh? At least Kerry feels bad about his war crimes. Me and Rache, we've been talking, man, and if Bush wins again, we're moving to Canada. I don't want to be hanging around when they start lining people up for the camps."

"I'm already worried the school board wants to fire me," Rachel said, coming over to the grill as Dahlia went inside.

"What?" Matt asked.

"It's the fucking Mormons," Mel said. "Fucking homophobic, misogynist bigots."

"There's concern about my *lifestyle*, but they can't fire me just for that. So I have to be careful."

"I'm saying sue their Mormon asses for discrimination."

"I just have to be careful. I can't say or do anything in class that could be construed as promoting, you know? So I can't even really talk about Mel. There've been some remarks and the administration's nervous."

"I'm telling you, man, fucking Canada," Mel said. "Or at least somewheres away from all these goddamned fundamentalists."

Dahlia switched on lights room to room, switched them off as she left, checking to make sure everything was at least superficially neat, no condoms in the bathroom wastebasket, no dirty clothes on the floor. She stepped into the bedroom and went to the dresser, opened the small cherrywood box on top, took the weed and pipe, slipped them into the pocket of her skirt. She turned back and looked across the smooth waves of the comforter over their bed, gray in the gray light, thinking of waking tangled with him this morning, or yesterday morning, or any morning, the comfort of his body in the sun, his pleasant familiar funk, all the nights that had become mornings, could she really let that go?

Sure, he's good, and soft, and comfortable. We're all comfy where things are, another summer gone, the wars drag on, tomorrow Columbus Day and nothing changes. He still thinks that project's—what? The future? And so listless lately, like he's thinking . . . Wendy? Hardly. He could but he won't. Anyone could do anything, but he's too . . . or if he did, she'd . . . Imagine: him reaching, drunk—he'd have to be drunk— her snide laugh, his wounded pride, and would I be hurt? By him doing it? Or by her turning him down?

You're terrible. Don't be terrible. He's a good guy. Not strong, but a good guy. Except for the fact you're drifting in a spin from today to tomorrow, and then what?

She'd have to turn the lights on soon. Something would happen. They'd be here soon and it was important to have a nice party. She put the flowers on a tray to take outside.

"I felt my ears burning," Dahlia said. "Y'all must've been talking about me."

"Naw, shit. We're talking about moving to Canada," Mel said.

"That's funny. We've been talking about moving too," said Dahlia.

"We've been thinking about it," Matt said.

"There's no real work for me here." Dahlia set the tray down and arranged the flowers and tabbouleh on the picnic table, then took the vegetables over to Matt. "Master's degree in anthropology and I'm pouring coffee at Redrock Bagels, sometimes a week running the river."

"I'll get you more days on the river, babe," Mel said.

"Thanks, sugar, but it's not that. I had plans."

"We talked about maybe moving when I finish my project."

"By then we'll be collecting social security," Dahlia said, laughing. "Don't you think you should start grilling, Matt? Start a little something, anyway."

Matt frowned, nodding, as the three women turned to each other and he turned to the grill, focusing on the vegetables and blocks of tofu. Had it really been two years out

here? And four years them together? It was funny to think
of, when magical 2000 had loomed so large for so long.
And they didn't get any Jupiter space acid, no starbaby, but
HAL had grown so vast and powerful we thought a time-
stamp glitch could destroy civilization. He and Craig had
laid in stores of bottled water, cans of beans, stacks and rows
of toilet paper, then themed their New Year's bash Beyond
the Millennium! with decorations put together from visions
of futures past: fins, chrome, glass tubes, and colored plastic. That night was the third time he and Dahlia had sex.
The end of the world came and went.

And what if every decision you made was a mistake?
What if computers had been a mistake and college had
been a mistake and cyclopiscope.com had been a mistake
and now Utah, too? The path had seemed so provisional,
yet at the same time somehow fixed—when his parents got
divorced and his mom got him a piano, his dad a Commo-
dore 64, what would you expect but that he'd sink into his
surrogate parental devices? He wasn't a recluse. You couldn't
say he was a recluse. He just spent a lot of time on his own,
developing an app whose main purpose was, jargon aside,
to predict the apocalypse. Yeah, totally fucking rational.

He lashed more marinade on the tofu. Had he started
another beer? Started and finished. The sun was down now
for real. The steaks, juicy red, sat waiting.

Somebody watching: a lean man at the gate with black
hair cut close, face taut and flat, lips compressed in a line
like a trick of the fading light. The man stared with eyes so
fierce, Matt's heart hung dry a beat and he stepped back,
fumbling his brush and dropping it. Say something.

Then Xena barked and Mel shouted "Wendy!" Matt scanned the ground, found his brush in the grass, bent to grab it, and when he rose again Dahlia was moving across the yard to the gate where Wendy stood with her man in the dusk, now smiling, composed of wholly other stuff. Matt noticed his black t-shirt printed in red—ENEMY COMBAT-ANT—and the way he held himself apart, like he wasn't sure how he'd be greeted.

Matt observed Dahlia smiling, skirt swinging, greeting the man, Wendy turning back and forth between them, Wendy with her dirty-blonde hair cut short in a feathery mop and high, tanned cheeks and fine-boned wrists and shoulders. She wore Matt's favorite dark green t-shirt that said:

CUBIC* cube
i think that square
is top of cool shape
in the world

Dahlia shook the man's hand and pointed over to Matt, who grinned stupidly and waved his grass-covered brush, remembering this must be Aaron, right, standing staring. The one who just came home.

"How you two want your steaks?" he forced himself to shout.

"Medium rare," Wendy said.

"Still mooing," the man said. "Thanks."

"Coming right up!" Matt said, his voice going high and brittle, hoping a fat smile would numb his unease. He cracked another beer and drank deep. He pulled the vegetables and tofu off the heat and wrapped them in foil, then laid on the salmon and Wendy's steak.

The man walked up and offered Matt his hand. His grip was gentle but strong. "Hey," he said. "I'm Aaron."

"Matt. Nice shirt."

"Thanks. Wendy got it for me on the internet."

"She's good at t-shirts."

"Yeah. She thought it'd be funny. She said you work with computers."

"Yeah, I code. I'm sort of . . . well, what I do now is part-time tech support for the county, but really I'm working on a freelance project, data-processing. Sort of global forecasting."

"Like stock markets and stuff?"

Matt chuckled, hating the self-deprecating note he struck. "Well, sort of. What I'm trying to do is use turbulence in complex systems to predict unforeseen events," he said, waving the barbecue tongs. "The problem with 'unknown unknowns' is that you don't know what you're looking for. Take 9/11 for instance, or the fall of the Soviet Union. The patterns were there but we weren't looking for them, and there was no way to know *in advance* which data points were the important ones. What we needed was a tool for monitoring data systemically, for helping us watch events not as points or lines but as flows and breaks. The program I'm developing uses chaos theory to visualize predictive data as a field. Then we can use those visualizations to shift our frame of reference so that something that *would* have been an outlier becomes something we're looking for: from an unknown unknown into a known unknown. It's about

letting chaos show its underlying order. I mean . . . Whoa,
I gotta flip this shit." He turned over the salmon and Wendy's steak, then reached for the last two steaks and threw
them on. "Hey D," he shouted. "Just a few more minutes
here. You wanna get the stuff?"

"Got it," she said, handing the weed to Rachel and going
back inside. Aaron nodded after her, his look lingering for
Matt's taste a second longer than was really necessary.

Rachel lit the pipe and passed it. They smoked. Chatted. Dahlia came back out with a pitcher and glasses. Time
slowed.

When did the porch light come on? Who turned the
light on?

"Fuck," Matt said, turning back to the grill and sliding
the salmon on a plate, forking the steaks and serving them
up, while Dahlia portioned out tofu for Rachel and Mel
and divvied up veggies and spooned out the vegan potato
salad Mel had brought. Everyone moved to the picnic table.
Matt lit the tiki torches and citronella candles and Dahlia
passed the tabbouleh. They tore into their food, washing it
down with beer, ripping into animal and vegetable flesh,
throats bulging. Their steak knives flashed in the light,
flecked with fat and blood.

They discussed: the virtues of cats v. dogs, as pets and generally, how best to marinate tofu, the election, how sick
they all were of the election, the curious nature of modern
life where it feels like part of you is connected via mass
media to this hyperlife that doesn't objectively exist but

functions entirely as "news," but what's news if not events yet the news isn't the event and you don't really experience the event but only the "*news*" of it, "yeah like 9/11," and how sometimes it feels strange when there *isn't* some disaster happening, like there's a gap in the matrix, and as Wendy parsed this phrase they talked about *The Matrix* and then other films commenting on Contemporary Life Post-9/11, and also music they'd been listening to like the new Wilco, then Rachel told a story about one of her second-grade girls who'd memorized all the lyrics to "Toxic" and had made up a dance to go along.

They compared tattoos: Wendy had a jaguar on her ankle—this was her Aztec horoscope, she said—and a fleur-de-lis on her lower back; Mel, a flaming skull with BORN TO LOSE on her left shoulder, a barbed tribal band around each bicep, and a complex floral design going down from her hip into the joint between her thigh and pelvis that she only showed the very top of, tugging at her jean shorts; and Aaron a crude circled A on his right shoulder, which he laughed off as his first tatt from back in ye olde punk days, an inverted cross on the inside of his left forearm, and then, pulling up his ENEMY COMBATANT t-shirt, sweeping across his muscled back a pair of intricate spiked wings, crested in Gothic script reading LONG IS THE WAY AND HARD. Neither Matt nor Rachel had tattoos. Dahlia had a dahlia, on her hip, which she didn't show anyone.

How it had gotten dark. How they made a circle with lawn chairs, smoked another bowl, and drank some whiskey out of plastic cups, the coals dying behind them, the moon rising into the stars. Their bodies hummed, satiated, lips slick with grease. Dahlia got a little cold and went in for a hoodie. Rachel got cold too, and Mel wrapped her in her leather jacket. Aaron lit an American Spirit. Xena chewed a bone. Balinese gamelan banged and gonged from the boom box.

"So, I have a story," said Wendy.

"Let's hear it," said Mel.

"Alright. Aaron already heard this one, but it's really weird, so I'll tell it again. Thursday night I was driving to Grand Junction. I was going to a poetry reading there. It was one of those days where nothing seems to quite catch, you know, like Mercury's in retrograde, like the universe is off-kilter." Wendy paused, casting her gaze into the distance. "It's like I wrote once, 'The fissure between the thought and deed, against the universal, the palsy in the hand of God.'"

"Nice," said Matt.

"The reading was this guy David T. Greene, who won the Yale Younger Poets prize last year with his book *Emblazoned Arcadia*. He's at once very classically concerned with craft and meter, but also super experimental, right, and he's working with hypertext and interactive poetics, doing things with New Media artists, and has a blog. So that's where I heard about the reading, the blog: he'd gotten a grant to drive across the country and write a sort of cyberpunk-Whitman long-poem meditation on America, blog it, and along the way he organized a series of readings. So he was reading at the Black Cat in Grand Junction, and . . ."

"Why didn't he read here?" Rachel asked.

"Well that's interesting. I asked him the same question myself. I told him about Eklectika and Back of Beyond and that there's actually quite a dynamic poetry scene here, but he said he had to leave early to make it to Salt Lake City in time for his reading there on Friday and then it was up to Washington and yadda yadda yadda. He seemed really edgy—his aura was totally broken up. He'd planned to have the readings be auxiliary to the experience of writing the trip, but instead he'd just been driving like crazy, barreling through to get from one reading to the next, and he hadn't even really had time to write the poem . . . But first, before all that, I was driving across the desert and do you remember the lightning storm Thursday?"

"Sure," Dahlia said.

"The sky was a 'charcoal smear livid with electric fire.' I watched it as I drove . . . I was halfway watching the storm in the distance, the way the light changed against the mesas, and halfway watching the road. You know how you do, especially when the highway's empty. I had an old mix tape Aaron made me years ago—I found it the other day and thought, wow, right before I get to see him in I don't know how long, here's this mix tape. And it was playing 'Teclo,' right, the PJ Harvey song, and I was very much in the moment, the speed and the storm and the rain flicking on the windshield and PJ Harvey sort of moaning right, 'let me ride on his grace,' and I flick on the wipers and then there's a coyote in the road and *bam!* I feel the car hit him."

"Oh my God," Rachel said.

"I slam on the brakes. But it had just started raining, right, and you know how all the oil on the road floats to the surface after a dry spell, and the car skids, slips sideways, and I panic. My foot's jammed on the brake and all I can think is 'They say steer *into* the skid but who are *they*? What do *they* know?' My mind is just whirling, right, but my hands do it, steering into the skid and I pump the brakes and the car slows and I pull over and stop. I'm like, shaking. In the rearview I'm so white I'm like dead and I remember thinking *maybe I am*, and then I felt like throwing up but just sat there, waiting, on the shoulder by the median—the wrong shoulder, you know?—and this Captain Beefheart song comes on . . ."

"'Clear Spot,'" Aaron said. "I put 'Clear Spot' on that tape."

"Yeah. 'Clear Spot.' I was like, wow. And the squealing fading in my ears and the shaking calming down and I think—what about the coyote? So I get out and walk back and I remember the sun going down, right, and the storm, and it's sprinkling rain like any second now the sky's gonna unleash the deluge and I walk back to where I started braking, and then I go back a little further and look and there's nothing. No coyote, no blood, nothing, and I climb over the median and check out the other side because you know, I thought, maybe the force of the car threw him clear but still nothing. So I run across the highway and check the other shoulder and there's still nothing, so that's when I think, oh my god: he's under the car. He must be jammed under the frame somehow. Maybe still alive. So I go back to the car, walking slow, trying to get hold of myself, and as I walk I watch the car and the road, looking for signs, drops or smears of blood, fur, anything. I get to the car and I so

much do *not* want to look underneath . . . but I work up my
courage and squat by the tire, sort of so I can hide behind
it if he jumps out at me, and I look underneath and there's
nothing. I can't believe it. I cannot believe it. Fender, grill—
no sign at all I hit anything, no contact with anything, no
remnants of flesh or blood, only the idea."

She paused, sipped her beer.

"Wow," Matt said.

"So what happened to the coyote?" Rachel asked.

Wendy held her hands open, palms up.

"Then what?" asked Mel.

"I threw up and felt a little better, then I got back on
the road. I was a few minutes late to the reading, so I
sat in the back—I mean, there were only like five people
there—and it was a great reading but my mind was still
on the coyote, on the absence of the coyote, and afterward,
I went up to thank David and say hi, and we got to talking
and then, later that night, when I got home . . ."

"You're leaving out the middle part," Aaron said.

"Oh, we had a drink, you know, and talked—"

"Talked," Aaron said.

"Anyway," she continued, "the important part is when I
got home. It was a weird night, weird energy in the air, and
there's that witchy feeling you get sometimes, that feeling
like there's a door open somewhere, right, like 'fragrant por-
tals, dimly starred.' So I got home and drove up the lonely
road to the driveway and came to my trailer and when I
make the last turn, my headlights sweep across the mesa
and I stop—because standing right there in the middle of
my headlights, right in front of my trailer door, is a huge,

mangy coyote, his enormous yellow eyes staring right at me. I'm so scared I almost pee myself, so I just sit there watching him and he stands there watching me. I leave the headlights on, because I'm not going to get out till he leaves and I'm not going to turn the lights off so I can't see him, and he just stands there, and then—and this almost made me start crying—he sits back on his haunches and starts panting, still just staring. Finally I sort of come out of it and think to honk the horn, but it does nothing. He ignores it. I roll down the window and shout and honk but none of it makes any difference, he just sits there, staring. I turn off the headlights. In the dark I can still see him there. I crawl in the backseat, check the locks, and go to sleep. When I wake up, he's gone. No prints in the dirt—nothing. Nothing but a faint smell, like an old dog, 'the scents of ghosts, the memory of lithic days.'"

"You think it was a ghost?" Rachel asked.

"Who knows?"

"That's really incredible," Matt said, wondering how much, if any, of the story was true and not really caring, because her telling had given him license to watch her lips move gleaming in the torchlight, her eyelashes flutter, her delicate fingers trace gestures in the air. Wandering his gaze over the curves and hollows of her body made him feel better about the energy he felt flowing between Dahlia and Aaron that he kept telling himself he was just imagining. People look at people, he thought, and that Aaron's knee had been resting against Dahlia's for the last several minutes was no sign of anything, no red flag, no indication of anything other than his own weed-stoked paranoia. It's all in your head, he thought, then again: say something.

Say what?

Dahlia felt him next to her, the pressure of his knee, the coiled power his body held, like he was about to jump on something. They're fucking, right? They had to be, Wendy and her war hero. Didn't seem to matter much to Matt, who looked at Wendy same as always: like he was gonna throw up on her shoes.

"Shit, babe, that's a crazy story," Mel said. "But what about this other wild animal you brought home? What's with Mr. Fox here?" She pointed her beer at Aaron: "Tell us something about yourself, Mr. Fox. What's your deal?"

His energy shifted, tensing. He smiled uneasily. "Not much to tell. I'm from Arizona, grew up near Tucson. I met Wendy in college. I'm just sort of traveling around right now."

"Vision quest?" Mel asked.

"Yeah, sure. Taking some time off. I was staying with some friends in Arizona, now I'm visiting Wendy, then I'm going to Colorado to stay with another friend, then maybe Montana or Washington. I'll probably head back to Tucson in December, get back in school."

"What do you study?" Rachel asked.

"I was doing history. Now maybe poli sci. Maybe something pre-law. Not really sure."

"Didn't you just get out of the Army?" Matt asked.

Aaron's smile hardened. "Still in, technically. But on my way out, yeah."

"What did you do there?" Matt asked. "I mean, if you don't mind my asking."

"You don't have to . . ." Dahlia said, touching Aaron's arm. "Matt spends all his time on the computer and forgets how to talk to people sometimes."

"No problem," Aaron said. "I'm what you call a Nasty Girl."

"A what?"

"Nasty Girl. It's slang for National Guard. I wasn't in the regular Army."

"Oh," Matt said. "Like the reserves?"

"Yeah, like that."

Mel leaned in. "So what was your MOS?"

Aaron sized her up. "Thirty-one Bravo. Yours?"

Mel shook her head. "No, man, I wasn't . . . My dad was in 'Nam, that's how I know MOS. He was a Fifteen Mike—a Huey mechanic in the Screaming Eagles."

"That's cool," Aaron said. "My military occupational specialty was Thirty-one Bravo. Corporal Aaron Stojanowski, 3rd Platoon, 858th Military Police Company, 850th Military Police Battalion, Arizona Army National Guard. Military occupational specialty Thirty-one Bravo One-Zero. They called me Sto."

"Sto?" Rachel asked.

"Like a nickname. Sto."

"Was that when you were in Iraq?" Matt asked.

"Matt," Dahlia said.

"Yeah," Aaron said.

"Wow," Matt said. "That must have been intense. Well, thank you for your service."

"Sure," Aaron said. "No problem."

"Was it dangerous?" Matt asked.

"Matt, please," said Dahlia.

"What? He doesn't have to answer."

Aaron lit a new cigarette from the butt of his old one. "You mean besides people shooting at me and shit exploding all the time?"

"I just, you know, I mean, all we know is what they show us on TV, right? I mean, we don't even know. I can't even imagine. We're totally ignorant of this situation, and I'm just wondering, is it really like how they say? Is it bad? Is it getting worse? Is it getting better?"

"I don't know what to tell you, chief. It's bad enough."

"But they can vote, right? They have democracy. That's better, isn't it?"

"Better than what?"

"I don't know. Better than Saddam? It just seems like such a waste if nothing good comes out of it."

"I don't know, man," Aaron said. "I was just a dumb grunt, you know. I don't know what to tell you."

"But, I mean, it's such a huge question now with the election and America's role in the world post-9/11, and we have this obligation, right, to try to make things better, but maybe it's really all about oil and . . . I mean, I don't even know what to think. Should we stay? Should we pull out? They say if we pull out, Iraq collapses into civil war. But it seems like that's happening anyway. What do we do?"

"Listen, uh, Matt? Matt, right? That's your name? Well, Matt, it doesn't really fucking matter what we do."

"But what about . . ."

"Things matter," Rachel said. "There are serious problems in the world, but people do things to make change
happen. We can hold governments accountable. Voices
matter. The election matters."

"That's exactly what I'm talking about," Matt said.
"Exactly. Should we stay? Do we have a moral imperative to
clean up our mess, bring democracy to the Middle East, or
what? I mean, we can't just leave, can we?"

Dahlia looked at Matt, her lips compressed. How many
beers had he had?

"Look," Aaron said, "Matt, Rachel, you seem like nice
people and this is a great barbecue. I'm gonna say this one
thing, then . . . Maybe let's talk about something else, okay?
Because Iraq's a fucking disaster. The whole thing. Staying's
a disaster. Leaving's a disaster. It's a fucking shithole. And it
doesn't matter what the fuck we think about it, because the
guys who run shit don't give a rat's ass what people like you
and me *think*. Or do. Or say. Unless we're blowing shit up
or donating money, they could give a flying fuck. So I don't
know what to tell you."

"That's a pretty negative world view," Rachel said.

"Yeah, well, I'm all traumatized and shit. You know what
it's like. You saw the movie."

"So why'd you go, then, man," Mel asked, "if none of it
matters?"

"Because they told me to."

"But why'd you join the Army?"

"National Guard. I was National Guard."

"Okay, man. Why'd you join the National Guard?"

"College money, patriotism. Service, challenge, honor. Nine-eleven. Same things as anybody else."

"But now you think it's all bullshit," Mel said.

"I think we all gotta make hard choices," he said, "and how you feel about shit doesn't really matter. You gotta do what you gotta do."

"And all you had to do was kill people."

Aaron laughed. "What?"

Rachel put her hand on Mel's thigh and squeezed. Mel brushed it off. "No, he made a choice. He wasn't drafted. All he had to do was kill people."

"Yeah, sure," Aaron said. "Not a bad deal, either. Easier than working for it."

"I just don't understand how you could do that, man."

"Mel," Rachel said. "Hey."

"You don't understand how I could do what?" Aaron asked.

"How you could kill people for money."

"Okay, you got me. I joined the Army so I could fucking kill people. Big secret: It's a blast."

"But doesn't it bother you at all?" Mel asked. "Aren't you ashamed?"

"Ashamed of what?"

"I mean, you know the war's fucking bullshit, but you go do it anyway. You know it's illegal, but you do it anyway. People die and you don't even fucking care. You could've not gone. You could've been a conscientious objector. You could've gone to Canada."

"I signed a contract. We had a job to do."

"That's all you got? You had a contract? A job to do?"

"This is real nice, Wendy," Aaron said. "I'm glad I came."

"Man," Mel said, "I just can't understand how you can take part in an illegal war that kills thousands of innocent people—*for college money*—and then act like it doesn't matter. Like you didn't choose. That's what seems completely fucked to me."

"Mel, honey," Rachel said. "Lay off."

"Yeah, Mel," said Dahlia, "let it go."

"Hey," Wendy shouted, "anyone else here see that movie *Eternal Sunshine of the Spotless Mind*? With that actor, whats-his-name, Ace Ventura? I watched it on DVD the other night and it was *so good*."

"Fuck that," Mel said. "This shit's fucked up. This shit's real. Don't you see that? Killing people for money? And then you wear that fucking t-shirt like it's all a joke. That's just *wrong*. I mean, if that's not evil, I don't what is."

"Are you fucking serious?"

"It's like the Nazis," Mel said. "Like some people do it just because other people tell them to."

"Mel, that's not fair," said Dahlia.

"No, really, man," Mel said. "Think about it. Loads of German soldiers were just doing their jobs. Loads of German people were just doing what they were told. They all thought it made sense, they all thought what they did was fucking justified, but it wasn't. They don't get to say it's okay. It's like that Eichmann book, man. Evil is evil."

"Call me a Nazi one more time," Aaron said.

Matt put his hands out: "Whoa, now—let's all chill out a little bit."

Mel stared hard at Aaron: "*Did* you kill anybody?"

His eyes narrowed.

"Well did you?"

His eyes closed slow, then he smiled and opened them. "No. I didn't. Not that it's any of your goddamn business, but no, I didn't kill anybody. It wasn't my job."

"But it was someone's," Mel said.

"I just held the camera."

"Hey, y'all," Dahlia said, getting up, "how 'bout some dessert? Mel, Rachel, you wanna help me with the pie?"

"Bullshit," Mel said. "I can't fucking believe I'm fucking sitting here with a fucking American Nazi I don't know what, and everybody's like, 'Play nice, Mel. Lay off, Mel.' Like it doesn't fucking matter. Fucking sheeple. This is why. *This* is why."

Aaron stood up. "I'm done here. Let's go, Wendy."

Mel stood to face him. "I know you. I know what you are. I can see it."

Aaron's voice went cold. "What the fuck do you want from me?"

"Admit what you did was evil."

"It's called reality. You need to grow the fuck up, bitch."

"Bitch? You fucking Nazi asshole!" she screamed, jabbing her finger in his chest.

"Listen up," he shouted, grabbing her wrist, "this shit"— then Xena—Mel yanking her hand away and whacking Aaron's arm, Aaron shouting in Mel's face and Matt leaning up going *whoa* and Xena—Xena barked, leaping snapping at Aaron who turned smooth and kicked the dog hard in the side, sending the animal rolling yelping and Mel surged, hitting Aaron in the neck and he caught her forearms in his fists and she kicked but then Dahlia was between them and Wendy and Rachel too, pulling Mel back, Aaron walking off cold, Mel held by Rachel, still raging, still flailing.

"Motherfucker!" she screamed. "Fucking motherfucker Nazi fuck!"

"Watch yourself," Aaron hissed.

"Easy now," Rachel said. "Easy."

"I'm gonna fucking kill you, motherfucker!"

"Somebody shut that bitch up," Aaron said, stalking back and forth along the fence line.

Dahlia went to Xena, the kicked dog hiding behind a bush near the back door, keeping an eye on Aaron the whole time. Rachel and Wendy whispered to Mel. Matt stood between them, near the barbecue again, feeling confused, until Wendy pointed at Aaron.

"Hey, uh, Aaron, you wanna go out front for a minute?" Matt asked.

"Fucking asshole!" Mel shouted after them as they disappeared. "Fucking fascist puke!"

"Mel, sit down," Rachel said, gently pushing Mel into a chair. "Calm down. We need to calm down."

"I think Xena's okay," said Dahlia.

Wendy took a step toward the gate, came back. "I'm so sorry about that. I didn't know—he seemed a little tense but I didn't know . . . That was completely insane."

"Mel, please, you need to calm down."

"Get the fuck off me!" Mel shouted, swinging at Rachel.

"Easy," Rachel said, holding up her hands.

"Whose fucking side are you on?"

Rachel took Mel's chin in her hand and pulled her face

up: "Melanie. You will calm down right now. You need to breathe. Breathe. You are not going to behave like this. You're a grown woman. Now breathe."

Mel took a deep breath and let it out with a shudder. Rachel knelt and held her. Wendy went over, then back to Xena, then stood alone staring up into the night sky. After a few minutes, Mel straightened up and wiped her bleary eyes.

"I'm alright," she said. "I'm okay. I just . . . I don't know what the fuck happened. With all the whiskey, I guess, I went a little sideways."

"You went, like, diagonal," Rachel said.

"That was crazy, Mel," said Dahlia. "You just called Wendy's boyfriend a Nazi."

"He's not my boyfriend."

"Well, he's not a Nazi either," Dahlia said. "He's a soldier who just got back from a war zone. He's a person."

"I know, man. I'm sorry."

"Honey, I love your political passion," said Rachel, "but goodness gracious. You might as well have just called him a baby killer. We don't *do* that anymore. You know how messed up your dad is."

"I'm know . . . I just . . ."

Dahlia stood between the flickering tiki torches in the dark, feeling the adrenaline course through her arms and legs, thinking who decides things? Who makes choices? You go do a thing, you commit to things, then something happens. Sometimes you just do things. Sometimes things just happen. "I'm going inside for a minute," she said to no one in particular, then slid away into the house, through the kitchen, down the hall and into the bathroom where the lightless gray and black wrapped around her like blankets. She locked the door behind her, felt her way to the toilet, and sat. She didn't want to see his eyes in the mirror. She didn't want to feel him. She rubbed her arms hard, trying to scour away the electricity, the gold flecks in his green irises, the way he sat too close, his chipped incisor, the way his knee bumped hers. His body pressing on her as she came between him and Mel, his arms, his muscled chest and shoulders. His smell that seemed to catch in her throat.

Why'd Wendy even bring him? *Some jerk.* He could do anything.

You have to stop.

But not if it happens to someone else. Who says I always have to be the same when I'm always different? Always different. *Pull yourself together.* Pull together what? Who? And what would it feel like?

Does Matt know? Is he gonna take you home?

I am home. You gotta get out.

Pull yourself together. You're the one who got her shit together. You make choices. You're the one who does what you do, this life, right now. Ride it.

babylon

between men and lions wolves and lambs

continued strong techniques, life's blood TV detainees
use of stress is essential
two CSHs with four sites out and OPERATION IRON HAM-
MER when these fail an Arab's honor can cause him to
react by interpreting the facts to suit himself or flatly
denying them. Therefore a Westerner should remember
the "yes" you hear does not always mean yes and might
mean no. That he answer "yes" whether it be true or not.
In the American world, a flat "no" signals you want to end
the very indirect approach toward corrective remarks and
include praise of any good points. Similar to this by grace
of God, our friend the Sheikh Talat, those rounds were
close. People demand we stay for lunch, continue past as
we turn along a street, pointless to question the political
blue decorating

the edge of Babylon
this point
aligned with the global lowest
art of an edge, heart of the city, the streets

blood TV
heart of the city

therefore about a minute use auditory stimuli hoods six
operating tables, some between us till mild physical contact
and mobile hospitals OPERATION PLANET X Department
of Defense by the grace of God global consensus my spear
Rumsfeld fully functional in 24 to 48 hours his story from
the bombs over OPERATION LONGSTREET and goes to work
for the US as a translator. As the insurgency mounts, he's
threatened by OPERATION RIPPER SWEEP to give them
intel and/or quit the Americans. Even as revelations have
been made and behavior exposed, oil policy throughout all
running a mathematician who doesn't know where action
might be warranted and

　　　　　　　　　　　　　　　　　　we see distinctions that
are not distinctions:

hides faith somewhere in Asia, perhaps Afghanistan, among
the symbols calling forth stages of military passage for
example opportunities lost indeed he's brought specifically
"graduated levels" and it stands sheikh danger
　　　　　　　　　"Humvees"

will be his lie and if CIA case officers local Hard Site
initiation of the abuse once the importance of a method
used at GTMO you (with) surely Allah facilitates OPER-
ATION VIGILANT RESOLVE majority of Iraqis are delta until
the government regardless, for example, appearances and

politeness automatically require an answer of "still check-ing" or something similar means "no," an indirect response also means "I am still your friend, I tried" therefore when dealing with OPERATION BULLDOG MAMMOTH polite way for an Arab to say no is to say "I'll see what I can do" no matter how impossible after the Arab concerning his suc-cess have fled to Iran from Baghdad works as a journalist. When the uprising begins in earnest OPERATION WARRIOR lives in the flood plain
heart of the TV
according to Military Intelligence

knowledge or implicitly of what will be yours my spear the Kingdom this day

I could hear the water I threw up
fall back on

the frequency of interrogations and the middleman's hands: having failed punishment of Allah to come victorious out of interlocking to circumvent public rage, buildings and the leashed hotel, pyramids naked, naked blood, heading off some report, the collective flattened and critically wounded patients sealed off from the responsibility made to spare those targets on the edge, the heart

your leader will
control your fire
(operation iraqi freedom, 2003)

i am an american, fighting in the forces which guard
my country and our way of life

i am prepared to give my life in their defense

The major in the lead truck took a wrong turn and we all
followed. We drove two miles down the wrong highway
before looping back to the intersection with the chipped
concrete barrier spray-painted MSR CLEVELAND *TO
BAGHDAD*.

We got lost again just the other side of the border and
wound up driving down a dirt road behind a line of tank
pits. Blackened hulks jutted up from the sand.

Later we saw our first Iraqis, a farm family thin as whip-
pets, standing outside their hut watching us go by.

We stopped and dismounted. All along the line, men clambered down and stood or knelt on the road or shoulder,
rifles aimed at the empty desert.

No radio traffic.

We stood in the sun while the wind whipped sand at
us. Waves of silica slid and ebbed across the blacktop like

the ghosts of snakes. Engines hummed. We watched the horizon.

The radio crackled and beeped twice. We looked to the truck in front and to the one behind. I wiped dust off my glasses. I drank water, then dug for an MRE. Chicken Cavatelli. Beef Teriyaki.

A few minutes later, the call came to roll out.

We crossed a bridge near a village, and on the far side, Iraqi kids ran at us waving knives.

"Watch those kids, Wilson," Captain Yarrow said.

"Roger, sir," I said.

Sergeant Chandler in the back leveled his rifle out the window.

"You buy!" they yelled. "Ameriki! You buy! Baynet!"

"Stay back!"

Men rose up behind the kids, grinning under mustaches and dragging coolers. "You buy, Ameriki," they sang out. "You buy Pipsi." They held up cans of red, white, and blue, wet with condensation, dripping ice. I could taste the sand in my throat.

The radio barked: "ALL ELEMENTS, DEEP STEEL THREE. BE ADVISED OF UNKNOWN CONTACTS BOTH SIDES. DO NOT STOP, DO NOT SAY AGAIN DO NOT BUY ANYTHING. SAY AGAIN, DO NOT STOP."

"Can I shoot one, sir?" Sergeant Chandler asked.

"*Balalalalalalala!*" Lieutenant Krauss shouted. The kids laughed and pointed. One of them jumped and danced, his knife shining in the air.

Captain Yarrow turned to me: "If they get in front of us, honk. And if they don't get out of the way, run him over. I mean it. Run him over."

I imagined the Iraqi boy's body dragged beneath the humvee's tires, three tons of steel rolling over his chest, squirting intestines onto the road.

"You buy! Ameriki! Baynet! Pipsi!"

Captain Yarrow double-checked his pistol. "Roger, Specialist?"

"Roger, sir."

When it happened, I thought, I'd speed up to make it quicker. I wouldn't look in the rearview at the stain of blood on the road. I'd keep my eyes straight ahead and not even from the corner would I look at the boy I'd killed.

Of course I'd look.

No. I'd watch the taillights of the truck in front. I wouldn't look.

Of course I'd look. I'd speed up—but would I even feel the body under the humvee's tons?

face the target, place the weapon to your shoulder,
move the selector lever from SAFE *to* SEMI

Night fell. Against the bruised and blackening sky, flames shot up from distant towers. Armored ruins lined the road in squads, charred corpses scattered in among the blasted metal. A dead Iraqi grinned where fire had burned away his face, leaving yellowed teeth in a black ring, eye sockets smears of shadowed flesh.

The convoy slowed.

Coils of wire bloomed along the highway.

A sentry directed us in, her pale cheeks washed in humvee light and smudged with dirt and soot. Refinery fires shone gold and red in her empty eyes. She swung her arm again in front, again, directing traffic.

To our left burned a great fire into which three joes shoveled trash. Beyond that some kind of rusting, latticed, industrial turret, erratically lit, rose in the dark. To our right loomed the shadows of the big green, lines of hemmets and trucks, machines rumbling low. Guided by soldiers with chemlights, red lines floating in the black until our lights hit them and they flinched, we circled along avenues of wire, down mazes of green steel. We stopped.

Word passed: stand by.

We dumped our gear and dug out MREs.

After eating I slung my rifle, lit a smoke, and walked down the line searching for someone to talk to. I found a bunch of guys standing watching three National Guard females changing their brown t-shirts. They'd climbed on top of their fuel truck for privacy but still we could see.

One girl was black or Hispanic, so timid she sat and all we could see was her forehead. Another was skinny like a boy, with buzz-cut hair, no tits, and a face like cratered rock. The third, she was our favorite. She had a nice face and brown hair pulled back in a ponytail—even in DCUs you could tell she was a woman. When she pulled off her sweat-soaked brown t-shirt, we cheered.

"Fuck you assholes," she shouted.

She had a gut, love handles, big tits. We adored her.

Someone shouted "Hey take off your bra" and she gave us the finger.

They pulled on their tops and the brown girl yelled down, "Show's over, shitheads."

Reading took this as an invitation to go backstage, but the rest of us scattered. We walked down the line, me, Villaguerrero, Healds, and Bullwinkle.

"I bend that white girl over the hood this humvee and fucking *bam*, right in the fucking ass."

"I want the Chicana."

"She black."

"No she ain't. She a hundred percent Puerto Rican. I can tell, I got spicvision."

"Wouldn't that be spicdar?"

"Beanervision."

"Beaners are from Mexico, motherfucker. I'm Puerto Rican."

"Beandar."

"You don't eat beans in Puerto Rico?"

"They fucking eat bananas."

"Anyway you couldn't even see her."

"Bananas and mangoes and shit."

"I could see her face and that's all I need, cuz that's what's I'm gonna have wrapped around my cock. Oh yeah, baby, oh you like it? Fuckin' eat it, bitch."

"Shit, I'll take two and make a Nasty Girl sandwich. Bread, bread, I'm the meat. Make my own mayonnaise."

"Fuck that. *I'm* gonna fuck the black girl. Y'all can fuck the dog."

"She a fucking dyke."

"Fuck, man, this point I put a MRE box on her head and call it even. I gives a fuck."

"Hooah."

do not let your imagination and fear run wild

I forced my eyes to the tires ahead, to the road, at the sky, to my speedometer, changing focus every few seconds. The greatest danger glowed in the yellow and red rear-bumper reflectors of the leading truck—watching them wobble and dip, sustaining their slow rhythms, blobs of dim, pulsing light undulating in the dark—only a matter of time and you wake up ditched, smashed, your humvee flipping, rolling, whatever.

I bit my cheek. I bit my tongue. I jammed my knee into a sharp edge of metal under the dash until my head cleared. I cracked hot Mountain Dew and chugged.

The line wavered and swayed as drivers dozed and awoke. We'd been driving for eighteen hours.

We turned off the highway down a dirt road running between a ditch and a wall, passing tall grass, palms, and farms. Things felt close.

Lights swam as I fought to keep my eyes open. My neck bent under the weight of its dumb head, like a cripple who can't hold his face up, like I needed a tube to talk with. We followed the convoy past a checkpoint and turned to the east fading ashen to white. In the distance, some kind of tower stabbed into the lightening sky. We turned again.

I saw great bands of painted Indians boil up out of the dark on steaming war ponies, ululating, attacking with tomahawks and Winchesters. I'd make my humvee jump like a frog: bounce over the burning wreck and over the ditch by the road, bounce across low scrub to the savages we'd land on and kill with a splat. Bounce, bounce, fuck.

"Wake up, Wilson."

The truck in front pulled off. I put us in gear. Too tired to care whether I'd fucked up or what, so I'd fallen asleep, so what. Fuck shit fuck whatever, cockfuck shitfucker asscunt.

"Where the fuck are we?"

I followed the five-ton onto an airfield. We stopped between two Black Hawks.

"We must be close," I said.

"I think so," said Captain Yarrow.

I jerked awake, pulling my seven-hundred-pound head up off the steering wheel. Captain Yarrow lay slumped against his door, drooling on his armor. Sergeant Chandler snored in back. The convoy was gone. The sky a cool and milky white.

We'd been left. Abandoned.

I slid into drive, honked the horn twice, then took off.

Captain Yarrow heaved forward. "What?"

"Hooah, sir."

"What? Where's the convoy?"

"Dunno, sir."

"They're what?"

"There." Intersection. In the distance, off to the right, the line of red lights.

Loaded with gear, we shuffled onto the plane and rode east, out of the sky, down the night.

Stewardesses brought our meal and choice of nonalcoholic beverage. I watched White Oleander *and slept through most of* A Beautiful Mind. *The screens all along the dim aisles flickered on the faces of sleeping soldiers.*

Dreaming valkyrie wings: we'd be FNGs at first but lickety-split start wasting hooches and fragging LTs, di-di-mauing back to the LZ, dropping bloopers into rice paddies, riding Hueys into the Shit, hog on our hip. We'd have hearts and minds sharpied on steelpot covers, tattoo our days down till we're short, wear our shit all fucked up and say, "Fuck the regs, man, this is Indian Country."

We'd prepared our whole lives for this. Bombed little brown people, helicopters swooping low, the familiar sight of American machinery carving death from a Third World wasteland. We expected nothing less than shell shock and trauma, we lusted for thousand-yard stares—lifelong connoisseurs of hallucinatory violence, we already knew everything, felt everything. We saw it through a blood-spattered lens, handheld tracking shot pitting figure against ground. We were the camera, we were the audience, we were the actors and film and screen: cowboys and killer angels, the lost patrol, the cavalry charge, America's proud and bloody soldier boys.

We stumbled blinking off the plane into the night's heat and crammed onto buses that drove us to a tent in the sand, where we downloaded bags into a box trailer. Shuffled to another tent to wait. Mustered into another where we swiped IDs, shunting through the green machine's hive mind, finally officially in theater. We got briefed on snakes and General Order One—no pork, no porn, no booze—then sent back to the tent to sleep. Then rousted again, onto buses driven by Arabs. We lumped in on each other in our gear, bitchy in the crowded stink. The sun rose over an empty desert.

At Camp Connecticut, a swath of tents pitched in the middle of nowhere like a mirage, we downloaded our bags from the trailer. We slept in piles like dogs. Not enough water. The high 114.

Lieutenant Colonel Braddock brought us to his tent for a PowerPoint presentation and speech.

"Men," he said, "tomorrow we embark on a most important and dangerous mission. We have trained months for this, and it is the epitome of our job as soldiers. I am proud to be leading you into our unit's first combat mission since World War II. I know you will acquit yourselves with honor and courage, because I know your leaders and they are the best leaders in the Army, and I know your sergeants and they are the best sergeants in the Army. Together we'll accomplish our mission and

follow up on our nation's great victory in Iraq with successful stability-and-support operations and a peaceful transition to democratic governance.

"I know many of you are too young to remember World War II, but I think this is a good time to reflect on the tremendous work we did stabilizing and securing Nazi Germany after the war and for fifty years protecting it from the Warsaw Pact threat. This was no mean feat, and if it seems overshadowed today by campaigns like D-Day and Anzio, then I will tell you this is a matter of perspective. Because winning the peace can be as hard, if not harder, than winning the war. We have our work cut out for us.

"In the coming weeks and months, we will be tested, challenged, and stressed, and there will come times when home will seem very far away. But let me remind you that we are Deep Steel, we are the tip of the spear, and home, men— home is here, with your fellow soldiers. We are each other's family. We're a band of brothers. Support each other, follow your leaders, listen to your NCOs, and we will overcome, we will rise up and grab that brass ring. We will succeed and we will be victorious.

"We are soldiers, the fighting men who man the ramparts protecting America from the insidious evils of terrorism and Islamic fundamentalism that now threaten our way of life. We're here because Saddam Hussein was a threat to America, his nuclear weapons and biological programs poised to be handed over to terrorists who hate us because of our freedom, who hate our way of life, and who have no compunctions about murdering your wives, mothers, sons, and daughters in cold blood. Because of the great bravery and professional dedication

of your fellow soldiers, Saddam Hussein is no longer a threat. Men, we're here to make America safe, and to make the world safe for America. I have the utmost faith that you will rise to the occasion and make me proud."

an arab worldview is based upon six concepts:
atomism, faith, wish versus reality,
justice and equality, paranoia, and the importance of family over self

No running water. No electricity. No AC. No grass, no carpet, no windows, no fans. Everyone in the world wears camouflage—the others talk gobbledygook and stare.

No running water means no showers, no sinks. No hoses, no faucets, no drains. No cold water, no ice. No laundry, no bath, no toilet.

We had a toilet. We had a plywood outhouse with three stalls. You sit on a wood O and crap in a washtub. Every day two soldiers pulled out the three tubs, poured in diesel and gasoline, and lit the shit on fire.

You stir the burning shit with a four-foot pole and drift around the smoke. You pour more diesel on the fire. You stir the shit. You gag. You stir. You eyeball the grunts in their hooch down the way, sleeping and playing cards, and mutter to yourself. The wind shifts and you circle, stir, pour.

■ ■ ■

No music, no TV, no radio. No magazines, no newspapers, no news. No internet. No books except the ones you brought.

The only information came in daily briefs: Fedayeen active in the area. Today two soldiers were killed in an RPG attack. Coalition Forces are securing the city of Baghdad. Watch for a white and orange compact sedan, suspected Fedayeen vehicle. Be on the lookout for a blue or white pickup. Saddam loyalists may be planning a series of coordinated attacks.

Giant camel spiders roamed our camp, some bigger than a grown man's palm.

One skittered across the sand at me on crazy legs and I stomped it. The thing reared back, inch-long fangs sawing the air, and lunged. I stomped it again, again and again, mashing it to yellow meat.

In addition to the camel spiders, there were brown recluses, black scorpions, mosquitoes, flies, fleas, biting ants, and, we were told, the deadly asp. There were cicada-like bugs in the trees as well, which didn't bite but sang all day in maddening skreeks. When they stopped, it was like going deaf.

Wild dogs prowled the camp at night. The muezzin five times a day.

reminder, you are a representative of the united states while in iraq

it will be important to use good judgment, tact, and diplomacy
in any dealings you may have with the people

Mail came, packages and letters from home. I inked a chess-board onto the bottom of an upside-down apple crate and made pieces from scavenged Russian commo gear: the king and queen glass diodes, the rooks resistors, bishops capacitors.

We started catching camel spiders and scorpions instead of just killing them. Did they burn? Drown? Could you poison them with laundry soap? Healds used his snips to cut the legs off one, leaving it hobbling on six, then five, then three. Down to two, it fell over wriggling. We thought about letting it starve then decided to burn it.

Operation Iron Bullet got underway. National Guardsmen and Iraqi workers came to load our bunkers' munitions onto trucks for transport to AHA Taji.

We were issued Humanitarian Daily Rations to give the Iraqis. Wrapped in tough yellow plastic, they were labeled A FOOD GIFT FROM THE PEOPLE OF THE UNITED STATES OF

America. The Iraqis brought their own lunches, flatbread with lamb and vegetables, and took the HumRats home.

They were a raggedy bunch, mustached and bony, wearing the same dirty clothes every day. We watched them with distrust and curiosity. Sergeant Chandler was the exception. Tasked with ferrying the work crews back and forth and guarding them during their shift, he got friendly. He ate their flatbread, gave them extra MREs, and bought their old dinars and army badges. Soon we did too. We bought the Pepsis they kept on ice in little coolers.

We captured a camel spider and a scorpion and Lieutenant Krauss announced a match. We fought them that night in a water bottle with the label peeled off. We cut the top off the bottle and cut another top off another bottle so it fit over the first like a cap. Several joes came to watch, huddled around us, and we dumped in one then the other. The camel spider skittered down to one end. We tilted the bottle so the scorpion fell on him.

Zang! went the black stinger. *Zang! Zangzang!* We cheered and shouted as the spider curled in death.

The next day, we fought this scorpion against another scorpion and he won again. The crowd multiplied and the shouts got louder.

The following day, though, our champion seemed sluggish. We were concerned. Did he need water? Was he depressed? We fretted and urged him to keep up his strength. We asked Healds but he snarled, "Dammit, I'm a medic, not an entomologist."

That night we fought our hero against another camel spider, this time in a new arena. We took the apple crate I'd
made into a chessboard and turned it right side up, covering
it with a sheet of acetate. It was delicate work: one person
held the arena and another the acetate and a third the water
bottles caging our gladiators, then we dumped them in one
by one, sliding back the cover, shaking the warrior in, fixing
the acetate quick. The second fighter was always trickiest.

Our champ beat the new spider handily and in honor
of his string of victories we dubbed him Saddam. The next
day, however, his stupor worsened, even though we'd left
him the spider's carcass to eat. We had another fight that
night, between him and a new, very large camel spider, but
he was too sick or listless to attack, and since the camel
spider's jaws couldn't pierce his thick exoskeleton, the fight
was a draw. We doused both in gas and lit them up. The
scorpion burned slow, sadly inanimate, but our camel spider ran, a skittering ball of fire, and crumpled outside the
hooch. We cheered.

We staged more matches, got good at it. The scorpions
were viciously territorial and fought both each other and
the camel spiders, but the spiders for all their fierce appear-
ance were comparatively irenic: they couldn't stand up to
those black stingers and wouldn't fight against each other,
no matter how much trash we talked. Scorpions were both
rarer and harder to catch, so after our first lucky string of
fights the battles grew infrequent. When we got a scorpion
we fought him against camel spider after camel spider until
he died in captivity or was killed by another scorpion. The
winner we named Saddam.

The radio crackled: MPs requesting assistance, moving in on a suspected cache, needed backup, wanted us, four or five humvees ASAP. The assault in two-zero mikes.

I threw on my battle rattle and ran into the CP, where Captain Yarrow, Lieutenant Krauss, and Sergeant First Class Perry stood pondering the sat-map.

"I think you can go out Gate 1 and down this road here, past, uh, what are those, houses?"

"Some kind of building."

"Past those houses, right, and you can turn down this road over the canal."

"Is that a bridge?"

"It's uh, I can't tell."

"Can we go around?"

"Around the canal?"

"I mean, you know, a crossing."

"You can go through BIAP but we'd uh, we'd need to get that route from somebody. I mean, we don't know. And it'd take forty-five minutes at least, just to get there, never mind the site."

"So down these roads here?"

"One of them must have a bridge."

"Sir, we should roll," Sergeant First Class Perry said.

"Can we take the map with us?" Yarrow asked.

"It's mounted to the wood, sir," Lieutenant Krauss told him. "And it's too big."

"Maybe we can fold it up."

"It's the only map we have, sir."

"Sir, we should go."

"Yeah, fine." He turned to me. "Wilson, you see this?" He pointed at the map.

"Roger, sir."

"That's where we're going. We go out Gate 1, we take the second left, then the second left after that. That should take us over the canal."

The smudge of tangled gray resembled a crushed spider.

"Roger, sir."

We headed out, headlights blazing, five humvees fully loaded. "Weapon status red," the BC called, chambering a round in his nine mil and grinning. "Lock and load!" My rifle's bolt slid forward with an exhilarating clack.

We rolled through the night past the first huts and trees and took the second left onto a dirt road bordered with thick vegetation. I strained to catch the twitch that would warn us of imminent attack.

"Turn down here," the BC said.

"That's the first one, sir."

"The what?"

"You said the second turn."

"I what?"

"You said the second turn."

"Hold on. Stop." He got on the radio. "Crusader CP, this is Crusader Six. Will you check the map here, we're at the first turn on the road but I think it's where the second turn should be. Can you verify?"

"CRUSADER SIX THIS IS CRUSADER CP. IT'S, UH, DIFFICULT TO DETERMINE EXACTLY."

"Crusader CP, this is Crusader Six, yes or no. Yes or no. Do I turn down this road or not?"

"ROGER, CRUSADER SIX. GO FOR IT."

We crept down the alley. Out of the vegetation on the left rose a stone wall eight feet high. On the right more vegetation and a drainage ditch and, further back, more walls, surrounding houses with brightly lit windows. The road narrowed. The wall closed in and on the right branches scratched at the windshield.

"Keep going," said Captain Yarrow.

Up ahead a donkey cart stood against the wall with a donkey tied to it. The road widened slightly, and on the right a driveway ran over a culvert and back into the palms about ten yards to a large, well-lit house. Just past the donkey, the road swung left around an angle of wall.

The donkey brayed: ahhhhhweeyhornk-yhornk.

"Can you get by?"

"Roger, sir."

"Keep going."

I passed the cart, feeling the dirt at the edge of the ditch crumble under the truck's wheels, and slid along slowly, closer and closer to the donkey now backing against the wall, panic flashing black in his eyes. The truck's front bumper brushed his trembling flank.

Ahhweeyhornk!

"We got people! I mean contacts!" Sergeant Chandler shouted.

I looked back at two Iraqis in robes standing in the driveway, smoking cigarettes and watching us. Sergeant Chandler trained his rifle on them.

"Watch the men, Sergeant! Wilson, watch that donkey!"

Ahhweeeeyhornk-a-yhornk-a-yhornk!

I edged the truck forward, brushing against the donkey's ribs. The truck behind followed close. I swung slowly around the corner of the wall. The road ended in a ditch. I stopped and looked at the humvee behind pressed against the braying donkey.

Ahhweeeeeeeyhornk!

"Fuck!" Captain Yarrow shouted. He got on the radio: "Crusader Attack elements, this is Crusader Six. Head back up to the, uh, back to the last route change, over."

Captain Yarrow and Sergeant Chandler got out. Lieutenant Juarez came up. The donkey kept braying and Sergeant Chandler kept his rifle trained on the smoking Iraqis. Yarrow and Juarez traded heated whispers while the humvees behind us backed slowly down the road.

The BC slapped the rear of the truck to get my attention

and started backing me toward the culvert and the drive-way, which, it turned out, wasn't wide enough.

"Are we backing up?" I shouted.

"We're turning around."

"I can just back up, sir."

"You're turning around, Wilson."

Okay. I watched the mirror, the back tires, the BC's hand signals, the wall on my left, the front bumper of the truck, and the increasingly freaked-out donkey all at once. The beast hopped up and down, convulsing, hooves stamping furiously. The bumper dragged against his rump.

The BC scowled and led me onto the driveway. The left rear tire started sinking. I couldn't swing the truck any tighter without smashing the donkey, and if I kept on like this I'd slide into the ditch. The BC swung me back, though, and farther, the left side sinking deeper and deeper. Just when I thought we couldn't go back any farther, the donkey maybe a foot in front, braying crazy-eyed in my headlights, the BC had me stop and turn hard left and pull forward. I went ahead until the brush guard rubbed the donkey's ribs. The BC backed me up again, this time to the right, then forward again, again left. Awheeeeeeyhornk-a-yhornk-yhornk! Four more times, tight back and forth, the back end sinking, the donkey braying, and at last we got the truck turned around. I pulled forward, scraping the cart with a creak.

The BC and Sergeant Chandler mounted up, and we rolled back to the rest of the convoy. Yarrow called up Lieutenant Krauss and chewed him out for giving us bad directions.

■ ■ ■

We took the second left. The next road was wider and ended in the overgrown courtyard of an abandoned building. We stopped and the BC called Lieutenant Krauss on the radio and yelled at him.

"This *is* the second turn," Captain Yarrow shouted.

"Uh, roger, Crusader Six. You check behind the building?"

"Yes. This is it. It's fucking palm trees. Look at the map again. Are you looking at the map?"

"Roger, sir. The map's right here."

"So you're looking at the fucking map?"

"Roger, sir."

"Then you can see. It doesn't go anywhere. It just stops."

"Roger, sir."

"So why the fuck you send me down here if you can see it just stops? What the fuck, Lieutenant? Can't you read a fucking map?"

"Roger, sir."

"Holy Christ. We're sitting out here like fucking . . . sitting ducks, and those MPs *need* us, they could be dying right now, and you can't even read a fucking map!"

"Sir."

"*What*, Lieutenant?"

"Sir, I think if you go back to the main road, turn left and stay to the right, break, just keep to the right and you'll come to some buildings, and keep to the right of those, break, there's a road that goes between the buildings and, uh, break, it looks like a small canal, break. Now you stay on that road until you get to another bunch of buildings, break, then

TAKE A LEFT AND FOLLOW THAT FOR, UH, BREAK, A KILOME-
TER, AND THERE SHOULD BE A BRIDGE OVER THE BIG CANAL.
How copy, over?"

"Stay to the right, go left, go over the bridge."

"Roger."

"Alright, Crusader CP. This better fucking work."

We passed more houses, lights burning bright in the darkness, more men standing in courtyards staring. Children
watched from balconies. At the next turn, we went right
and Lieutenant Juarez's team went left and we rolled down
the alley to what looked like a cul-de-sac.

"There, there!" the BC shouted, pointing to a gap
between a house and a small canal. "That's the road."

"We can't get through there, sir," I told him. The path
was no bigger than a walkway.

"Don't *fucking* contradict me, Specialist! Drive down that
road!"

Grinding teeth, I poked the truck into the alley. The right
side dipped precipitously down the canal's bank. Left tires
against the wall, my right tires churning mud at the water's
edge, undercarriage dragging, I inched forward as the path
narrowed and the slope steepened. I stopped the truck so I
could shift into low-drive.

"Keep going! What are you stopping for!"

I eased the truck forward. The path narrowed and the
right side sank deeper into ditch muck. Soon there wouldn't
be any path at all.

"Sir."

"Fine, I see! Fine!"

I put the truck in reverse and backed out. Thankfully the drivers behind us had waited, so it was a straight shot back to the cul-de-sac. Mud flung up from the tires.

The BC called up Lieutenant Juarez. His team hit a dead end, too. The BC radioed Lieutenant Krauss and told him to ask the MPs for directions. We reformed the convoy and returned to the CP.

Lieutenant Krauss radioed just as we were coming in Gate 1 and told us the MPs had started their assault, but they still needed us. He told us they had a route that went around BIAP. We were to go through Checkpoint 7 and take the first right.

"Do you mean go in through Checkpoint 7 or out?" the BC asked.

"Uh, out."

"Alright. Let's roll."

We drove out Gate 2 and headed for Checkpoint 7. Just before reaching the checkpoint the BC told me to turn off the road. We drove between two closed-up vendors' shacks into a rough field of hard furrows. The humvee bumped up and down.

"I don't think this is a road, sir."

"Keep going, Wilson."

We came to a low berm separating the field from a flooded pasture.

"Fuck," Captain Yarrow said. "Alright, turn around."

We got back on the road and went through Checkpoint

7. The BC had me hug the right side, searching for the route over the canal. We eventually hit a dirt road that led off into the dark. The BC told me take it.

Lieutenant Krauss radioed that the MPs had secured the site but still needed help. They were undermanned and unable to handle security, processing prisoners, and chasing down fleeing targets all at once. Captain Yarrow told Krauss we were on our way.

The road rose onto a wide berm running along a canal. We drove down one side until it stopped, then doubled back to a bridge we'd passed and crossed to the other. We followed the berms, a maze in bas-relief, not sure where we were going but definitely headed the right general direction.

Eventually we came to a dip where the road led off the berm and through a depression. We followed it down then up around a low hill onto another berm, lined on one side with concertina wire, running northeast by southwest along an even larger canal. *This* was the canal we had to cross. There was no way across. We stopped.

"That's the house right there," the BC said, pointing out a low, distant building surrounded by trucks. I looked with my NVGs: Martians making the green scene, maybe six hundred meters away.

We mounted up and drove until we came to a Bradley parked across the berm. Beyond the Bradley rose a wire-topped wall, BIAP's outer perimeter. Captain Yarrow scowled. He got out to talk with the Bradley commander, who didn't think there was any way across the canal from this side.

"You've gotta go around north," he said, "through Gate 7."

Captain Yarrow came back to the truck. "Head back to the CP," he said. It was nearly midnight.

He radioed Lieutenant Krauss and told him find another route. Lieutenant Krauss said he thought he had one that went through Abu Ghraib, west along the highway, but that he had to show him on the map.

As we pulled through Gate 2, Lieutenant Krauss radioed and said the MPs had called off the request. We pulled up to the CP and Captain Yarrow ordered senior leadership into the hooch for an After-Action Review. Everyone else was dismissed.

I unloaded my rifle, stripped my battle rattle, and bummed a smoke from Healds. We had little to say. The whole thing was too dumb. All I could think about was how soon I'd take off my boots, crack open my cot, and rack out.

Halfway through our smoke, Lieutenant Krauss came out and started digging in the humvee, at first leisurely then with growing panic.

"Wilson, you see the BC's sidearm?"

"No, sir," I said. "Why?"

"You sure?"

"Not since we rolled out. *Why?*"

"You might wanna get your gear back on."

He ran back into the CP. Healds and I put our gear back on. A few minutes later the BC, Lieutenant Krauss, and some other soldiers mounted up and we took two trucks, C6 and C5, out the gate.

"Lock and load," the BC said flatly, his empty white hands in his lap.

■ ■ ■

He decided we'd start at the last place we'd been, so we drove all the way back through Checkpoint 7 out to the berm, going the whole way at walking speed so we could search the road with flashlights.

My helmet bit into my temples. Next to me, Yarrow's neck was tight with tension, his mouth set in a grimace.

We drove up to the Bradley, inching across the sand, then came back. We stopped so Lieutenant Krauss could kick at shrubs and poke in shadows. We drove back to the field outside Checkpoint 7 and parked in the furrows, policing them on foot. Please, I prayed, somebody please attack us.

We drove back to the other side of BADW, back among the houses, scanning the ground at a creep. The moon had set. It was after three. I was too tired to care anymore. We stopped in the cul-de-sac and searched the ditch on foot. The Iraqi men came out to watch us again.

We drove back down the alley with the wall on the left and the vegetation on the right, the first place we'd gone, and there, next to the donkey cart, was the Battery Commander's pistol, its lanyard splayed in the dust. It still had a round chambered.

The BC smiled as he holstered his sidearm. "Good work, men. Let's head home."

Prerecorded bugles pierced the dark. "Crusader Rock!" Mondays and Wednesdays out the kaserne gate, running up past the Edelsteinminen into the wooded hills or down through the cobbled streets of Idar-Oberstein. Muscle-failure Tuesdays, push-ups, sit-ups. Thursdays training. Fridays the "fun run," the whole battery, straight down the hill to the Bahnhof then suffer back up.

Mondays were Preventative Maintenance Checks and Services, Tuesdays and Wednesdays Army business, Thursdays Sergeants' Time Training, and Fridays motor-pool closeout. Clockwork.

Omens foretold action, if not an invasion at least serious bombing. Global drama, weapons inspections, secret reports.

Good. Yes. We don't want the smoking gun to be a mushroom cloud.

Meanwhile, we grunted through the week, waiting for Freitag, aching for pilsner. We'd start a little on Wednesday night and sometimes Thursday too, and by the weekend hit full swing: hefeweizen, fräuleins, döner and schnitzel, jäger and techno, hazy days, hazier nights. There was Café Carré down the hill, our informal battalion pub, and there were The

Matrix and the Q and a dozen others, and oh, the herman girls. If you got sick of the barracks sluts at The Matrix, the ones who knew more guys in the unit than you did, you could always take the train to Köln or Saarbrucken or a cheap flight to Prague or Berlin. There was the Savoy, too, where for eighty euros you could relieve your tensions with a Thai girl, and Rot Frankfurt, only an hour away, a red-lit sex bazaar of six-story whorehouses, titty bars, and erotik-shops, jam-packed with Japanese businessmen. Or, like my roommate Villaguerrero, whose girlfriend was back home in Queens, kill the weekend with Grand Theft Auto.

Rumors said we're deploying, rumors said we're not. Ultimatums were issued. Bullwinkle said there's no fucking way we're going. Sergeant First Class Perry shrugged.

Briefly, after settling into the routine but before we knew we were going, I came back to myself. After the shocks of Basic Training and moving overseas, months of pure action, I began to see myself again and wonder who was this strange and stronger man in camouflage. The past clung fragile, like dying moss, barely felt. I kept in touch with my old ex-girlfriend but didn't tell her about Julia and Sabine, didn't tell her much—what was there to say?

What was I now, a soldier?

Fuck no. All a sham. I'd tricked them, and I'd ride these four years till I got out and made a new plan. I'd drink the pilsner, salute the butterbars, and hop to it, pretending I cared. I'd wear the stars and stripes on my shoulder and intone the soldier's creed. Too easy.

We're not going, Bullwinkle sneered. Of course we're not going. That's fucking retarded.

■ ■ ■

The president made a speech. Captain Yarrow told us be ready.
That Friday we had battalion formation. The colonel said we'd
be in the second wave, relieving the units currently moving in,
either to finish the war or more likely for SASO. We had a ten-
tative ship date at the beginning of May. Things'd be hopping
and popping till then, but the colonel insisted we'd all get a
week's leave.

We spent that weekend drunk—calls home to tearful moth-
ers—tense discussions with wives and kids—and Monday
started the paperwork, packing, predeployment logistics clus-
terfuck. We got issued new gear. We got ceramic SAPI plates for
the vests, but only two sets per battery. There weren't enough
desert boots. The DCUs were all the wrong sizes.

We watched the war on TV. We tracked Fox News, Nasiriyah
and Basra, the Old Breed, Rock of the Marne, the Screaming
Eagles. A few days later, we were told we'd have the next week
for block leave. I called my ex-girlfriend and asked her if she
wanted to come to Paris. I said I'd pay for everything.

squeezing the trigger releases the hammer,
which strikes the firing pin,
causing it to impact the primer

I woke to a dull sky, the air not yet warm. Early sun shot between massive apartment blocks to the east, gleaming off the turquoise dome beyond the north wall of Camp Lancer, gilding palm leaves, turning the streets to light. I crammed my patrol bag in my stuff sack and folded my cot.

I went out through the X-taped glass door to the balcony overlooking the courtyard. At the near end were two plastic chairs, and at the far end Captain Yarrow on his cot in a sleeping mask. I sat down, lit a smoke, and watched the sky brighten behind the mosque's minarets.

The city slept. To the north, an orderly middle-class neighborhood, a grid of streets, houses and yards, cars parked in driveways, shaded sidewalks. Kids played soccer there. To the east and west, thoroughfares lined by shops, market stalls, and cafés. Farther east stood high-rise apartments, but to the west the neighborhood thinned to a desolation of half-built homes and vacant lots bordering the UN compound at the Canal Hotel. Beyond that lay the borders of Sadr City, a warren of low wires and bristling aerials ruled by Ali Baba and Shi'a militias. To the south, beyond the defunct cigarette factory, the city stabbed up: minarets and smokestacks, the Green Zone's palace spires, Ba'athist icons, cyclopean dream-sculpture. In the distance a great blue egg hung against the sky like a fallen planet.

This was the only time all day the city breathed softly, evoking in the pale, slanting light imagination's Babylon, letting me feel for a moment like the poet I'd once been.

Later the temperature would top 115. Later I'd chamber a round and prepare to kill. Later the heat and stink of the day, the yelling faces, rancor, noise, and fury broiling and thrumming in waves off the blacktop would make me both want and fear needing a reason to pull my trigger, to feel my grip buck in my hands, to tear jagged red holes in men's flesh.

But for a moment, I had white-gold serenity glazing still arcades. I prayed in the morning's ease for grace, that I might find it somewhere out there over the wall and down shadowed alleys, under arabesques of purpled gold, beneath the hovering sun now glaring like a blooded eye.

Downstairs I showered in a makeshift stall between two ponchos. I put on the same sweat-stiff DCUs I'd worn the day before. I checked my combat load, made sure I had the BC's MP3 speakers. I did daily maintenance: oil, coolant, transmission fluid, belts. Struts, CV joints, tires. I checked the undercarriage for leaks.

■ ■ ■

Healds, Porkchop, and I headed for breakfast, walking through the shattered central hall of the bombed-out six-story ruin that stood between us and the DFAC. Wires and collapsed supports hung from the ceiling like vines. Holes blasted in the floor dropped into stinking sub-basements full of soda cans and rot, pits yawned in dusty corridors littered with rock and paper, the scent of things long dead wafting up from below. Stories of crushed stone loomed overhead, gashed rebar jutting and bristling rust-red through tunnels of light burrowing into the sky, broken granite, twisted metal. Sometimes chips of stone clattered down rubble-choked stairs and we'd flinch, imagining the whole thing collapsing in on us.

We came through the shade into a flash of light outside the DFAC where three sergeants lounged smoking cigars. We cleared our rifles and went inside. We got our food and coffee, slathered our plates with Texas Pete, then sat in plastic chairs at plastic tables and watched Fox News on a widescreen TV.

Glory. The salt and pepper shakers, the napkins and plastic forks and Styrofoam plates, the bad food, the worse coffee, even the ketchup packets and juice boxes glowed sublime, transcendent, essential. I cherished it. I needed it. I relished those eggs and that coffee and the witless ballyhoo on the satellite news, dizzily feeling for a moment like a man in a world where people had *opinions* about *events*, a world of APRs and Dow Jones numbers and mortgages and "thinking outside the box," a world where celebrities had breakdowns and we complained about cell-phone service and no one was trying to blow my fucking legs off.

A humvee burned, caught in the TV's frame like a votive. Honorable Secretary Donald Rumsfeld came on and said we'd reached a turning point. He was followed by a man with mousse in his hair standing on the roof of the Palestine Hotel, then a commercial for Viagra.

The *Hagakure* reads: "The way of the samurai is found in death. When it comes to either/or, there is only the quick choice of death. It is not particularly difficult. Be determined and advance . . . If by setting one's heart right every morning, one is able to live as though already dead, he gains freedom in the way."

I checked my weapon, patted down my armor plates, reminded myself that I was a soldier and this was my fucking job and I would damn well try to die with a little dignity.

Beyond the gate, the roads were already thick with cars, the skies hazy with smog. The chaos out there, the crazy Arabic writing and abu-jabba jabber, the lawless traffic, the hidden danger and buzz and stray bullets and death looming from every overpass pressed down on my soul like a hot wind. On the streets, eyes scanning trash for loose wires, I sank into the standard daily manic paranoid torpor: trapped in a broiling box with big targets on the sides, damned to drive the same maze over and over till somebody killed me. We rolled down Canal Road, our escorts weaving in and out of traffic, our hemmets and Iraqi semis chugging behind.

"Whatcha wanna listen to?" Captain Yarrow yelled over the engine.

"Whattaya got?" I shouted back.

He waved his MP3 player at me. "All kinds of stuff," he shouted.

I shrugged. He pushed a button. The Pet Shop Boys blasted from the speakers, singing "West End Girls."

whenever possible, you should avoid kill zones
such as streets, alleys, and parks

Driving the edge of Sadr City through bumper-to-bumper afternoon jam, I heard Lieutenant Krauss behind me yell, "Weapon on the left."

"What, where?" the BC shouted.

"Pistol. Pistol left side. Blue shirt. Pistol left."

Captain Yarrow grabbed the hand mike and I looked left, taking the scene in a glance. First it was a mass of bodies on a corner then I picked out two people arguing, a blue shirt, a pistol. Captain Yarrow said something into the mike and Lieutenant Krauss shouted, "He's aiming! He's aiming!"

Then two loud bangs behind my head. Brass dinged off my Kevlar and fell burning down the back of my shirt.

In my periphery, movement: Iraqis scattered and dove to the ground.

"There he goes!" shouted Krauss and fired two more times. I scrunched my head into my shoulders like a turtle, closing the gap between my helmet and armor. His empty shells plinked off me.

More shooting, ours, into the crowd. Across the street I saw a woman in black jerk up and swing to the ground.

"Cease fire, cease fire!" Captain Yarrow shouted. "Keep driving! Keep driving!"

Our windows wide, we sucked down exhaust, refinery smoke, propane, and the reek of sun-baked sewage. Crowds and traffic, buildings looming, cars and stucco, and we come up out of the mess onto the expressway, flow at a dead stop. Honking cars clogged the lanes, bumpers scraping fenders, brown faces glaring. Up ahead we could see American soldiers blocking the road, gun trucks and air guards, some big Army goatfuck.

"IED?"

"Didn't hear anything."

"Maybe it hasn't gone off."

"Could be a checkpoint."

"I think it's an IED."

Ahead on the left, Iraqis cut through a gap in the guardrail where a tank had rolled through. We moved slowly forward, filling the space opened by the fleeing cars.

"If it was a checkpoint, we'd be moving."

An Iraqi car started backing toward us, angling for the gap, and I laid on the horn. The driver stuck his head out of his window and pointed where he wanted to go. I flipped him off and goosed forward, ramming his rear. His hands flew up in anger.

"Good job, Wilson."

"You want me to go for that gap, sir?"

"No, we'll wait it out."

Twenty-five minutes later, broiling between the sun and the engine, I asked him again about the gap and he said yes. We edged over, nudging Iraqi cars out of the way with the brush guard, then swung around and took off back the way we came.

Captain Yarrow scanned the thick red and blue lines on his street map of Baghdad. He gave me directions across the 3ID bridge and into the Green Zone, but we got lost and wound up driving down a quiet, tree-lined boulevard along the Tigris. We passed a building spray-painted IRAQI COMMUNIST WORKERS' PARTY and a looted bank. Iraqis ambled along like it was Unter den Linden: couples holding hands, businessmen talking, heads bowed like mendicants. The smell of the trees cut the stink of exhaust, and in the dappled shade, it seemed we'd fallen through a rabbit hole into some alternate Baghdad, an oasis of brotherhood and peace.

Then we came up on a bridge and into the burning sky. Refinery fires licked the horizon.

A couple days later was the Fourth of July, and to celebrate they had a barbecue at the DFAC, hamburgers and hot dogs, and a *Star Wars* marathon in the compound's decrepit movie theater. After dinner, as the sun went down, Healds and I and some other guys went up on the roof of our building and smoked.

The upper six floors were off-limits because of snipers. The first few times, we went cautiously, for souvenirs.

Someone found a framed photo of Saddam. I got a hadji calendar and a picture of some guy getting an award. We also found what the Marines had left, a pile of shit, half-eaten MREs, and graffiti, FUCK IRAQ! and FIRST TO FIGHT!

Now we went up to watch the city: Sweeping cloverleaf interchanges, satellite dishes, pileups and traffic, six million souls watching DVDs and blogging, texting each other, hurrying through markets past sheep carcasses hung to bleed, spice sellers, bags of black, dried limes and reed baskets and old women haggling over okra, children running between stalls and down alleys, faces flickering in brass. Up out of the ancient garden of Sinbad's Baghdad and the nightmare of Saddam's Ba'athist dystopia grew the fiber-optic slums of tomorrowland, where shepherds on cell phones herded flocks down expressways and insurgents uploaded video beheadings, everything rising and falling as one, Hammurabi's Code and Xboxes, the wheel and the Web, Ur to Persepolis to Sykes-Picot to CNN, a ruin outside of time, a twenty-first-century cyberpunk war-machine interzone.

We watched cars zoom by below while Kiowas whickered overhead. An RPG went off in the distance, yellow sparks shrieking up at the helicopters ceaselessly circling, and we cheered. Tracers rose and fell across the sky like burning neon.

"I can't believe how much this place looks like L.A.," Burnett said.

Foster flicked a butt over the side. "You up here last night?"

"Naw."

"Wicked firefight."

The sun bled magenta across the horizon and the lights of the shops and cafés carved tiny scallops in the purple night. Cars without headlights flew down the road, weaving crazily. No traffic lights, no cops, no streetlamps. We waited for collisions, explosions, gunshots.

"This stupid fucking place," Burnett said. "I don't know why we don't just nuke it."

"What, Burnett, you wanna miss this? This is your *war*, man."

"Yeah. I wanted to meet interesting and stimulating people of an ancient culture and kill them."

"Shut your fucking face, Pyle, you sick piece of shit. You do not deserve to survive in my Corps."

"You ever notice Bullwinkle looks like Pyle?"

"Better watch out. He might shoot you in your underwear."

"He better fucking kill me if he thinks he can take my underwear."

"C'mon Burnett. I know you're a secret hadji lover. You blow your wad every night dreaming of some fat-assed hadji bitch riding your cock all *belelelelelelelah*."

"See that bitch today in the blue jeans? Shit hot. Just like a fucking American girl."

"Ass cheeks like melons. Honeydew melons."

"That's what I'm talking about, some sweet hadji ass."

"Fuck that. Hadjis stink."

"Shit, they wash up like normal people. Besides, you stink too."

"Yeah, but I ain't gonna fuck me."

"Unless you get some hadji twat, you're the only thing

that's fucking you. Just let yourself go for a few weeks till you're *really* filthy. Then you won't even notice."

"Negative. They're probably fucking diseased or some shit. Catch some freaky Mohammed clap."

"The Black Syphilis."

"Hell yeah. They got diseases here you ain't even heard of. I heard the PA say watch out for leeshamaneesis. What the fuck's that? We shoulda just fucking nuked this fucking fucked-up fuckhole from the fucking start. And then we come back and take the oil whenever we want."

There was a flash in the distance.

"Oh shit you see that?"

"Looked like an IED."

An Apache swung low over the gray cloud rising where the flash had gone off. We lit cigarettes as the last of the light faded, watching the Apache dip and swing like a giant angry wasp.

we are heroes in error;
what was said before is not important

The road bent away from the river and climbed a low berm. Oil glimmered purple in the sun in puddles, leaking through the berm's sandy skin. To our left stood hovels wreathed in wires and clotheslines and a flock of raggedy children, shoeless, hooting and pointing. Far to the west lay the outskirts of Baghdad, smudged with haze. We turned past a wrecked BMP slouched inert on the shoulder.

"It's right up here somewhere."

We passed some blown-out tanks half hidden in the palms to our right, then hit a road leading around the village toward the city. The BC pointed and I turned and we drove by the husk of a building, just two ruined walls standing in the shimmer like sundial hands.

"It should be right here," the BC said.

I scanned the earth for telltale fins, black mounds, glints of aluminum casing.

"Pull off over there."

The BC and Lieutenant Krauss got out. C27 pulled aside

and Staff Sergeant Smith joined them. I dismounted and stood smoking, watching the perimeter.

Two older hadjis in man-dresses walked toward us from the village. The flock of children from before overtook them, rushing at us.

"Ishta," I shouted at the kids.

They jabbered back. "Mista, Mista! MRE!"

"Uskut," I yelled. They laughed and capered.

We didn't have a proper translator, but the manager of our hadji work team spoke a little English. The BC called him over and tried to ask the two villagers if they could help us find the ammo cache.

"Boom-boom," Captain Yarrow said, gesturing with his hands.

The two villagers spoke. The team manager listened and nodded and smiled. "Is bombs no here," he told Yarrow. "No bombs. People good, Bush good. Saddam bad."

"No, not people's bombs," the BC said. "Old bombs. Saddam bombs. We're here to clean them up. Tell them we're here to take the old bombs away."

"Oh yes, yes. Okay good. No problem." The team manager turned back to the two men and they chatted back and forth.

"Mista!" one of the kids shouted at me. "You give me dollar!"

"Fuck off," I said. "Ishta."

They laughed and pushed each other toward me.

The team manager turned back to Captain Yarrow. "He say no bomb. Bomb bad. No bomb. He say Saddam bad, no bomb. He say al-Ameriki come, go bomb."

"Go bomb?"

"Go bomb, bomb." The team manager mimed hauling something off.

"Take bomb?"

"Yes, take bomb! No problem!"

"What about the tanks? Is there anything over by the tanks?"

"Tank?"

"The tanks." Captain Yarrow hunched his shoulders and rocked his body back and forth. "Brrrrrrrrrum," he growled, swinging his head side to side.

"Ah, tank, yes. No. Yes. No problem."

The kids edged forward and I waved my rifle at them. They shrieked and scattered, then reformed in a mass. They laughed and pointed.

"Mista, you give me."

"Mista, MRE."

"Ishta," I said.

"Ishta, ishta!" they shouted back.

"He say yes, bomb and tank, yes. There, there. No problem."

"Great," said Captain Yarrow. "Tell him thank you, and to keep his people back while we're working. Tell him it's very dangerous."

We drove back up the road, where we found a small cache of tank and mortar rounds in the palms, hidden behind a berm. It took about two hours to clear everything. The kids kept running over and we had to keep chasing them off.

■ ■ ■

Driving down the road something exploded behind us, shaking our truck, then something else exploded and the radio squawked: "GRENADE GRENADE CRUSADER TWO-ZERO-THREE WHAT'S YOUR STATUS?"

"STATUS GREEN OVER."

Captain Yarrow stuck his head out the window, trying to see the convoy behind us. He told me pull over.

"Sir?"

"Pull the fuck over, Wilson!"

I eased off the gas and slid to the shoulder. Shots to the right, AKs, close.

"FIRE RIGHT SIDE! RIGHT SIDE!"

Healds's rifle went off pop-pop-pop.

"I can't see," Lieutenant Krauss shouted.

"Keep going, keep going!" the BC yelled.

I swung back onto the road and took the convoy up to fifty. The shooting kept on, mostly us, then petered out.

Captain Yarrow got on the radio and called for a status report. Everyone responded except Two-zero-two. Yarrow screamed into the hand mike: "Crusader Two-zero-two, Crusader Two-zero-two, what's your status, over? Respond! Respond!"

No answer. I exhaled, staring at the road. The world was clearer now, numinous, drenched in light.

"Crusader Two-zero-two!" Captain Yarrow shouted. "What's your status, over? Respond!"

My armor plate lay on my chest like a lover's head. I needed a cigarette.

"Any Crusader element, this is Crusader Six, does somebody have eyes on Two-zero-two?"

"CRUSADER SIX, THIS IS CRUSADER TWO-ZERO-FIVE

NOVEMBER. WE HAVE EYES ON TWO-ZERO-TWO, STATUS GREEN, BREAK. THEY DON'T HAVE A RADIO. OVER."

"Well make sure they get a goddamned radio," Captain Yarrow shouted into his mike. "Somebody give me a sitrep."

"SIX, THIS IS ONE-SIX NOVEMBER. TWO GRENADES FROM THE OVERPASS, BREAK. ONE FELL WIDE AND THE OTHER BOUNCED OFF THE BACK OF TWO-ZERO-THREE."

"All Crusader elements, this is Crusader Six. Keep a tight eye on your twelve. Watch those overpasses and don't take any chances. Let's get this load of ammo to Wardog."

"You see who was shooting at us, Healds?" Lieutenant Krauss asked.

"Uh . . . honestly, sir?"

"Yes."

"Not really."

At the next overpass I saw two hadjis crossing above so I swung wide right to keep the convoy from passing beneath them. As we drove into the shadows under the arch, I heard the trucks behind open fire.

*desiring democracy and modernization immediately
is a good example of what
a westerner might view as an arab's "wish vs. reality"*

Sergeant Chandler read *Maxim*. Lieutenant Krauss and
Captain Yarrow watched *Braveheart* in the captain's room. I
sat listening to this mix CD a girl had made me and rereading the letter she'd sent. Rifle fire popped off close. Sergeant
Chandler flipped a page of his magazine.

Lieutenant Krauss stomped in, weapon in hand. "What
was that?"

Sergeant Chandler shrugged.

The LT went downstairs, then returned a few minutes
later and went back to *Braveheart*. Healds came in and asked
me if I wanted to smoke and I told him I'd just had one.

I read the girl's letter again, amazed at how far away it
came from, how ignorant she was of my world. I picked
up a pen and paper to reply but found myself struck
dumb, washed in a frustration humming like great
engines.

■　■　■

The next day we got a late start and by the time we hit the streets, the shooting was heavy. A shot every few seconds, every minute or so a long clatter of fire. Some close, some farther away. Sometimes we'd hear the ping of nearby ricochet, though it didn't seem like we were being targeted.

We pulled off onto a frontage road, searching for the first cache. Captain Yarrow peered at the map, at his GPS, then back at the map, sometimes giving directions. For myself, I watched the tree line, the buildings in the distance, the earth and sky, eyes wide for the spray of impact or a muzzle flash. I felt preternaturally alert and also numb. Shots cracked out all around us.

Captain Yarrow directed us into a wide, vacant lot, about a block off Canal Road.

"Fuck this," Healds hissed.

"You guys nervous?" Lieutenant Krauss asked.

Loud zing of ricochet.

"Fuck no, sir. This is bread and butter. I love it when the world goes batshit and everybody's shooting all over the goddamned place."

"You worry too much," the LT said.

There was an overpass to the west and a cluster of half-built three-story homes to the north. Beyond that, northwest, lay Sadr City.

"Stop here," Captain Yarrow said. He and Krauss got out and Healds and I stayed in the truck.

"You see anything?" Yarrow yelled as he and the LT stomped around searching for shells.

"No, sir."

"Follow me," he said. We circled the field, shots popping

all around us, then the two officers got back in the truck. Another zing, another ricochet.

Captain Yarrow had me drive northwest toward Sadr City. As we neared the ghetto, the shooting got louder and louder until we swam in the noise of it. Shots and echoes and ricochets wrapped us in a cacophony like industrial dance. I waited for the first rounds to puncture the windshield or the canvas roof.

The next site was a larger lot, five blocks long and two blocks wide, full of stagnant pools and blackened muck. Driving in circles through the filth we eventually found several hundred mortar and light artillery rounds scattered in and around a stinking puddle. Fins stuck out of the oily water like dead metal sharks. Most of the rounds were scattered, black, and misshapen, the obvious remains of an explosion. Captain Yarrow marked the site on his map and had me drive the corners. The shooting let up for about half an hour then redoubled, manic, the sky raucous with metal.

The BC had us drive to the UN compound at the Canal Hotel. We parked our trucks around back and went in for lunch. Weapons and armor were prohibited, so we left everything with Foster, who volunteered to stand guard if we brought him a plate. On the way in, we passed fleets of bright blue, brand-new SUVs marked in day-glo orange: UNHIOC, UNHCR, UN, UNESCO. We'd seen them driving the streets, clean and shining, stunning colors blazing against the city skelter.

"Remember," Captain Yarrow said, "we're representatives of the United States of America. Be on your best behavior."

The doors opened to beatitude: clean and quiet, chilled, orderly, bureaucratic assurance washed in light and AC hum. A woman wafted by in a skirt, trailing eddies of designer scent, and our heads turned together following her gold earrings, her swinging curves and lean calves, her high heels clipping along the stone. A man in a jacket and tie passed the other way, carrying thick files in soft pink hands.

Captain Yarrow led us to the cafeteria, where again we stood dazed, this time by the heaps of food on the serving line, the gleaming elegance of the white tablecloths and smiling servers. They had roast chicken and fresh salad, rice and hummus, bread and fruit and sauces, all on porcelain plates with metal servingware, drinks in glass tumblers and—impossibly—ice cream.

We piled our plates high and feasted like jackals.

I wondered as I ate: maybe when I got out I could do this, be one of these people, get the thrill of war without all the Army bullshit. I could be a war correspondent or maybe some kind of humanitarian. It'd be perfect: I'd get the adventure but I'd get to bathe, eat well, and drink cognac with beautiful, intelligent women. I'd have the internet, cynical-wise conversation, and the warm fulfillment of knowing I was doing something *good*. For the *world*.

My mouth full of chicken, I flushed with obscure yearning, loneliness, and the sudden desire for these people to see me as one of their own, to see how enlightened I really was beneath my salt-stiff DCUs, how different from the thugs I'd come in with. I wanted to talk with these business-casual

cosmopolitans about human rights and cultural program-
ming, Michel Foucault and Zadie Smith. I wanted to
corner the woman in the skirt, take her hands in mine, and
convince her: I used to read *Whitman*. I used to read *Joyce*.

After finishing our ice cream, a few of us wandered down
the hall to the café to smoke. There were more men and
women there, more UN types drinking tea and coffee. A
talking head on the TV said that Uday and Qusay had been
killed.

the primer ignites the propellant in the round

gas from the burning propellant
pushes the projectile along the weapon

Captain Yarrow watched *Black Hawk Down*. I stood in the
doorway behind him, eyeing the jumpcuts flashing Holly-
wood prettyboys acting tough.

"You don't get enough war during the day, sir?"

"What's that, Wilson?"

"I said you don't get enough war during the day, sir?"

"I'm watching for pointers. This is tactical review."

"Sir?"

"Yeah. Good lessons learned. Like, bring water. See, if
they'd done that, they would've been in much better shape.
Their NCOs needed to be doing better precombat checks
and inspections. You can learn a lot from this, Wilson.
You'll be an NCO yourself someday."

"Roger, sir."

"Pull up a chair."

"No thanks, sir."

I went back to the common room. I looked around at the
same tired, dirty faces I saw every day, then sat and flipped

through the letters I'd saved up from girls back home—artifacts from hyperspace. Who were these women doing roller derby in Wisconsin, meditating, hiking mountains? Who were they to say they missed me and hoped I was safe? What the fuck did they know about it? Where were their hands, their smells, their voices? What would they think if I shoved my rifle in their faces and screamed at them, "Kif! Oguf!"

I did fifty push-ups then went downstairs to smoke.

Geraldo had lit a plastics fire in a trash barrel, filling the courtyard with toxic fumes. I walked past him, out through the yard toward the wall, thinking I could go right over—escape into the night and find some nice Kurdish family to take me in who wouldn't cut my throat in my sleep. I could walk around in regular clothes, sit in a café and bullshit about politics. I could even turn hadji, learn to read the Koran, grow a mustache, wear a man-dress, glare at Ameriki humvee. I could learn to breathe again.

I made my way back toward the barracks. I brushed my teeth, went upstairs, took my cot out onto the balcony, and unrolled my patrol bag. Shots rang out. I listened to *The White Album* for a while, then took off my glasses and closed my eyes.

Used to date a beauty queen, olee-olee-annah. Now I date my M-16, olee-olee-ann-ah. Oh-lee-ohhhh, olee-olee-annah, oh-lee-ohhhh, olee-olee-annah. Used to drive a Cadillac, olee-olee-annah. Now I hump it on my back, olee-olee-ann-ah.

We tumble off the bus in the night, screamed at by a redheaded specialist who briefs us on what we're forbidden and gives us two minutes each in curtained stalls to dump out all our chewing gum, candy, novels, magazines, CD players, nonprescription medication, booze, cigarettes, drugs, video games, and whatever else we thought we could sneak past the drill sergeants. We're warned this is our last chance. We're told someone will think they're the exception. They're wrong, the specialist says. They will be the example.

On Monday morning, just like in a movie, our first round brown breaks the dark shouting and banging a can. We muster, go to chow, and it starts: forms, shots, ID cards, briefings, initial uniform issue. Somebody tells the drill sergeant there's no hot water in the showers and he puts on a concerned face and says he'll check on it. Thursday we take our initial PT test: thirteen push-ups, seventeen sit-ups, run a mile in eight thirty.

Three guys fail out and get recycled to Fat Boy. The next morning the rest of us post with our bags in the yard.

Then the real *drill sergeants arrive. Heads shaved to bullets, eyes dooming searchlights, boots gleaming liquid pain, they lunge at us in their Smokey Bears lucid, swift, and terrible. At once they're on the attack, herding us into cattle cars, and we stumble in on each other, dazed and sweating.*

Inside the cattle car hot and close with the stench of fear, I watch the fort roll by through a tiny window. We stop and they scream and we fall out and form up. There are legions of them and all they do is yell. You flinch, move, wobble, mutter, blink—Wham—there's a fucker on your eyeball like you just raped his mom. We line up and get helmets and rucksacks and laundry bags full of equipment. As we waddle with our gear into lines in the sun, the drill sergeants lash into us. They form us back up and issue precise instructions for the arrangement of our equipment, this goes here, that there, you have thirty seconds and what the fuck are you thinking, Private? You have completely jacked your entire day and do you think . . . Are you eyeballing me, Private? Are you fucking eyeballing me?

We're loaded back on the cattle cars panting. The trucks cross to the training side. We stop and they're on us again, faster Private you wanna die, you gonna die you move that slow, you think this is summer camp, you think I'm here to—you best move Private—Are you eyeballing me?

They start simple: stack things this way, you have thirty seconds. You fail, get down and push. Move over here, stack everything that way, you have thirty seconds. You fail. Get down and push. We get some kind of speech. Get everything up to the barracks, pick a bunk and stow your gear and return to the drill pad. You have two minutes.

You fail. Get down and push. You have to learn the value of time, Private, you must learn the value of time. A lot can happen in two minutes.

The lunatic fascist fuck in the funny hat who made us call him Drill Sergeant gathered us around him in a small circle, forty stinking boys, and had us one by one say our names, where we're from, and why we joined the army.

His name was Drill Sergeant Krugman. He was our supreme fistfuck, a light infantry sniper, and I still think back fondly to our first day there, his big black boots shining in my face as he walked up and down the line, the pain in my arms and chest and hips, the puddle of sweat on the floor under my chin. Down, he said, and we lowered ourselves to the level of his rippled boot soles. Up, he said, and we pushed past the toe gleaming like a vulcan mirror, past the ankle where the boot narrowed, up the leather along the leg where it widened, the laces taut and strong, hide smooth, to the very top, where snugly bloused trousers slid into the leather like a hand into a glove.

Three-five, Drill Sergeant, we gasped, weak and broken. We did not deserve his love. Down, he said. And we went down.

Now his eyes scanned the circle of shaved skulls.

"How about you, pinhead? Why'd you decide to pollute my army?"

The googly-eyed private looked up. "Uh, my name's Jimmy Wuckertt, Drill Sarnt, and I'm from Bahstan. I, uh, joined ah, you know, ah, nine-eleven. Drill Sarnt." The truth: a long night of the soul, in jail for possession with intent to sell, when he realized that if he kept dealing and smoking, it was sooner rather than later he'd be doing way more than ninety days. Of course you're not supposed to be able to get in the army with drug offenses like that on your record, but there's a waiver for everything.

"And you, Carruthers, you fat fuck?"

A brick-headed troglodyte: "Jason Carruthers, Drill Sergeant! I'm from Indianapolis, Indiana, hooah. I joined the Army to shoot stuff! Jump out of planes and kill people! Drill Sergeant!"

There were a couple hooahs.

"We'll see. And what about you, Thorton?"

"Hi." Thorton waved at us. He was a big guy with an ape's face and monstrous ears. "I'm Albert Thorton. I'm from Nebraska, but I was actually living in Illinois. Uh, well, actually I joined the army for a couple of reasons, Drill Sergeant. I was a teaching assistant, working on my PhD in history, on the one hand going further into debt and on the other, after September 11, it sort of seemed . . . I mean, it felt like I wasn't doing anything with my life. I wanted to do something important. Something meaningful. So, I felt like I should . . ."

"Shut your cakehole, Thorton. You're a fucking college professor?"

"Well, I was teaching but . . ."

"Alright, Professor, shut your goddamned mouth and push."

Thorton was confused.

"You better dad-gummed start pushing right now, *Private."*

Thorton dropped to his hands and pushed himself up and down.

"*You.*" *Drill Sergeant Krugman turned, pinning me with his cold blue eyes.*

I saw myself as he saw me, skinny-necked, bird-beaked, blinking anemically from behind clunky-framed Army-issue Basic Combat Glasses, and wanted nothing more than to erase myself from his vision, erase my poems, my hippie past, erase everything but the camouflage BDUs I wore and my determination to make it through.

"Nine-eleven," I shouted, "Drill Sergeant!"

most iraqis see themselves as a persecuted people
and hold the coalition forces, as the occupying power,
responsible for resolving all personal and national problems

I sat in one of the ratty chairs scrounged to furnish Sergeant First Class Perry's "reading room" and opened my MRE: Charms, Cappuccino packet, Country Captain Chicken, Pasteurized Jalapeño Cheese Food Spread, Wheat Snack Cracker, and Noodles with Butter Sauce. The Noodles and Charms went in the trash. The entrée I deboxed and slid in the MRE heater bag, into which I poured some water. Then I fit the bag and entrée back into the box and placed it all, as per instructions, "against a rock or something." I leaned back, listening to the heater's chemical hiss, my transistor radio's crackle, and the BBC announcer's accent, so *civilized*, doing cricket scores.

A boom sounded somewhere in the city and I jerked. Voices, talking, nothing—I wanted to be on mission or I wanted quiet. Sergeant First Class Perry was the same, which is why he'd commandeered this room, closed off as it was from the gymnasium that housed our new barracks.

The gym was a vast bedlam, divided into rough thirds by battery, about two hundred joes all told. The main areas were subdivided into loose platoon AOs, squads, and individual cubicles carved out with plywood and poncho liners.

A guy in Bravo Battery named Pizza had started walking around naked. When he got up one afternoon and pissed all over the floor, he was put on suicide watch. He screamed in the night, eerie piercing howls of terror. Villaguerrero punched some dude from Alpha, got his rank taken away, and was tasked to DIVARTY. Bullwinkle crashed a hemmet into the compound's main gate, tearing open a fuel tank and spilling gas everywhere. Lieutenant Krauss had started talking to himself.

The Iraqi Governing Council was appointed. General Abizaid said our enemy was waging "a classical guerrilla-type campaign." Rumsfeld said we'd turned a corner. The Jordanian embassy got hit by a suicide bomber—foreign insurgents, they said, probably al-Qaeda.

We were told to be on the lookout for an orange and white sedan.

I took out the entrée bag and cut it lengthwise. The smell of cheap curry and preservatives made me gag. I set the entrée aside to cool and squeezed Pasteurized Jalapeño Cheese Food Spread on a Wheat Snack Cracker.

Anxious music cut the cricket scores: "Breaking news at the BBC. Just minutes ago the UN headquarters in Baghdad came under attack. We go now live to Baghdad . . . Adrianna?"

"Hello, David. We're live from Baghdad. US forces have sealed off a sizable area around the UN headquarters here in response to what initial reports seem to be saying was a suicide car bomb attack just moments ago. There's no word yet on any casualties sustained inside the compound.

"The bomb was heard throughout the city, yet another in what has become a typical series of daily explosions. United Nations representatives and American military personnel have so far refused to confirm speculation as to the number of casualties or how the attack may have penetrated security, though it is worth mentioning that in recent days the UN had reduced its security profile and decreased the number of American soldiers stationed there."

"Have any groups claimed responsibility for the attack, Adrianna?"

"No, David. Representatives have so far refused to speculate on which group if any might have carried out the attack, and there have not as yet been any statements made claiming responsibility. I can tell you that unidentified sources say the attack was committed with a truck bomb loaded with high explosives, and that the driver used an unguarded access road to enter the compound."

I thought of the woman in heels trailing her complex scent. I ate my Wheat Snack Cracker.

"Adrianna, can you describe the situation there?"

"Well, David, it's difficult to get close to the scene. US forces have sealed off the compound and are blocking the main roads with battle tanks. Soldiers are patrolling the area and there's clearly an emergency plan in operation. It seems from here as if one corner of the UN building has collapsed entirely. Military personnel are currently searching the rubble for survivors."

Sergeant First Class Perry came in the door and glanced at the radio. "What's up, Wilson?"

"UN got bombed, Sergeant."

"That so?"

"Suicide truck bomb."

He grunted and sat on his cot. I ate my Country Captain Chicken.

aline the front and rear sight with the target
and squeeze the trigger

Our days at CAHA Wardog began when the hadji semis
arrived. We worked them in pairs. One soldier would
sling the other's rifle and guard the driver. The other
would climb into the cab and tear covers off seats, sweep
through knickknacks on the dash, pull up floor mats,
shout down, "What's this, huh? What's this for? What's
in here? You fucking hiding shit, huh? You think you'll
get over, do ya? Hey, look at this guy. He thinks he's a
fucking exception."

After the cab, we'd search the truck's exterior, checking
the wiring, the engine, and the underside of the trailer bed.
We'd check their fuel tanks. Finally we'd search the driver
himself, patting him down along his man-dress, turning
him around, making him take off his kaffiyeh.

"Do a complete search," shouted Staff Sergeant Smith.
"Check their junk. They could be fucking hiding bombs in
their taint."

The hadjis stank of old sweat. We made fun of them,

scowling, shouting, laughing. We pointed at a fat one, mimed his belly, and asked, "Baby? You have baby?" His friends laughed and he blushed, frowning.

At the end of the day, we searched the hadji workers as they left. "What the fuck is this, you little fuckwad?"

I looked over. Burnett, towering over one of the hadjis, held an MRE bag in his fist, shaking it. He shoved the hadji, who stumbled back and put his hands up. "No Mista, no," he bleated.

"This fucker's got nine-mil rounds in his MRE bag. Trying to fucking steal from us."

"Lock 'em down," shouted Staff Sergeant Smith.

I threw my helmet on and grabbed my rifle.

"Mista," one of them said. He put his hands out in supplication.

"Shut the fuck up, bitch! Uskut your ass!"

"Mista, Mista," he said.

"Uskut, bitch!" I shouted, sticking my rifle in his face.

To my left, one of the hadjis got up and Burnett forced him back. There was a clack on my right as Stoat chambered a round, then a series of clacks as we all followed suit. The hadjis got panicky.

"No, Mista," one said, climbing to his knees.

"Sit the fuck down, bitch!" I shouted, bringing my rifle to the ready. He sat back down.

One of the hadjis on my right whispered something to another and Stoat jumped at him: "No talking!"

Lieutenant Krauss called higher, waited for higher to call

back. The shift foreman spoke some English, so they tried to use him to talk to the hadjis. We waited.

"Sit the fuck down!"

"Deep Steel Three November, this is CAHA Wardog."

"Roger Deep Steel, CAHA Wardog standing by."

"He say no Ali Baba," the foreman said. "He say mistake, mistake."

"Fucking mistake is right. Biggest mistake he ever made."

"No Ali Baba, Mister."

"Shut your fucking dirty mouth."

"Roger Deep Steel, CAHA Wardog standing by."

"He say for to melt. To make for, eh, car?"

"Bullshit."

"No Ali Baba, Mister."

"You fucking Ali Baba if I say you Ali Baba. Now shut your fucking face."

"Roger Deep Steel, CAHA Wardog still standing by . . . Roger Deep Steel, this is CAHA Wardog. We've got a . . . Roger . . . Roger. Roger. Roger. Standing by."

"No Ali Baba, Mister."

"This is the last fucking time I'm telling you to shut your goddamned mouth."

One hadji jumped up and ran for it. Duernbacher tackled him. They twisted his arms behind his back and zip-stripped his thumbs together and left him face down in the sand. Duernbacher slapped him in the back of the head. "Silly fucking hadji. Trix are for kids."

Eventually Battalion sent instructions, and we picked five hadjis to take with us back to BIAP: the one who'd tried to steal the rounds; his brother, slightly younger; the guy who'd made a run for it, a badass in a Def Leppard t-shirt; another, in a man-dress, who seemed to be trying to ignore us; and lastly the crew foreman. We lined them up, except the one we'd already tied, twisted their arms behind their backs, and zip-tied their thumbs together as tightly as possible. We blindfolded them with abdominal bandages and tape. We loaded the thief and his brother in the back of a humvee and the other three in the bed of a hemmet. We sent the other hadjis home and told them not to be late to work tomorrow.

At Battalion we stood in the parking lot half-watching the hadjis, joking and fucking around while they were taken in one by one to be interrogated by S-2. We untied their blindfolds and cut their zip-ties. There were dark circles around their thumbs and blood where the plastic had cut into their skin. Burnett and Stoat took an order for Burger King and got us all dinner. I sat on a Jersey barrier with my gun in my lap, chowing on my Whopper, watching the hadjis in our humvee.

The light faded and the sky darkened to purple. The temperature dropped and BIAP's streetlights buzzed on.

"Mista," one of the hadjis said, "Mista." He made a gesture like he had to pee. I waved him out, he climbed down, and I walked him to the porta-john.

"You try anything, I'll shoot you in your face," I said.

He went in and came out a few minutes later. I walked him back to the truck.

It was dark now and hard to see in the back of the humvee,

so I cracked a chemlight and tried to hand it to the hadji. He wouldn't take it. I shoved it at him. "Take it," I said. He shook his head and waved his hands.

I tossed the chemlight in his lap and he shouted and jumped back, brushing it away with the back of his hand. We all laughed. He crouched back and brought his palms gingerly up to the chemlight, as if it gave off heat.

Lieutenant Krauss came out later. We blindfolded and zip-tied all the hadjis again and took off. We tried to take them to Camp Cropper, BIAP's prison complex, but the MP said we didn't have authorization.

"We have authorization from the mayor's cell," said Lieutenant Krauss.

"That doesn't matter, sir," the MP at the gate told him. "I need paperwork from Division."

"Okay, stand by." Krauss got on the radio to Battalion. After a few minutes he came back to the MP.

"Alright, I talked to our S-2 and he said we're supposed to bring these prisoners here to Camp Cropper."

"Sorry, sir. I need authorization from Division."

"But we're supposed to bring them here."

"No can do, sir. I need paperwork."

"Well, what are we supposed to do with them?"

"Play duck-duck-goose for all I care, sir. There's a POW processing station down the road. Why don't you take 'em down there."

"We were told to bring them here."

"Like I said, sir, I need authorization from Division. High-value prisoners only."

"But these aren't POWs."

"POWs, enemy combatants, civilians, doesn't matter. Just take 'em down the road to the MP station and they'll help you out."

"Where's this station?"

"It's just down the road on the right. Before the airfield."

We drove down the road and went past the airfield, then turned around came back the other way took the first left and wound up driving down this alley though a cluster of deserted buildings. Then we came back out to the main road and turned right and drove past the airfield and down the road until we came to 123rd MSB, which was the first right after the airfield but clearly not where we were going, so we turned around again and this time took the next left after the left we'd taken before, which led to a guarded compound with a locked gate which the guard wouldn't even tell us what it was much less let us in, but he did give us directions to the MP station, so we drove back down the road and found the right turn and pulled into a brightly lit compound, the largest section of which was surrounded by nested chain-link fences topped with triple-strand razor wire. Hadjis in orange jumpsuits and ankle cuffs shuffled chained in trios through the yard inside the fence.

We parked and downloaded the prisoners and took off their blindfolds. Lieutenant Krauss went in to talk to the Sergeant of the Guard. Our hadjis shivered in the chill.

"Probably fucking insurgents and shit."

"Even if they sold the rounds, they'd get used on us anyway."

"Fucking hadjis."

Burnett spit on the ground in front of the one in the

Def Leppard t-shirt. The hadji glared up at him. "You want some?" Burnett barked. "Eyes on the ground!" Burnett pointed. "Put your eyes on the ground!"

The hadji glared up.

"Get your eyes down, shithead." Burnett grabbed the man by the back of the neck and pushed his head toward the ground. "Watch the dirt."

Lieutenant Krauss came out and asked Staff Sergeant Gooley and me to follow him inside to help with the paperwork. He had a list of the hadjis' names along with the info that came up in interrogation, and we filled out two double-sided forms for each one, going over *address of suspect* and *identifying marks/tattoos*. Mostly we filled in *unk* and *n/a*.

Eventually we finished and handed the forms to the SOG, who stacked them in the corner with a pile of other forms then turned to a lanky, dark-haired corporal. "Hey, Sto, go grab some guys and process these EPWs, would you?" We stood outside watching the first two get processed—screamed at, kicked, manhandled, handcuffed, then led away to get their very own orange jumpsuits. Burnett and some of the others clapped.

"I wonder what's gonna happen to those guys," I said.

"They'll be processed. There'll be an investigation," Lieutenant Krauss said.

"What the fuck do you care?" Burnett glared at me.

He was right. What the fuck did I care?

wars are not won by machines and weapons
but by the soldiers who use them

As the fall wore on, the weather got colder. Gray clouds swept in, obscuring the sun. Porkchop regaled us with tales of going home on leave, how much he drank, how hard he fucked his wife. Most of all, he talked about his 'Vette and its mods. He got nitro, new tires, fat rims. He got a new tattoo, too, on his calf, an eagle wrapped in the stars and stripes, clutching bloody rags in its talons. A single tear fell from the eagle's eye; behind the bird rose the smoking silhouettes of the Twin Towers.

"You like that, huh?"

"Nice," I told him. "Real classy."

"The rags are like ragheads."

"Yeah, I get that. Very multicultural."

Porkchop squinted at me and tucked his trouser leg back in his boot. "Why you such a faggot, Wilson?"

"'Cuz I hate freedom, Porkchop."

He told me to go fuck myself.

■ ■ ■

We took our work team to the stables. CAHA Wardog had been one of Saddam's equestrian clubs before he'd decided to turn it into an ammo dump. There was hay and horseshit and garbage everywhere, which we had hadjis clean up with shovels and brooms.

The hadjis worked slow, taking long breaks and half-assing everything, so I'd go through the stables and shout at them: "Work harder! Get back to work! Shovel that shit! Git 'er done!" They glared at me and my rifle and I glared back, praying for an excuse. "Fucking get to work!"

"Man"— Sergeant Chandler shook his head—"you gotta relax."

"Somebody's gotta make sure they keep working," I said.

"You're gonna give yourself a heart attack."

"Yeah," Porkchop said. "Why you such a slave driver?"

"I told you, Porkchop, I hate freedom."

"Fuck you."

"No, fuck you, Porkchop. Really. Anytime."

I headed back through the stables. I found a hadji squatting in one of the side rooms, resting against a wall. I shouted at him to get the fuck back to work and he glared at me like he'd cut my throat if he could. I shouted again and stared him down till he picked up his shovel and got back to the horseshit.

"You give me cigarette," one said to Bullwinkle one day while we stood around watching them work.

"You give me blowjob?" Bullwinkle said back.

The hadji smiled.

"Blowjob?" Bullwinkle said, making an O with this mouth and jerking his head back and forth over his rifle barrel.

The hadji kept smiling. "No, Mista. No mota. You give me cigarette?"

"You ficky-ficky?" Porkchop asked him.

"No ficky-ficky," the hadji said, still smiling.

"Fuck off," I shouted, waving the hadji away. "Get back to work."

"No ficky, Mista," he said, ducking and grinning.

"You ficky good, huh?" Porkchop asked him.

"Get the fuck back to work."

The hadji glared at me and slunk off.

I knew better.

This wasn't who I was, who I was meant to be. I was *sensitive*. I'd been a *poet*. The solution seemed obvious: if I just shot a hadji, it'd all be okay. If I just killed one hadji, anyone, someone, then all the black bile, hatred, and fear would flow out of me like blood and water pouring from the wounds of Christ. I'd be transformed, transfigured. Please Jesus, I prayed, let me fucking kill somebody.

We came back each night and spent a couple hours relaxing, drinking vodka and Gatorade and watching *Sex and the City*. Samantha fucked a fireman, Charlotte got married, Carrie dumped Mr. Big and went out with Aidan, then got back with Mr. Big.

We downloaded crates of water and crates of MREs. We swept the barracks, swept the compound. We watched hadji bootlegs of *The Matrix Revolutions* and the new *Texas Chainsaw Massacre*. Some guys redeployed back, some other new guys showed up. Staff Sergeant Reynolds, Cheese, and Reading played *Halo*. Cheese begged us to quit calling him Cheese, and Burnett said he'd punch him in his fucking face if he didn't shut his goddamn cockholster.

I was driving and Staff Sergeant Gooley was saying to me how all of us who'd been out last night clearing the CAHA shouldn't have to be going out there again today because none of us had gotten enough sleep, then there was some shooting close behind the convoy, and the truck radio crackled: "FIRE FIRE. SHOOTERS ON THE BUILDINGS."

"Stop!" Staff Sergeant Gooley shouted. We heard M16s and SAWs answering AK fire, then the low thump of our .50s.

"CRUSADER THREE-SEVEN, WE'RE TAKING FIRE."

"Turn the truck around!"

I started to pull a three-point turn and as we swung the other way the trucks behind us started turning too, so we had to wait. There was more shooting from the highway. All the trucks turning around at once in the alley made a slow chaos of bumps and shouts. One of the trucks tried to drive out in reverse, its driver screaming, "Just back up! Back up!"

Staff Sergeant Gooley grabbed the hand mike. "This is Crusader Three-seven, gimme a sitrep!"

"ALL CRUSADER ELEMENTS CONVERGE ON THE NORTH-EAST BUILDING," Staff Sergeant Smith barked.

"This is Crusader Three-seven, somebody tell me what's going on, over," Staff Sergeant Gooley shouted into the radio.

"ALL CRUSADER ELEMENTS RETURN FIRE ON YOUR TARGETS."

More shooting, the *tock-tock* of our .50s. As we rolled slowly behind the other trucks back to the highway, we could see the rest of the convoy scattered between the alley's mouth and the nearest overpass. Crusader 5 sped down the highway on the other side, through a gap in the guardrail onto the shoulder toward a three-story building, Staff Sergeant Smith leaning out his window shooting wild with his M16. Figures ducked behind the wall up on the roof of the building and others ran along the overpass. One .50 traced a slow arc along the road, lobbing fat gobs of metal through the air, knocking chunks out of concrete. Porkchop rode the second .50, firing at the top of the building, his body shaking at one with the gun: "Yeah, get some! Get some! Fuck yeah! How you like it? Get some!"

"Over there," Gooley pointed, and I drove to the cluster of trucks by the building where Staff Sergeant Smith stood shouting.

"You three secure the rear of the structure, everyone else come with me." Staff Sergeant Smith rammed his shoulder through the front door. Men followed. Staff Sergeant Gooley told me to stay with the radio, then ran in after.

More shots came from the overpass and I swung open my door and slid sideways in my seat, pulling up my rifle and taking aim at the shadows ducking between the concrete supports. I hissed, exhaling, squeezing my trigger. I was surprised by the ease of it: just pull. My hadji ducked behind a support then dashed for the next, making his way toward the trees at the edge of the overpass. I fired again, aiming higher this time, the top of my iron sight to his right, above his head, leading but missing again and gritting my teeth and firing. Breathing.

"Crusader Three-six, this is Crusader Six. I need a sitrep."

My rifle bucked into my shoulder. The .50s punked away. It was like a carnival, a shoot-em-up stand on the midway, but as I fired again I felt light-headed and distant, third-person somehow. The figures on the overpass ducked from pillar to pillar, dodging fire, and finally disappeared off the far side. Porkchop shifted fire to the trees at the edge of the highway, dumping rounds into foliage.

Staff Sergeant Gooley ran out of the building and grabbed the hand mike. "Cease fire, cease fire, this is Crusader Three-seven say again cease fire."

"Crusader Three-seven, this is Crusader Six. I need a sitrep."

"Crusader Six, this is Crusader Three-six." Lieutenant Krauss broke through. "We're, uh, taking fire but, uh, it's under control now. Standby for sitrep. Break. All Crusader elements, this is Crusader Three-six, return to the highway and give me a perimeter."

"Three-six, this is Three-seven, we need to clear these buildings," Staff Sergeant Gooley said into the radio.

"Three-seven, this is Three-six, give me a perimeter, now. Out."

So we drove back down the highway and set up a perimeter, blocking traffic both ways.

Staff Sergeant Smith walked up to Lieutenant Krauss. "We gotta clear all them buildings, sir. They're out there."

"Sergeant, we're not prepared to cordon off a whole . . ."

"Sir, we need to clear them fucking buildings," Staff Sergeant Smith shouted up at him.

Krauss backed down. "Alright, Sergeant. Take some men and clear the buildings."

We spent the next two hours waiting while the clearing teams went through the cluster of buildings along the highway, kicking in doors and screaming at hadjis. They didn't find any weapons. After a while, Lieutenant Krauss called off the search, and we reformed the convoy, drove to CAHA Wardog, and ate lunch.

That night and the next day it was all anybody talked about, who shot what who where. I didn't feel any better and my soul didn't bleed like the wounds of Christ. What happened was the days got colder. I drew new rounds to replace the ones I'd fired. We ran patrols. We set up TCPs. We watched more *Sex and the City*, cleaning our rifles and arguing about who'd give better head, Charlotte or Carrie, and who we'd like to fuck up the butt.

We got a speech from Captain Yarrow telling us what a great job we'd done. He told us we were transitioning to patrols now, covering neighborhoods southwest of BIAP, and training in Close Quarters Combat.

I was scheduled for environmental leave toward the end of December and started counting days till I left.

We practiced kicking in doors. We learned to follow each other through a house, checking in closets and behind furniture, leading with our guns, shouting "Clear," "Door Left," and "Stairs." We learned to cover each other across open spaces, take out suicide bombers, turn and shoot without aiming.

On Thanksgiving President Bush came. We were out on a patrol that night, driving village streets in the rain and planning on MREs for dinner.

We watched *Top Gun*, *Pumping Iron*, and *The Shawshank*

Redemption. We wrestled, played pool and ping-pong, played touch football in the parking lot, argued and laughed and got in fights. Reading kept playing "Gimme the Light" and that "Birthday" song.

One day I walked up to the CP and First Sergeant Beaman came out grinning. "They captured Saddam," he said. "Caught like a rat in a trap."

"Great," I said. "We can go home now, right?"

"It'll be a real turning point," he said.

I nodded. "Now all we gotta do is find those WMDs."

"Hey, Wilson," he said. "Get down and push."

"Hooah, First Sarnt." I dropped and pushed until he told me to stop.

I decided to quit smoking. Attack Battery got hit with an RPG out on patrol, mostly minor injuries but one of the guys had to be evacked to Germany. Somebody in another unit was run over by a tank. I cleaned my rifle and waited for Christmas.

4 to 71 at 122nd. 9:59. Take the 10 to the 15, change down-town to the 77 and get off at 21st. 10:12.

I talk to my ex-girlfriend and we decide to try again. The trouble starts almost immediately, with my car's clutch grinding out as I drive in over the coast range from Newport. I make it to my mom's in Corvallis, but going to Portland the next day the clutch drops with a thunk, *and I have to get the car towed back to town, where it sits in my mom's driveway growing a skin of brown needles.*

It's a sign, of course—the sky full of signs that fall.

Things don't improve in Portland. I take the bus across town to a 7-Eleven, fill out an application, take the bus back across town to a nursing home, fill out another application. Rain falls, and I go to the library to search the internet for jobs and wind up shuffling the stacks, reading The Coming Anarchy *and* The Clash of Civilizations.

4 to the 72 at 82nd. 11:37. 12:19.

We go to a dinner party with some friends of hers. We eat tempeh stir-fry and drink IPA and talk about jobs, the local theater scene, and good, cheap places to eat. After dinner we pass a joint and the conversation gets grim, somebody says they can't stop thinking about on TV those bodies falling. Did we think everything had changed? Would they attack the Mall of America? We talk about blowback and globalization and how, yeah, on the one hand it seemed maybe we'd sort of caused it. Maybe we wanted it to happen. We talk about troop movements in the Hindu Kush.

3:58. 14 to 9 to 60th. 4:09. 5:23. Home.

I make pasta. We drink wine. The money dribbles away. I apply at Goodwill, Burgerville, Powell's, Denny's.

Thanksgiving comes and goes and Christmas too. Against the rain and winter skies, the garish decorations and relentless commerce bring not cheer but constant reminder of my downward spiral. No joy, no carols, not even Santa can save me.

One day, after spending two hours filling out a personality test at Walmart, I go down the strip mall to an Army recruiting office. The recruiter starts my packet. He asks me about drug use and criminal record. He tells me about bonuses and college money. He asks me what I want to do and where I want to go.

babylon

wounds to the stomach, prosecuted—many have moved to the cities, particularly Mosul, Kirkuk, and Sulaymaniyah Operation Resolute Sword divided into the Shi'a majority in the south and the Sunni who live mostly in the central part of the country around Baghdad have not been assimilated into the population are "Marsh Arabs" who inhabited the lower Tigris and Euphrates urban centers with Baghdad being Iraq my spear

population of two already pleaded to be those targets on the edge of the gallbladder and transverse colon; only those acts which can be said to be half measures, the national Kalashnikovs

with a gunshot wound through the rectum; and two with possible war seen war that will be fourteen more casualties arrived Operation Sidewinder CIA secret prisons at the military's Iraqi Advanced Trauma Life Support protocols for the administration of Bush's decision was over the last six

sometimes they arrested all adult males present the US citizen

military must adhere wholly by the low-value treatment
often including pushing Saddam

punching and kicking and striking with rifles heart of the cover
of darkness OPERATION IRON SABER after 2130, the White
House by remote control, we've ravaged disarmament in the
early morning hours Thursday they're apparently exploiting
the Arab fear of dogs and you, the city and two key avenues,
DETAINEE-14 and a totally widowed mother—he, Astya-
nax, which meant the questions of the local Coalition less
than a meter across and devoid of any more but the dainti-
est and choicest of morsels

                                                            surgical
burned down tired and went to sleep, he would lie
knowing neither want nor care, whereas the version here is
not simply the General might salvage judged (myself) and
I do not make
            filled with water, linking unstable
My spear! Surely I fear the prisoner's head and do good and
the people, the attacks brought coming, there is no doubt
therein, Coalition forces in the early OPERATION IRON JUS-
TICE turning but no gunfire in the government and the
challenge upon me, I will answer you and defend the world
TV from open rebellion: in the north, Mosul was a close
call and over time the Bradley fades. The US-trained Iraqi
police enter hell abased. Allah is striking selected targets
of wounded and many dead. He urges them to surrender
OPERATION IVY NEEDLE the west seems nervous, boys,
most surely the opening stages

police stations   other small attacks   intense heat

center and the Pentagon, he and his team Allah, your Lord, Babylon where the rebellion is Operation Red Dawn another road

the fall
(baghdad, 2003)

Saddam smiled, white teeth shining. A common picture in a common frame, by law others like it hung all over. Thought or feeling made no change—hating the picture was like hating the sun. Even here, Qasim thought, in our musty office: Saddam Saddam Saddam. This one's old, brown and fading, creased along one edge, the frame's glass cracked at the corner. Surely we should have it replaced. The picture, the desks, the floors, the walls.

The office was windowless, unventilated, stale. Three desks crammed against each other left a narrow perimeter for chairs. Qasim sat alone, leaning, pencil in his mouth, staring at Saddam, the Americans' deadline barely a week away.

Home? Or stay? For the forty-ninth time, Qasim heard Professor Hureshi tell him, "Go if you must, but I can't promise you anything. You know I have done everything I can to keep you on, but if you leave before defending, I would be very hard-pressed to justify holding your teaching position when there are others whose service recommends them. Who have advocates. You have been given every opportunity, Qasim—"

"But Professor, my wife . . ."

"You have been protected like a son."

"Let me . . . let me talk to my uncle. Please, Professor. Just a few more days."

And your wheedling worked, *again*, and Hureshi gave you till Wednesday, the last day of classes before the deadline. And now? Give up everything after working so hard . . . or stay here, cut off from Lateefah and mother, while . . .

Qasim twisted the end of his mustache, replaying the hours of teaching uninterested students, the longer hours grading, the years of study, tutoring, working odd jobs, doing accounting for his uncle, all the effort he'd put into the dissertation. And now when he phoned Lateefah, drained to the point of hopelessness, she only made it worse. Punishing him with her silence. Blaming him.

Maybe going back would give us another chance. You don't have to be a mathematician. Take some job in the Ministry of Water, teach high school geometry. It won't make up for . . . but maybe Lateefah—maybe she and I . . .

The door swung open and Adham flew in, throwing down a pile of manila folders, slumping into his chair: "What, my cousin, can you tell me, is so bloody hard about turning in your homework?" Adham raised one hand to heaven and covered his heart with the other. "I understand yes, the end is coming. I understand, yes, the Zionist crusaders are going to bomb us to rubble. I understand—am I not understanding?—that there is a better than fair chance almighty God in his infinite compassion has willed that our beloved university will be destroyed, our city wiped from the face of the earth, our friends and relatives charred to ash so that even the vultures and rats will be left starving in a waste so total it will make the Mongols' sack of the libraries seem like Eid al-Fitr, but my cousin, my brother, my friend, as a fellow mathematician and as a fellow teacher, let me ask you: is that any reason to not turn in your homework?"

"Well . . ."

"Do you know how many of my students turned in their work this week? Two! Barely half the class even bothered to show up! And Mundhir Hashir, the deputy minister of education's miserable bastard, you know what he says to me? Professor, please, can I get an extension till next week? Next week! Because he has drill with the Hizbis. Oh sure, Mundhir. Whatever you like. Just the way I passed you on the midterm. Whatever you want, just don't sic your daddy on me."

"Adham . . ." Qasim twisted his mustache and squinted meaningfully at the third desk, where their colleague Salman worked and—if department rumors were true—kept files on nearly everyone.

"Pfah! Have you even seen the birdwatcher today?"

"No. No, not yet. Cousin, I know what you mean. Every class gets smaller and the ones that show up barely pay attention. But there *is* a war coming."

"And those who cannot dance complain the floor is crooked. They're students. They should attend class and turn in their homework. It's very simple. Determination is the key to everything."

"I can understand their trouble. I haven't touched my dissertation in weeks."

Adham jabbed a bony finger at Qasim. "Then the carpenter's door is loose."

"But the Americans . . ."

"But! But! There is always something! Nowhere in the Qur'an does it say life will be easy!"

"Well maybe the Qur'an can help me decide whether or not I should return to Baqubah."

"'Righteousness does not consist in whether you face east or west. The righteous man is he who believes in God and the Last Day, in the angels and the Book and the prophets.'"

"So?"

"So listen for the voice of God and the prophets."

"Right. Of course. And you? What have God and the prophets told you?"

"Oh, I'm going home. My father insists on it. He says things will be much safer in Fallujah."

"But your teaching . . ."

"I talked with Hureshi, and he told me to take all the time I need."

Qasim blinked slowly and gritted his teeth, thinking, *goatfucker!* You backward, camel-riding bumpkin with your *book* and your kaffiyeh! You who maybe, yes, you're in the party, but you don't even believe in a secular state! *You?*

"Your wife is in Baqubah, isn't she?"

Qasim exhaled through his nose. "Yes. My Lateefah. And the rest of my family."

"Who's taking care of them?"

"My uncle Jibril, my cousin Faruq, who lives in town, my little brother—I don't know. There are too many of us."

Adham spread his palms. "Cousin, it's simple: Go. In times like this, you must lead your family. 'Consider those

who fled their homes in their thousands for fear of death. God said to them, *You shall perish.*'"

"But if I go . . ."

"Yes?"

"Nothing. Just . . . My sister-in-law will be there too. With their children."

"Not your brother?"

"He's in the army. He drives a tank."

"God grant him victory."

"God!" Qasim barked. "The same God that put him there on the front lines? The same God that brings the Americans?"

"Don't be blasphemous, cousin."

"No, Adham, please. Tell me what we've done to deserve this."

Adham leaned forward, crossing the desk so his gleaming face hung before Qasim's, his words harsh whispers. "Let me tell you, cousin, about what I believe. The fate God weaves is a song of many voices, and things that seem to be disasters today may be openings through which God's hand will pass tomorrow. There are many of us who wait for the day when we will lead our people back to the virtues of our fathers, back to the Book and the Caliphate, to the days before petrodollars and satellite dishes and nationalism. Sometimes, cousin, a storm scatters our tents because it's time for us to move on. When the wind blows, you ride it."

"Well, I think we're done for."

"Fine. That is what you think." Adham turned to his students' papers. "Your pessimism is a tool of the deceiver."

Qasim snorted and stood, grabbing his satchel. *Tool of the deceiver!* I cannot *believe* the things that come out of his mouth. I need to get out of here. I should see when Luqman is leaving—God willing, soon, so I can call mother and make arrangements for going to Baqubah.

Is that what you're doing now, Qasim, going home?

Yes. No. Yes.

Maybe.

The blind man stood in the courtyard feeling the sun on his face. He was very old and very frail, and where his eyes should have been were two pale and clotted scars. Hair like white wire sprouted from his brows, from within his ears and nose, from his cheeks and lips and chin, thickening over his neck in a tangled wave. In one hand he held his stick and in the other, his book and pen. From his bony shoulders hung a threadbare dishdasha.

"Ah-ham," he croaked to himself and nodded, shuffling toward his bench along the wall. Soon, yes, he could feel it, coming from the sky. His little birds knew. Didn't they always?

"Ah-ham," he croaked, reminding them.

Near his feet, the one-legged half-wit echoed back "Aham!"

The blind man smiled and nodded. When a wound is tired of crying, it will begin to sing, he thought, sitting on his bench and listening to the life of the yard around him: the three men arguing, the others slapping down dominos, the idiots and cripples and crooks. He could just make out the voices in the women's yard beyond the wall, and the sound of lunch being prepared in the prison kitchen.

The old man laid his stick across his thighs and then his book atop it. It was a large book and its leather was worn by years of handling. He'd written through it many times, each cycle over the one before, until the pages held all he'd ever known or thought or felt—or nearly all. The end was coming, but it wasn't there yet. There was another sura to write.

He felt for the ribbon between the pages and opened to where he'd left off, his fingers skimming the lines, tracing the scant indentations of yesterday's pen. In a day it'd be flat like the others and return to blankness, but for the moment it held the impression. He read yesterday's verses and then again, remembering, reciting, then took the cap from his pen and began on the left his verse for today. He wrote slowly and with great care words he would never see and only briefly know, the same words or different, the one song in many verses.

Sometimes he'd pause and stick his pen in his mouth. He'd jab at the pen with the jerking stub that was all that remained of his tongue, remembering how many years ago, in a dark and stinking hole he could only barely now envision, a cold blade had been forced between his teeth and his mouth had filled with blood.

Qasim took the phone up onto his uncle Mohammed's roof, where he sat in a plastic chair and turned east to face the prayer call from the loudspeakers of Um Al-Tobool.

The sun sank behind him, a red burn against darkening violet, the last light flaming on the mosque's dual minarets, their paired domes, the delicate twinned crescents.

What would come of it all?

God's will, as the call closed with the Fatiha: "Guide us in the straight path, the path of those whom Thou hast blessed, not of those who have incurred Thy wrath, nor of those who have gone astray."

Silence opened across the city. A dog barked below. Qasim dialed his uncle Jibril. His cousin Bahira answered, and Qasim asked to speak with his mother.

"Qasim?"

"Peace be upon you, Mother."

"Upon you be peace, little fox."

"How are you?"

"Allah carries us in his palms. The children are putting tape on the windows. Izdihar is such a precious lamb, she drags a chair in from the kitchen to stand on. She can't reach all the way up, so she puts little designs in the corner. She wrote her name on the one in my room. Little Izdihar. Written in tape. Did I tell you Afifah and the children are coming? Your brother Darud, his division is near Basra, they say. Jibril says we will crush the Americans even more quickly than we did last time, God willing. Are you praying, little fox?"

"Yes, Mother."

"Are you coming home for Ashura? Jibril has put his foot down like every year, but Rahimah and I are going to celebrate and it's for the children, anyway. It's important. You always tell the story of Ali Husayn so well, little fox. Won't you be coming home for Ashura?"

"I don't know, Mother."

"You'll be home before the infidel comes, I'm sure."

"Mother, I need to talk to you about that."

"What do you need to talk about? Your father, God preserve his soul, would want you home. If not for me, for Lateefah."

"How is she?"

"Her heart is like fire on you. What do you expect? What's she supposed to do while you waste your days in Baghdad? She can't make a child. She can't make a home."

"Did she quit her job at the school?"

"No, not yet. But it blackens her face to work like a girl with no husband."

"Mother, you know I'm working."

"You left a fine job your father would have been proud of to live like a beggar."

"Father would want me to finish my degree."

"Your father knew what needed to be done and did it. He would not have run away from his family. He would never have left me alone as you have done with Lateefah."

Father would have found a way.

Long ago, Faruq had planned that after Qasim completed his bachelor of science at Baghdad University, he'd be sent abroad for a doctorate. Money was put aside, crucial favors were done for certain well-placed officials. Then came the war with Kuwait. Faruq got Qasim a draft deferment and Qasim finished near the top of his class; few of his peers were so lucky. The peace, though, turned out to be almost as bad as the war: continued bombing and crippling sanctions ruined the already weak economy. Business stopped, trade stopped, the dinar plummeted against the dollar, inflation surged—it was as if Faruq's savings were being eaten by rats. At the worst of it, they spent their cash in stacks and wads; a month's salary might buy a chicken or a few dozen eggs. Then, in the purges and paranoia following the Shi'a uprising, Faruq's delicately nurtured connections died on the vine. Those few friends still hanging on to power wouldn't stick their necks out. Nevertheless Faruq found a way, somehow, scraping together enough hard cash and finessing enough shady deals to send Qasim to Heriot-Watt University in Edinburgh. With some help from the school, there was just enough money to get him started; Faruq impressed upon his son the necessity of finding funding.

Qasim had been north only a few gloomy months—cold, humiliating months full of unnerving lessons in the limits of his talent; dismal months of constipation, headaches, and a constantly running nose; lonesome months where the English he so struggled to master always seemed to bend back on his tongue into gibberish; nightmare months where he wandered the streets in a muddle, baffled and awed by the strange stone city around him and the cruel, doughy faces of the Scots who lived there; despairing months where each night, curled under his duvet with the door shut against his roommates, he struggled desperately to keep from weeping, to keep them from hearing him weep, despondent for home and exhausted from working so hard and falling behind and the unending gray skies pissing rain—when at last the phone rang and his mother told him in a stern, quiet voice that his father was ill and the doctors did not expect him to survive the winter.

Qasim flew back to Baqubah, elated to be home until he saw his mother's haggard face, his father's withered body. Over the next year, Faruq slowly shrank, crumpling and shriveling in the grip of the cancer. There was no going back to Edinburgh, even if Qasim had wanted to, there was no money left for anything, yet on his deathbed Faruq demanded his son's promise: finish your schooling. The machines beeped and hissed. Faruq's dry, fleshless fingers burned in Qasim's palm. I promise, Father. I promise.

"Do you hear me, Qasim?" his mother shouted. "Are you even listening? Qasim, you must come home!"

"Mother, I'm staying in Baghdad."

"What? Qasim, you can't. You must come home."

"If I want to keep my place here teaching, I have to stay."

His mother snorted. "Ridiculous boy who thinks he can tell his mother about his great responsibilities. Little boy who can't even take care of his wife, who isn't even a father, who leaves his family to be murdered by the infidel."

"Mother . . ."

"A fine man, a fine hero, devout, brave . . ."

"Mother, please."

"A real Saladin."

"I'm not coming back to Baqubah. That's my decision. That's the end of it."

"Fine. Then I live with the shame of having given birth to a coward."

"Mother!"

"At least your brothers are men."

"Put Lateefah on the phone!"

"Remember, Qasim, that a man who cannot tend his wheat will eat his barley."

"Mother, put Lateefah on!"

He heard the phone hit the table and his mother curse him as she walked away. A moment later, Lateefah's voice: "Qasim?"

His knees went weak. His voice went weak. "Lateefah."

"You're not coming," she said.

"Lateefah . . ."

She said nothing. He listened to her breath and thought he might die from it. Breath after breath. Sometime later—Qasim couldn't say how long—he heard her set the phone down. His uncle Jibril picked up.

"Your mother says you're staying."

Qasim exhaled. "That's right, Uncle."

"Well, listen, Nephew, women don't always understand the choices we have to make. If it were up to them, we'd never leave home. I'm sure you have your reasons, and becoming a professor is a great service . . . How is your dissertation coming along, anyway?"

"I'm working through some difficult spots right now. It's a bit of a maze, you know, but . . . I'll find my way."

"Good. Maintain discipline. That's a great source of strength."

"Have you heard from Darud?"

"He's near Basra, that's all I know. They can't say any more. He'll be one of the first to repel the invaders."

"My brother's very brave."

"Not all of us are warriors, Nephew. The nation needs scholars, as well."

"And accountants."

"And engineers, like your father."

"He fought. So did you."

"And so did Aban and so did Bishr. Don't forget about them, and don't forget that heaven isn't so pretty for a man's widow and his fatherless children. God grant your sister-in-law doesn't have to learn that lesson."

"I pray for my brother's victory."

"Listen, Qasim. I want you to know your mother and wife are safe here, and they will be as long as I can lift a rifle. If you have to stay in Baghdad, I trust your reasons. But if there was any way you could come to Baqubah, I know your wife and mother would be relieved. They worry about you." He paused. "I'm sure you have your reasons. Your family is my family. They are safe in my home, always."

"Thank you, Uncle."

"Your father would be proud of you, Qasim. God your pardon and protection."

The sun had set and lights had flickered on across the city. The weekend had begun. Qasim heard a grunt behind him and turned to see Mohammed coming onto the roof with something in his hands.

"Are you off the phone?" Mohammed asked.

"Yes, Uncle."

"Good. Mother will have dinner ready soon. Here. She finished mending your trousers." He handed Qasim a folded pair of slacks. "She says you should take a dance class."

Qasim smiled. "She's very patient with me."

"Yes, she is. And what about you? Have you decided?"

"I told Mother I'm staying here."

Mohammed looked out over the city. "It's a beautiful night," he said. "This is my favorite time of year. We leave the rains behind, but it's not hot yet. It's a pleasant time to be in Baghdad."

"It is," Qasim said.

"You know our family has always shown determination in the face of trouble."

"I do."

"I would hate to think that anyone could say our family couldn't take care of itself . . . That anyone in our family would turn away from his obligations."

Qasim felt heat rising in his cheeks. Mohammed scuffed his sandal on the roof.

"It's difficult," Mohammed said after much thought, "as a young man, to know how to balance your responsibilities. Your wife, your family, your tradition . . . the nation, Islam, your work . . . A man must see what follows from the recitation of his soul." Mohammed shook out a cigarette and lit it. "It's not always easy, especially in at time like this. A man must act with strength, but humbly. God does not love the proud."

"Yes, Uncle."

Mohammed turned toward Qasim, his gaze full and measuring. "Go thank your auntie for sewing your trousers. Tell her I'll be down soon. After dinner, I need you to come with me to the office to go over some accounts."

Qasim stood and nodded, watching his reflection—a tiny speck in the dark of his uncle's eye—dwindle and fade into nothing.

■ ■ ■

"Thank you all for coming. I know things are difficult now, and that time spent here is time away from your family during these crucial last days." Qasim considered his class, barely half full. With the deadline only two days away, many classes had already been "temporarily" suspended, and all across town offices and stores were closing up, sending everyone home except the last few needed to board up windows and lock doors. He had almost canceled class himself, but it was his favorite, and he wanted to see them all one last time.

"I don't know when we'll reconvene, or even if we'll be able to finish this semester's work. The uh . . . Well, I hope al-Sahhaf is right, and we destroy the Americans quickly." He paused for a moment, thinking how best to phrase this, knowing at least one student in his class was a Ba'athist.

"Professor al-Zabadi."

"Yes, Amr."

"Professor . . . If we don't . . . I mean if we can't . . . make it back to class . . . I'm from an-Nasiriyah, and I'm going back home . . . If we can't come back to university this semester, will we be able to withdraw without a failing grade?"

"Yes. If we're not able to reconvene this class, I'm going to recommend everyone be given the grade you've earned to this point, for an hour and a half of credit. But, no, Amr, I'm not going to fail anyone because—" He stopped, watching Amr's face twitch, his shoulders shudder, and his chest explode, spewing bits of bone and gore all over his classmates. What? I'm not going to fail anyone because they're crippled? Because they're dead? He remembered the last war, the trucks and tanks full of smoking corpses. "I'm not going to fail anyone because they can't make it back to class. The worst that will happen, the absolute worst case, is that you'll take a withdrawal." Pray God, the absolute worst. "But what I plan . . ."

There was a knock at the door. Professor Hureshi poked his head in.

"Professor al-Zabadi, a word."

"Class, you'll excuse me." Qasim smoothed his mustache and followed Professor Hureshi out, closing the door behind him.

"I wanted to catch you before you left this afternoon. Have you reached your decision, Qasim?"

"Professor Hureshi . . ."

"Qasim, I need to know on whom I may depend. We must assume, God willing, that things—"

"I'm staying," Qasim said. "I'm staying. I'll be at my uncle Mohammed's."

Hureshi blinked and flashed his teeth. "I am pleased to hear it."

Qasim thought of Lateefah—alone in the hole he'd dug her. The pain he caused. His mother's shame. And when the war came? Could he stand it?

He hugged Hureshi and kissed his cheek.

"I'm glad to serve," he said.

Salman sat smoking. He'd taught his elementary statistics class that morning and was now going through his students' tests, but his mind kept wandering back over what he'd just seen. On the way down from Hureshi's office, he'd noticed that weed al-Zabadi in the hall talking quietly—even intimately—with Anouf Hamadaya. Perhaps the way they were standing so close and whispering so ardently meant nothing. Perhaps it was merely class-related. She was one of his students, after all. But Salman had learned over the years to trust his suspicions: even if they weren't always right, they almost always suggested opportunities.

Salman kept an eye open for opportunities. Unlike Adham, who came from a wealthy family in Fallujah, and Qasim, whose middle-class family stood solidly on their construction business and their date farms in Baqubah, Salman came from people little better than peasants. What was left of them, anyway, after the 1991 Shi'a uprising. Salman's father, his two brothers, three of his uncles, and most of the rest of the men in his extended family had either died in the fighting or been butchered after Karbala fell. Salman himself, sixteen at the time, only barely escaped with his life. For nearly a week, while Republican Guard soldiers roamed the streets dragging men off to be executed and dumped in open graves, Salman lay hidden in a shattered groundwater pipe, drinking fetid water, dizzy with hunger, his heart thundering every time a jeep or tank rolled over the road above. When at last he crawled out, nearly dead from dehydration, he was the last living man in his immediate family.

He hated the men who'd murdered his brothers and uncles and father, it was true, but it was an abstract hatred locked so deep within himself that it was no more than a cold violet idea, having little to do with his day-to-day life. He'd recognized early that the strong and forceful climb to the top, and since he was neither, his only hope lay in cunning. Justice was for the mighty; Salman vowed to survive. So when his draft notice came up, he dutifully went away and served in the infantry, and when Lieutenant Azimaya approached him about serving the greater glory of Iraq, the only question in his mind was how far it would take him.

It got him all the way to Saddam University, and after he finished his BSc with a dual major in business and maths, it got him into the Economics Department at Al-Mustansiriya University to work on a master's. While taking economics classes he worked as a TA in the maths department, but even what he got for teaching, added to what he got paid for informing, didn't quite make ends meet. Not only was he supporting his mother and sisters back home, but he was trying to save up for a wife, so he drove a taxi three, sometimes four nights a week, and could be found for certain odd jobs if the price was right. He'd hoped when he finished his MA to get a cushy government position—maybe join the Party—then find himself a bride.

The upcoming invasion made a mockery of all that. He knew he'd survive, no matter what, maybe even thrive in the chaos, but nobody wants war except soldiers and fools, and Salman was neither. Salman was shrewd. Salman was observant.

Anouf, for example, he'd been watching for a long time, and not just because she had a face like an Egyptian movie star and a figure to match. The other students gossiped about her because of her modern clothes and her blue jeans, but also because of the men who picked her up from school, whispering that she supported herself as a prostitute for high-placed government officials and was an informer for the Mukhabarat besides. Salman had wondered himself, at first, but the truth, which he'd uncovered in time, was that her brother was of one of Baghdad's biggest embargo cats—the loose gang of black marketeers and smugglers who made their money supplying people with everything prohibited by the UN and Saddam. The thuggish men who picked Anouf up from campus every day were her brother's runners.

Salman doubted Qasim's interest in Anouf had anything to do with her brother. Frankly, it was a miracle Qasim managed to get out of bed every morning without cracking his head open. He certainly wasn't tough enough to hang with the likes of Hamadaya. Perhaps he needed something, though, some paperwork, a visa, or maybe with the war coming . . . what? Maybe it went the other way: he worked as an accountant for his uncle, so maybe Anouf's brother was having trouble with his books? Most likely, it was just school drama. Qasim had a crush on Anouf or vice versa. Al-Zabadi wasn't handsome, manly, or distinguished, he wore glasses, he had a crooked nose and a ratty mustache, he was unkempt and awkward, but for some baffling reason, his female students were always having crushes on him. Pity, Salman suspected—the same gush of emotion they'd feel for a sick cat.

So maybe they're flirting. Maybe Anouf has a crush. Maybe Qasim has finally grown tired of living apart from his wife. Maybe he's more of a man than he seems. Whatever it is, we'll see. We'll see what it's good for.

■ ■ ■

Qasim barely caught Luqman as the rotund physics pro-fessor blew out the door for home. His wife had called, said the Hizbis were digging a trench right next to their house, and demanded he do something. She said they'd even threatened to lock her up. Lock her up! Luqman didn't know what he could possibly say, but he hoped when he got home, somebody would listen to reason. It was too bad the Hizbis had picked his house to set up next to, but what could he do? They had guns! They were Hizbis!

"I will be glad, nephew, when the Americans have freed us from this plague." Luqman turned down the radio, which was playing a patriotic song from the war with Iran.

"You really think it'll work?" Qasim asked, staring out the window at the city streaming by in a blurred mosaic of brown and gray.

"Nephew! Look at MTV. Look at CNN. We'll vote, we'll have a constitution, we'll elect our president. Think of it! No more Hizbis! No more secret police! No more Abu Ghraib! It'll be like it was in the seventies, before the Mother of All Morons attacked Iran. I'm telling you, everybody had a new car and nice clothes. Not this shit I wear now, but good stuff from Egypt."

"You don't think they just want our oil?"

"*Of course* they want our oil! But they don't want to steal it, they want us to sell it to them, just like the Saudis. They just want to make sure we're loyal. Okay, then. We'll be loyal. We'll be good, loyal friends, and with the US behind us, we can stand up to the Zionists, we can stand up to the Persians, we can stand up to those pricks in Kuwait. And we'll all have satellite TV. Freedom, Qasim. Freedom! And satellite TV! We won't have to hide anymore!"

Qasim loved how Luqman was, outside of work, willing to say anything. One day he cursed Humam Abd al-Khaliq Abd al-Ghafur, the minister of education—or, as Luqman called him, "the rancid curd of a faggot sheep's syphilitic foreskin"—for twenty minutes nonstop. Yet despite Luqman's hopeful levity, Qasim's mind kept returning to the coming bombs, his problems with Lateefah, and his strange conversation with Salman. Why had Salman asked him about Anouf? And could it be true what he'd said, that her brother was a gangster?

He'd noticed her the first day of class. As beautiful as she was, there was no way he couldn't have. He was shy, though, and considered himself a professional, so he tried to put her out of his mind. When she started making cow eyes at him and laughing at all his dumb jokes, he thought it was just because he was her teacher. He remained stony, unresponsive—for the first few assignments, at least, until she proved she could do the maths and wasn't baiting him for a grade. After that . . . well . . . *She must know I'm married*, he thought, so he never told her. He assumed she was single and available, so he never inquired.

Anouf would wait after class, hovering at his desk to ask him about some knotty algebraic conundrum, her skin rich and luminous, her eyes quick like oil in the sun, her face delicate and open. One time their hands had brushed, and a terrific shock lit through Qasim's belly. It took everything he had to keep from grabbing her wrists and pulling her across his desk.

Yet he restrained himself. He had as yet dishonored neither himself nor Miss Hamadaya and had no intention of so doing. With the war coming, though, sometimes things just happened. Maybe he and Anouf would be caught in a bombing raid. She'd come to him for help . . . rescue . . . trapped in a dark basement, alone, while bombs fell above, her hands sliding down his shirt to his belt, her heaving bosom crushed against his chest, her breath slow and warm on his neck—

But Salman said she was leaving. Why, then, did she say that she's staying? And why would she tell me to call her and let her know I was safe? Why would she smile so happily when I told her I was staying, too? Was it all some trick? Or was Salman lying? One of them was, that's for sure. And what was that about Munir Muhanned, the gangster Salman said her brother worked for? Cheating on your wife, that's one thing; besmirching a gangster's sister was something else entirely. Salman must be lying—but why?

Qasim interrupted Luqman's monologue. "You ever heard of Munir Muhanned?"

"The gangster?"

Qasim's heart sank. "Yeah."

"Oh, some. You know. They say he's like Abu Alich from *Wolves of the Night.* I heard one story about him, about some cop who wouldn't take his payoff and started locking up his men, putting the squeeze on him, so Munir Muhanned paid off the cop's boss, then just killed him."

"The boss?"

"No, the cop."

"And they didn't do anything?"

"There was a stink, but Muhanned greased all the right palms and they left him alone. The best part is, they took the cop out into the desert and buried him up to his neck. Left him for three days. When they came back, *he was still alive.* He'd almost dug himself out. So they tied him to the bumper of their truck and drove home to Baghdad. By the time they hit Firdos Square, all that was left was the rope."

In Qasim's mind, he became the cop and Anouf's brother was Munir Muhanned—Qasim pictured a cross between Saddam and Al Pacino. "I ain't gonna kill you," he said, slapping a wrench in his open palm, "because that wouldn't hurt enough. But you're gonna pay for what you did to my sister."

"I didn't do anything!" Qasim hissed.

"What?"

"Nothing."

"I'm gonna drop you here because I gotta run," Luqman said, pulling off across from the Yarmouk gas station. Traffic was sparse: the Ba'athists had set up checkpoints all over, discouraging people from going out. "The wife is having fits about these Hizbis. God keep you safe, Nephew."

Qasim watched Luqman pull away into the dusk and turned heavily toward home. He walked slowly across Jordan Street, dodging a truck full of sheep, two taxis, and a passenger bus with no lights on, then went around the far side of the gas station to avoid the long line of cars waiting to fill up. Aside from the gas station, the neighborhood was quiet. Lights were coming on in the upper stories of the houses, glowing warmly through latticework window screens and ugly taped Xs, but nobody was out, nothing seemed to be happening. It felt as if the city had curled in on itself, waiting, afraid. It wasn't far to his uncle's, only a few short blocks along some old railroad tracks and through a vacant lot, but it seemed that night as if he were crossing a vast cavity, an eternal lostness.

What would happen to his city, his country? Every farewell stuck in his throat, each goodbye seeming, in some way, the last, because in a week nothing would ever be the same again, even if, God willing, Luqman and Anouf and Lateefah and his uncle Mohammed and everybody important to him survived. It was as if the calendar went up to the deadline and stopped: everything after, blank.

Except it won't be blank. It'll be terror and death and fire from the sky. It'll be like before, with power outages and burst water mains and no food and police crackdowns. The UN will come in with their humiliating aid and we'll stand and beg for a bag of rice.

Something snarled, so close he seemed to feel it more than hear it, and he spun hard, his pulse banging in his temples. Maybe six meters away—two dogs fighting over a pile of trash. One was much smaller than the other, and sicklier too, but appeared that much more vicious.

Qasim watched as they growled, circling, then the little one pounced. The big one went low and came up under the other, tearing at its chest with his teeth. The little one bit at the bigger one's ear, his shoulder, then leapt back bloodied. The big one stepped forward and the little one ducked right and went for the neck. The big one met him jaw to jaw and the two merged in a tumble of fur and teeth, standing on their hind legs, snarling furiously and pawing like boxers. Qasim's heart pounded in his hands.

The dogs came apart again, the little one jumping back limping. Both were bleeding, but the little one was clearly getting the worst of it. Their tongues lolled between their shiny white teeth, their eyes flashing like stainless steel.

The big one leapt, going for the kill. The little one dodged left, but the big one was faster, clamping down on his neck and shaking him by the throat. Qasim picked up a rock and threw it, hitting the big dog on the flank.

"Hey," he yelled.

He picked up another rock and threw, this time nailing the big dog in the head. The dog's jaw opened and his victim fell free.

"Hey! Piss off!"

He let fly another rock, which the big dog ducked, then another and another. The dog turned and loped a few meters away, then stopped and growled at Qasim, who threw again, hitting the dog square in the side and sending him fleeing.

The little one lay in the garbage, panting heavily, bleeding from its side, throat, and muzzle, one eye slashed and oozing, paw twitching. Qasim crept up, rock in hand, closer and closer to the wounded dog. It seemed oblivious, its good eye unfocused. Qasim thought it must be dying.

He crouched above the tiny beast, his nostrils full of blood and trash and dog scent. The dog's body heaved with breath, moist and red, its fur darkly matted. Qasim reached out his left hand toward the gaping wound on the dog's neck, toward its head.

The dog jerked up and snapped down. Qasim flinched and screamed. The dog bit harder, and Qasim stumbled back, lifting the bloody dog in the air. He shrieked and shook his arm, but the dog hung on, legs wriggling. Then Qasim swung and smashed the dog to the earth, knocking it loose. It pushed unsteadily to its feet, snarling and wheezing at him. Qasim stumbled back and kicked. The dog limped out of the way. Holding his bleeding hand, backing up staring at the dog, Qasim cursed wildly. The dog growled and barked. Qasim watched it as he backed away, both of them now silent, and when he was far enough, turned and walked off, checking twice over his shoulder, down the street and around the corner to his uncle's.

He pushed open the gate with his shoulder, holding his bloody hand to his chest, dizzy with the waves of pain now shuddering up his arm. As he went in through the front door, he heard gunfire and an explosion and thought for a split second *it's started*, before he realized it was the TV in the living room and Arnold Schwarzenegger saying "Now daht's a vake-up kahll!"

His aunt Thurayya called from the kitchen: "Is that you, Father?"

"No, Auntie," Qasim said. "It's me."

He stumbled through the parlor into the back room where his cousins were watching TV, then into the bathroom. He put his hand in the sink and turned on the water. His dizziness swept in waves, now pain, now cold. His auntie came up behind him.

"Are you alright, Nephew? You sound upset."

"I hurt myself," he said, turning away.

"Let me see." She grabbed at him.

"It's fine," he said, wrapping his hand in a towel. "I just need a bandage."

Aunt Thurayya was quick for a middle-aged woman, and tenacious, but Qasim was tall enough and the bathroom cramped enough he could keep her out.

"Let me see, Nephew."

"It's fine. I just caught it on some metal."

"You need the tetanus."

"I had the tetanus."

"It's not a vaccine! You need it each time."

"It's fine."

"You'll do it wrong. Let me see if you need the tetanus."

"I don't need the tetanus!"

"You need the tetanus!"

Qasim swung on her and shouted, "Leave me alone, old woman!"

Thurayya backed up a step and stretched to her full height. "You will not speak to your uncle's wife in such a tone."

"Enough meddling! Go!"

"Mind your tongue, boy!"

"Woman, leave me be!"

Thurayya glared at him, then turned and swept into the living room, storming in front of the television and yelling at Maha, Nazahah, and Siraj. She shut off the movie and made them go do chores. Qasim was shaking again and could barely hold himself up. He went to the kitchen and found a bandage.

The bite was deep, jagged, inflamed. He couldn't find any antibiotic cream, so he just put some cotton pads in the wound and wrapped it up. It was unwieldy work, but he managed to cover the gashes. Thurayya stood in the living room glowering. His cousins sulked at their chores, well aware who'd caused their misfortune.

"I won't be having dinner," Qasim said, taking a piece of flatbread in his good hand. "I need to work."

Upstairs, he sat at his desk and looked out the window. His mind had gone remarkably clear, and though his hand ached wretchedly, he felt crisp, even refreshed. He munched his flatbread, for a few minutes blessedly free of thought, enjoying the brilliant coruscations of the streetlights through the palms.

When he'd finished eating, he put on his headphones and pulled out his dissertation. Against a background of chirps and beeps, riding a delicate synthesized wave, David Bowie moaned out, "Nothing remains . . ." Qasim let the music ease him into the pure spaces, the gently shimmering universe of thought called mathematics. He flipped through his notes with his good hand, recovering lines and curves, weaving arcane connections, coming back after an exile too long to his comfort, his true home, his love.

Salman drove up over the Al-Jumariyah Bridge, catching the outdoor fires from the masgouf restaurants along Abu Nuwas Park flickering orange in the black waters of the Dijlah, and descended into the subdued hustle of Yafa Street, passing the Parliament building and the Assassins' Gate. Aziz liked Salman to meet him in a particular shisha café in Mansour, to which he was now driving in an unusual mood, enjoying the easy feel of nighttime Baghdad yet planning, calmly and just below conscious thought, his tactics for dealing with Aziz. He was almost certain he was going to have do something unsavory and probably dangerous, but he just hoped it didn't involve his notional status as a reservist.

Salman couldn't remember the last time he went to drill, but even he knew the situation was bleak. Maintenance didn't happen, training was a joke, and morale wretched. The Sunni officers despised the almost wholly Shi'a ranks, and vice versa, and everything was infiltrated by the Mukhabarat. No camaraderie, no sense of unity: each man looking out for himself, which means you're always looking over your own shoulder. Not that it would have mattered much even if they did all work together. The armored corps were still devastated from the last war, the air force nonexistent, the artillery bombed to pieces—even after Iran, things had been better. The troops were digging in as they'd been told, but no one had any illusions about what would happen when the shooting started.

As he turned along Zawra Park and passed the Baghdad Zoo, noting soldiers setting up antiaircraft guns under the lights of the Dream Park's Ferris wheel, Salman realized he couldn't care less who won. Someone would always be on top, and the guy on top has to step on everyone else in order to stay there, so what's the point in getting worked up over who it is? There has to be a sheikh. Sheikh Hussein or Sheikh Bush, it didn't matter. Power flowed the same no matter who wielded it. And if you weren't on the side of power, you got out of the way.

He parked around the corner from the café and walked up. Rubbing misbaha beads between his fingers, he wished he'd changed from shirt and slacks to a dishdasha. The robe would have been so much more comfortable. Most important, he had to keep from being put in a fight Iraq was bound to lose. Salman definitely didn't want to ride around Baghdad in the back of a Toyota pointing a machine gun at curfew breakers. Maybe if he told Aziz he was investigating somebody—something vague and hard to check up on. He could say he needed to collect evidence, do some surveillance.

The café had a grand entrance that always pleased Salman's eye: high and wide, dark wood hung with scimitars, shelves and tables busy with archaic-seeming bronze lamps and ornate, multicolored shishas. Peer too hard and you'd see how chintzy it all was, but in the dim light and thick, fruit-scented smoke you could pretend, imagining yourself in some Abbasid harem—sticky dates and slippery olives, the lingering odor of spiced tobacco, veils and low-lit lamps half-concealing firm and youthful flesh. Salman found Aziz sitting alone in a corner in the back, drinking chai and smoking—not a shisha, but a Marlboro. The red and white pack lay ostentatiously on the table. The two men exchanged greetings, shaking hands softly and touching their hearts, and when the server came, Salman ordered chai.

"Still they haven't voted on the resolution," said Aziz, flicking ash. Salman noticed, as he always did, that the two smallest fingers on Aziz's left hand were missing. They'd been lost to shrapnel in the Iran War, but even crippled, the man's hands were powerful, brutal hands that knew a lot about killing, and Salman watched them to keep from getting caught in the operator's deep, hooded eyes. "There's talk of a veto, Russia, China, France. The world may yet stand with us against the Zionist aggression."

"The Americans won't be happy until they've got all Islam under the lash. It's always been that way, they're just using their own guns now. We'll have to fight them sooner or later."

"We've struggled a long time against the Zionists."

"God willing, we'll destroy their armies on the field of battle."

"Insha'Allah," Aziz said flatly. "How is your mother, Salman?"

"She's preparing to celebrate Ashura. Privately, of course."

"Ashura." Aziz took a drag from his Marlboro. "I'm wondering, Salman, if you've thought much about what happens after the war."

Aziz was a hard man, a shadowed man, and although Salman didn't know exactly where he stood in the Mukhabarat hierarchy or what he did, he suspected Aziz would have no compunctions at all about cutting Salman's balls off with a dull knife and stuffing them down his throat. He might even enjoy it, if the man ever felt joy. Either way, Salman was confident that in the clandestine webs sure to be spun in the postwar chaos, Aziz would remain one of the nastier and more important spiders.

"I am your servant," he said. "And a soldier of the Revolution."

"We expect the war to be a long one. We expect the Zionists to make great gains, initially. But there are plans for what comes after. Salman, you have always served us very well."

"I'm honored to do so."

"But not everyone is so loyal. We expect many Shi'a to collude with the Zionists."

His father gunned down by helicopter, his brothers dragged off to be shot like dogs, the mass graves and burning bodies, his tunnel that was almost a tomb—Salman imagined a boot stamping the images out. "You will need information," he said.

"Yes. The Saddam Fedayeen and Mukhabarat are prepared, in the event of the Zionists' temporary success, to fade into the desert and carry on the fight. We are Arabs, after all. We shall scatter like the Bedu and strike at the Zionists from the dunes, as we once fought the Turk and the British. We'll raise a jihad against the Americans and bleed them the way the Afghans did the Russians. We'll cut them four thousand times for every time they cut us. It may take years, of course, but patience makes all things possible."

Salman saw where this was going. "The Americans will need collaborators. Translators."

"Your English is good, no?"

"Fair. Mostly economics terms. But it's passable."

"Work on it. Here," Aziz said, putting a satellite phone on the table. "This is how you maintain contact. The phone has two preprogrammed numbers. The first is to call me. I may or may not answer, and if I do, I may not have time to speak. Use it only when it's most urgent for you to pass on information. The second is strictly for emergencies. Strictly. But if you need it, don't hesitate. You will be all but on your own. We will call when we need you. Keep the phone close by. You understand?"

That all sounded fine, so far as it went. A bit like planning your own funeral. "Yes."

"Good. Now we must come to a more urgent topic."

Salman raised his eyebrows. Here it is, he thought, and struck first: "If I may, sir, I have something to tell you." Aziz showed no response. Salman went on. "I've heard Munir Muhanned may be selling information to the Americans, via an agent in Kuwait."

"You have evidence?"

"Not yet. But . . . I have a line. I think one of my colleagues is working with Muhanned's men to encode the messages."

"What's his name?"

"His name?"

"Yes."

"His name."

"Yes, Salman."

"Of course. Qasim al-Zabadi."

"I see. Well, we'll take care of it. For now, I need you to deliver a package." He slid a folded piece of paper across the table. "Go here and ask for Naguib. He'll have instructions for you."

Salman palmed the paper. "Is that all, sir?"

"Yes, for now. You have university work, don't you, that exempts you from emergency mobilization?"

"Of course."

"Good. You'll be well placed, if you manage to make it through the next few weeks. Don't do anything stupid."

"Yes, sir," Salman said, and left as calmly as he could, elated to have been exempted from reserve service. He'd needlessly used up his "suspicions" about that weed al-Zabadi, but that was fine. There would always be another Qasim.

Ashura had come and gone, unobserved, the Lament of Husayn forbidden on state radio. Qasim got up early all the same and prayed, irritated and guilty, thinking of his mother and Lateefah. Of more interest to the rest of the family—mostly Sunni—was the impending UN vote and the threat of veto, the worldwide protests, and the upcoming deadline. Indeed, the house buzzed like a newsroom. All day long, Al Jazeera and BBC ran on the TV in the living room and Iraqi radio played in the kitchen, while the family talked constantly. The chatter eased and obscured the fear behind their preparations.

The generator had benzine and the lines were hooked up. Extra propane tanks had been bought for the kitchen gas, since no one knew when the filling stations would reopen. The windows were taped. Mohammed had drilled a well, but the foot valve was leaking, so Mohammed's son-in-law Ratib was out in the front garden trying to fix it. Ratib's eldest, Siraj, worked in the garden with him, digging a hole for the benzine cans and propane tanks, and little Abdul-Majid, barely out of diapers, pretended to help, poking at the dirt with a stick till Siraj sent him running with a smack. The little one ran in the house wailing, snot-faced, crying for his mother, Warda, who was rifling through the living-room closet collecting candles—citronella candles, scented candles, beeswax candles, all jumbled together in a box.

Warda knelt and wiped Abdul-Majid's face while he cried and told on his brother Siraj. She kissed his head and gave him some candles to carry, picked up her box, and led him into the kitchen, where Thurayya's widowed sister, Khalida, was preparing the midday meal: chicken with red rice, salad and pickles, shineena, with golden vermicelli for dessert.

It had been a year since Khalida had come to stay with her sister. She'd once been an editor at a respected publishing house specializing in trade books, and her husband had been a policy coordinator for the National Progressive Front. About four years ago, he'd disappeared, but she kept working, living alone, waiting for him to come home, until one day her spirit just gave out. By the time Thurayya and Mohammed took her in, she was a scarecrow: withered to a stick, hair unbrushed, nails chewed to ragged nubs, darting eyes flashing out at a world full of hidden enemies. She was a bit better now, but the run-up to the war was wearing on her nerves.

"Hello, Auntie," Warda said.

"God bless," said Khalida, wiping her hands on a towel. "And what have you got there, little man?"

"Some candles," Abdul-Majid said, sniffling.

"And what are you going to do with them?"

"We'll light them with matches."

"That's right," Khalida said. "We'll light them with matches."

"And they'll make light," he said.

"That's right! They'll make light! So that your auntie can see your beautiful face!"

Thurayya turned from her shopping list, warmed by the joy in her sister's shy voice. She smiled at Khalida, Warda, and Abdul-Majid, her daughter Nazahah sitting next to her slicing cabbage, her precious family, her beautiful home— then scowled as she remembered the snake upstairs.

"Nazahah," she said, "pay attention to what you're doing."

She still couldn't believe Mohammed had refused to turn his back to the ingrate, brother's son or no. After all his shiftlessness, all his laziness, and finally this, this disre- spect—Thurayya had given up on him. She never thought her sister-in-law Nashwa had been hard enough on the boy anyway, especially after Faruq's death, and now . . . stay- ing in Baghdad, leaving his wife in Baqubah, during a war . . . unimaginable. Then, to talk to her as if she was a child! What did you expect from such a one? Those who haven't learned from their parents will learn their lessons from the days and nights. And for her own husband to nurse this viper . . . Mohammed left her no choice but to snub him at every turn, to cast a pall of tension over the house so thick, they'd suffocate till she got her way.

Yet what good was hardening your heart when they'd soon be huddled together praying for mercy? What did you gain by adding trouble to trouble? It was almost enough to make her want to forgive him—but the thought of his smug smile enraged her all over again, and she reminded herself that to show weakness with men was to submit to endless trampling.

"What are you doing?" she yelled at Nazahah. "Cut thin, thin! Shred the cabbage, don't chop it!"

"Yes, mother," Nazahah said. She knew Mother wasn't

really mad, not at her, anyway. Thurayya doted on her daughters, and her corrections usually took the form of good-humored exasperation or gentle scolding. Only in the most extreme circumstances did she lose her temper, and when that happened there was no mistaking. Mother would volcano, throwing plates, screaming, turning the house topsy-turvy until the violator collapsed in a shamble of tears. The last time that happened was when Maha got caught with a French magazine—Heaven knows where she got it—full of shirtless male models. "That was so worth it," Maha said after, her face still puffy and red. They had, Nazahah couldn't deny, been exceptionally beautiful men.

Nazahah often enough found herself a target for her mother's irritation, but never her rage. She did what she was told, said please and thank you, and hardly argued with anyone. Her eldest sister, Warda, was well behaved, too, though stubborn as a mule, very much in her mother's mold. It was poor Maha who was doomed to be the sower of strife: daring, cruel, walking through life with a feather on her head, always fighting the flies in front of her face. She terrorized Nazahah, who cowered before her older sister like a beat dog.

Nazahah's comforts lay elsewhere. On turning thirteen, she'd fallen in love with God, and since then she'd floated through her days awestruck, contemplative, the world around her a tremulous vision. Every thing, every moment quivered with weight and substance, perfection, symmetry, and beauty, since all was the will of God, the one and only: every thrush, every wren, every cloud, every fear, every slice of cabbage, every word her mother shouted, every shifting emotion vibrating though the house, even the coming war. All. Her only problem was reconciling Michael Jackson, whom she understood to be somehow vaguely yet irrevocably not halal, possibly even haram. She would not let him go, however, and solved her conundrum by ignoring it. Michael and Fatimah sat side by side on her tiny shrine, holding the Prophet between them in harmony.

"Wake up," her mother snapped, slapping the table. "You'll cut your fingers off."

Nazahah smiled at her mother.

"When you finish the salad, go see if your brother-in-law needs anything out front," Thurayya said. "I'm going upstairs to check on your sister."

Maha was Thurayya's lamentation. She was too pretty by half, for starters, and she knew it. Then her temper! And the airs she put on! Thurayya's plan was to get her married as quick as possible. They needed someone from the right kind of family, though, someone attractive, with good prospects . . . and young. Maha was picky—haughty—frankly, impossible. There was no shortage of available men, but the problem was that they needed a real Prince Charming, someone handsome and brave, sweet enough to treat her well but strong enough to control her. God willing!

Thurayya went up to the girls' room, where Maha lay on her bed listening to a bootleg CD of Brandy's *Never Say Never* and flipping through an Egyptian movie magazine. She watched her daughter daydream, wondering where she got her pride and her insolence, but loving her for it too. Maha would be a queen someday, when she found her prince. Thurayya smiled, then said, "Daughter."

Maha flipped the pages of her magazine.

"Maha! Go downstairs and help your auntie with lunch."

"But Mom . . ."

"No buts! Downstairs!"

Thurayya watched Maha stomp down the stairs, then circled back to her bedroom, where Mohammed was showing Qasim how to work his AK-47. Qasim held the weapon's barrel awkwardly in his crudely bandaged left hand and struggled to pull back the charging handle. The weapon kept slipping from his grip.

"Here," Mohammed said, "put the barrel on your foot and let the weapon pull down—not on the ground! On your foot. If you get dirt in the barrel, it'll blow up in your face."

Qasim tugged on the charging handle, and this time it slid back and clacked home. Mohammed found himself wishing, again, as he often did, that the boy had served his time in the military instead of getting the deferment Faruq had wrangled for him.

"Are you staying for lunch, my dearest husband, great and wise lord of the home?" Thurayya asked.

Mohammed frowned. "No. Is Ratib still working on the well?"

"I don't know anything about wells, my noble sheikh of infinite courage. I'm just a silly woman who isn't even given due respect in her own house."

Qasim turned in time to catch Thurayya's cold glare as she left.

"We need to talk," Mohammed said to Qasim. "But first we have to finish cleaning out the office. Go start up the van."

Qasim rode the bolt forward on the Kalashnikov and handed the rifle to his uncle, then headed downstairs. So he'd snapped at her—so what? Was he supposed to feel bad now, or pretend women got to boss him around? What could she do about his stupid hand? It was fine. Okay, it was oozing pus, developing a yellow crust around the hot, raw wound, and it hurt more every day. It might even be infected, but he was sure it would heal soon. A little bite, nothing he couldn't handle. He certainly didn't need a gaggle of women honking over him.

He started the van and slid his bandaged hand over the wheel, letting himself slide into the pain aching up his arm. He would master the pain. That would be manly.

Mohammed got in the passenger side.

"You can drive with your hand like that?" he asked.

"Yes, Uncle. It's nothing. The bandage is just to keep it clean."

"Let's go, then. First stop is Zubair's, then we'll go get Othman."

Qasim honked the horn and Siraj ran over and opened the gate, then stood aside while the van backed into the street. As they drove off, Mohammed noticed a black Mercedes pull out and follow them.

Mohammed had two offices, one in the Karrada, where he met with clients and handled paperwork, and one in a warehouse out in Baghdad Al-Jidida, where he kept the trucks and machinery. Earlier that week, they'd gone out to the warehouse and secured the outer wall with barbed wire and spikes, bricked up the windows, and locked up the equipment. Mohammed's chief foreman, Yaqub, lived near there; he promised Mohammed he'd keep an eye on things. The Karrada office, on the other hand, Mohammed had decided to empty. He, Othman, Qasim, and two employees with a pickup spent the afternoon hauling out all Mohammed's files and personal effects and as much furniture as they could manage, then securing the building.

Qasim laid mortar, bricking a window, while Mohammed sat at his desk going over outstanding contracts. Othman double-checked the file cabinets to make sure they were empty.

"I think," Othman said, "it's a great opportunity. I think they really mean democracy."

"Nonsense," said Mohammed, not taking his attention from his papers.

"It'll be like Russia, I think."

"Russia, huh?"

"Iraq's a great nation, my friend, but we sow and weep under the lash of a tyrant. Our wheat is salted with tears of oppression. After the war, we'll be free to farm how we like. Our fields will sprout with joy." Othman's fine, soft hands spread to mimic tears falling on the wheat, then sprang up to show the new harvest.

Qasim thought the poet a silly old man, but Othman had been Mohammed's best friend since they were boys. The two men were oil and water, Harun al-Rashid and Jafar, Don Panza and Sancho Quixote. Whereas Mohammed was an engineer, a pragmatist, and a nationalist, Othman was a poet, romantic and cosmopolitan. Whereas

Mohammed had never left Iraq, Othman had traveled to Cairo, Paris, and Moscow, and had spent two years in exile in Beirut. Mohammed built houses and offices; Othman wrote poetry and had translated Hart Crane's *The Bridge* and Lautréamont's *Les Chants de Maldoror*. Mohammed was broad-shouldered, with a square, handsome face that in a good light looked like Omar Sharif's; Othman was dumpy and pear-shaped, with a long, sloping nose—he looked more like Nour El-Sherif. He wore thick glasses, through which he peeped out at the world with eyes that always seemed to be laughing.

"You're a poetizing fool," Mohammed said, slamming down his pen and sitting up. "Iraq is a great nation *because* we have a strong leader. You'd rather have madness, revolution after revolution, like the sixties? You'd rather a plague of crusaders? Because that's what they'll be, Othman, these Americans, just like the British. A plague. They're going to come in like pharaoh and put their foot on the neck of Iraq."

"They'll take Saddam's foot *off* the neck of Iraq, is what they'll do," Othman said, "and you'd see that if you weren't so old and set in your ways."

"Set in my ways? Listen, brother, I know you're an ignorant old skirt chaser who doesn't know from a handful of lentils, but you must have been taught a little of your nation's history."

"I know 'His watchdogs have corrupted the land,'"— Othman recited, quoting his teacher al-Bayati—"'stolen the people's food, raped the Muses, raped the widows of the men who died under torture, raped the daughters and widows of his soldiers who lost the war, from which, like rabbits in clover fields, they had run away, leaving behind corpses of workers and peasants . . .'"

"Then you know we're a nation of peasants," Mohammed interrupted, setting his contracts to one side. "A nation of ignorant hill people in the north, dull-minded farmers in the south, and superstitious tribesmen in the west. We are, like most Arab nations, a backward and troubled people. And yet we've modernized more than any other. We beat the Iranians, we beat back the Americans, we've kept our nation together and hauled our peasants screaming and wailing into the twentieth century. And how, my brother, did this happen?"

"The curse of oil?"

"No. By having a strong leader. A strong leader who believes in *unity*, who believes in a powerful, secular state—a *nation*—that can stand up to the Zionists and lead the Arabs into the future. We're an Islamic *civilization*, not merely a *people* or a *religion*, and it takes a strong leader to keep us moving together. Without Saddam, Iraq will shatter into a thousand pieces."

"I read Aflaq too, my educated friend." Othman perched his wide rump on the edge of Mohammed's desk, offered Mohammed a cigarette from his pack of Miamis, then lit one himself. "Of course we must put sectarian squabbling behind us. On that, I walk with you today and tomorrow and the day after. But for our Father Leader and Daring and Aggressive Knight, the Hero of National Liberation, unity was always only a word. Four thousand times, he played the Kurds against the Sunnis and the Fivers against the Twelvers. He doesn't heal the rifts between Muslims—he manipulates them. Whereas in a democratic Iraq, an Iraq where every voice can be heard, with the Americans here to help . . ."

"To take our oil, you mean. What does your Al-Bayati write? 'The hourglass restarts, counting the breaths of the new dictator . . .'"

"They want us to modernize. You see how they are with the Persians. With the Wahhabiyya."

"Speaking evil from the left side of their mouth while flattering out of the right. Denouncing the mujahedeen with one hand and shoveling cash at them with the other. Yes, I see. The Zionists and the Persians have always conspired together."

"You're too cynical. You always have been. You've always been too willing to accommodate yourself to power."

"You didn't seem to mind much when I used my 'accommodation' to get you out of jail."

"For which I am forever grateful, my friend," said Othman. "You saved me."

"And I would do it a thousand times. But to save you, I had to have power. Brother Othman, listen: power must be held. It must be used. Listen: this has *nothing* to do with democracy. We're under attack from the Zionist crusaders because we stood up against them—because bin Laden stood up against them. It's the same as it was with Kuwait. Someone dares to stand up to America, and they're going to punish whoever they can put their hands on. Listen: Saddam is the only thing that has kept our nation together for the last thirty years. When the Kurds took up arms against us, who stood against them? When the ayatollahs started rioting and rebelling even here in Baghdad, who stood against them? When the Persians bombed our cities and cut us off from the Shatt al-Arab, who stood against them? And when the Kuwaitis started murdering innocent Iraqis and then that snake George Bush, who I spit on, invaded our lands and butchered our brothers, when the entire world lined up to see us broken—who stood against them?"

"'Carpenters and ironsmiths, hungry and burned under the autumn sky, all forcibly led to slaughter, killed by invaders, alien and homegrown . . .' My friend, the same man who runs Abu Ghraib, who gassed the Kurds, who disappeared your own brother-in-law. How can you stand by this dictator as if he stood by you? He cares only about al-Tikriti. He cares only about Hussein. For all his strength, he has no more honor than a dog. And his sons! Think of them. You know the stories."

"Rumors. Your tribe sit around the Writers Union like Scheherazade, making up gruesome fables to shock each other."

"Not fables. You see the disco boats. You know what happens to the women—the daughters they take. Scheherazade's not far off."

"Listen, Othman, sometimes the powerful must be cruel. If we have to torture people to save lives, so be it. If we have to spy on people, so be it. If my grandsons are to know a peaceful and democratic Iraq, unified not by force but by law and honor, it will only be because we built strong foundations to secure that future. Is Hussein perfect? No. Is the party perfect? No. There are excesses. There are lies and evils. But the choice, Othman, is not between perfection and imperfection. We must choose, as always, between the lesser of two evils: a powerful leader or anarchy. And if you choose the Americans, you choose anarchy."

"Maybe Bush will be strong," Qasim said from his bricked-up window.

"What?" Mohammed turned, incredulous.

"Maybe Bush will be a strong leader. Maybe *he* will keep Iraq strong."

Othman chuckled. "Your nephew sees things differently, brother."

Mohammed stood up, spitting and stomping his foot. "Fuck Bush," he said.

"But if Bush can beat Saddam, doesn't that mean he *is* stronger? And maybe he'll make Iraq strong again. Then we can build our democracy."

"You see, Mohammed," Othman said. "The young have hope. They're not frightened of the future like you are."

"Bush—strong! You heard about the protests. Against Bush. In his own country. He can't even unify his own nation, and they have it easy. They're rich. Fat. Decadent. Not only that, their women . . . You see how it was with this Hillary Clinton and now that Condoleezza Rice . . . Their women practically run the country."

"Mohammed, surely you wouldn't oppose a woman's rule . . ." Othman said with a grin.

"At home. At home. There is a very strict line."

"I see. So because Thurayya hasn't yet made an assault on your office, you consider it well defended," Othman said.

"True enough," Mohammed said, wiping his hands and

holding up his palms. "And she won't ever try, God willing. Now, if you two are done vexing me with your daydreams, let's finish up and get out of here."

Qasim wiped his trowel on a brick and dropped it in his tool bucket. Mohammed tied up the last pile of contracts and set them on a corner of the desk. Othman closed up the last empty cabinets. Mohammed sent Othman to check on the other workers, then turned to Qasim. "Nephew, a word."

Qasim faced Mohammed. His bad hand ached, and he felt feverish and dizzy. "Uncle, I know I was short with Aunt Thurayya."

"Yes."

"It's just that . . . It's not just her. I can't take all this feminine meddling. My mother, Lateefah, Aunt Thurayya . . . I have to make important decisions, and all their fussing is . . . they don't understand. They have no right to question me. They're just women."

Mohammed rubbed his mustache. "It's true, nephew, that women are women. And it's true that you must be firm with them. You can't let them treat you like a boy. But a man's wife . . . Well, things aren't always so simple."

"My wife is my Fatimah, Uncle. She's my servant."

"No, Nephew, you are hers. Lateefah is the one who will bear your children. She's the one who carries your family in her hands. In her belly. You must protect and cherish her. You must stand by her."

Qasim winced. "Now *you* are meddling!" he shouted.

Mohammed stepped across the room and slapped Qasim hard, knocking him back against the bricks, sending his glasses clattering to the floor. Qasim cried out, tears leaping to his eyes.

Mohammed exhaled through his nose with a snort. "I've nearly had my patience with you, boy," he said. "Indeed, were it not for my obligation to your father, I'd have sent you from my house a long time ago. You blacken your father's face. If you want to stay, if you want to curl your tail and hide in my home, then I will suffer it because your father was my brother. But don't think you get to call yourself a man in my home. I know what you are, and I know a man who abandons his wife out of fear and pride is nothing but a dog. When we get back home, you'll beg your aunt's forgiveness, or you'll leave. Now clean yourself up and meet me outside."

Some hours later, Qasim sat at his desk fuming, trying to puzzle out a particularly knotty equation, unable to focus. He'd called Baqubah earlier to talk to Lateefah and it had gone disastrously. His mother wouldn't speak to him, and when his wife picked up the phone, she wouldn't answer. Qasim was solicitous at first, gently asking questions, but each time Lateefah refused, his anger redoubled. When he finally asked, "What's wrong with you? Why are you silent?" she said, "I'm grieving because my husband has abandoned me." Qasim exploded, screaming into the phone, berating her faithlessness, and calling her names until she finally hung up on him.

Qasim told himself he'd called to entreat her, to comfort her, to promise her he'd send for her, and that it was her unrelenting selfishness that had provoked him. Sitting in his room, going through the same handful of variables over and over, his mind raced along the well-worn track of his indignation, chronicling the story of how put-upon he was, how beleaguered by fate, how neglected and how beaten down. His pained hand, his headache, and the fever in his ears made it all that much worse. From the Gulf War to his exile in Edinburgh to his father's death, from his meddling aunt to his bullying uncle to his thankless wife, his life appeared to him as a succession of struggles against a despotic fate that had unfairly singled him out among all the others, he, Qasim, son of Faruq, for tribulation.

There was a knock at the door.

"I'm working," Qasim shouted.

The door opened and Qasim turned to glare at Nazahah, who meekly watched at the floor.

"Cousin . . ."

"What? What do you want?"

"There are men here to see you, Cousin."

"What men?"

"They say they're from the university."

"From the university?"

"Yes, Cousin."

Qasim stood. "I'll come down."

"They said they'd see you here. They'd like to speak to you privately."

"Well, alright. Send them up."

Nazahah bowed and left, closing the door behind her. Qasim faced his chair into the center of the room. Two?

He supposed both could sit on the bed, or one at the desk. He smoothed his blanket and arranged his papers and pencils.

There was a new knock at the door and as he turned, it opened. One man scanned the room and sat easily on the bed, the other closed the door behind him and stood in the corner. Qasim knew at once they weren't from the university.

"I . . ." Qasim began, but was interrupted by the sitting man, who waved his hand and clicked his tongue. He looked around the room again, taking in Qasim's modest furnishings, his many books on his few shelves, his bureau, the picture of Lateefah he kept near his bed, his handful of shirts and trousers hanging in the open closet. Eventually the man turned and looked at Qasim like he was measuring the size of the hole he'd need to bury him in. Qasim realized he was trembling, his skin turning clammy, his mouth going dry.

The man looked away, past Qasim, through the window to the darkened city outside, the distant lights of the Um Al-Tobool Mosque. "Nice view," he said. Qasim jerked back over his shoulder, looking in surprise at the same view he looked at every day, then turned again to face the man.

"You . . ."

The man waved, clicking his tongue. He turned to Qasim's nightstand and picked up the photo of Lateefah.

"That's . . ."

"Shut up," said the man by the door.

"Professor al-Zabadi," the sitting man said, still holding the photo of Lateefah.

"Speak when you're spoken to," said the other.

"Uh . . . yes, sir."

"Professor Qasim al-Zabadi."

"Yes, sir." Qasim thought he might throw up.

"Please sit down," the man said, turning to Qasim, who sat, looking from one man to the other. "This is your wife Lateefah?"

"Yes, sir."

"She's not here?"

"No, sir."

"She's in Baqubah?"

"Yes, sir."

"You know, Professor al-Zabadi, we're not from the university."

"Yes, sir."

"Do you know where we're from?"

"I think so, sir."

"What do you think?"

"I think you're from the police."

"Why is that?"

"Because you seem fearless."

"Is that it? Or is it because of what you know?"

Qasim's ears began to ring. The air seemed to be leaking out of the room. "What I . . . I don't know what I know."

"Professor," the man said, "you have not joined the Party, is that correct?"

"I . . . no. Not yet, sir."

"Why is that?"

"I wanted . . . I needed to finish my dissertation. I'm not . . . I'm not one for politics, for all those political . . . things. I'm just . . . a mathematician. Just maths. So, I thought, what do politics and maths have to do with each other? I'll join later, of course, but I didn't."

"Just maths."

"Yes, sir."

"I see. And who do you do maths for?"

"I don't understand."

"*Who* do you do maths for?"

Was this about his uncle? Was this about the accounts—the bribery, black-market deals, shady negotiations with officials? It was all run-of-the-mill stuff, the only way to get things done. He couldn't believe they'd be here about that. Had his uncle made enemies? Was he going to have to . . . ? Qasim blinked. The room dimmed and blurred.

"Just . . . just my uncle Mohammed . . . he's down . . . stairs . . . "

"We spoke with him. He's a very honorable man. But there are so many questions."

Qasim choked back a belch of vomit. He sweated cold sweat, his good hand clenched in a fist and his bad hand throbbing. The man stared, watching and measuring. Qasim said nothing. With a great internal wrenching, he decided to answer only direct questions and speak as little as possible. He couldn't lie, that was beyond his strength, but he could keep himself from giving away anything more than what they forced from him.

"Your uncle is very honorable," the man said. "He takes care of his family. He takes care of you."

Qasim coughed.

"It would be a pity if something happened to him."

Qasim looked from the one man to the other.

"Do you understand what I'm saying?" the one asked.

"I . . . think so."

"What I'm saying is that we're interested in certain kinds of information. But we're very busy men, you know. We have only so much time. So if we're looking over here, maybe we don't have time to look over there. Or vice versa. You see?"

Qasim looked at the man, confused.

The man sighed and stood up. He stepped over to the desk, leaned over Qasim, and flipped through his papers. Qasim felt him at his shoulder, a menacing blur in his peripheral vision.

"What is this?"

"My dissertation, sir."

"What's it about?"

"Harmonic analysis. It . . . it has to do with permutations of Fourier series. Fourier transforms."

"Transforms?"

"It's . . ." Qasim gritted his teeth. "It's very abstract. It has to do with series of numbers, with periodic functions. You would need several years of higher mathematics in order for my explanation to make any sense."

"Why don't you try?"

"It has to do with—simply put, what I'm trying to do is develop a harmonic analysis of certain non-abelian groups to explore whether or not we can analyze them topologically. I think I've been able to establish these groups as locally compact in certain cases, but I'm still working on applications of the Peter-Weyl theorem. The problem is, they're not always locally compact—which means . . . well. It's . . . it's a bit ambitious."

"I see. And these equations, they're good for making codes?"

"What?"

"Somebody gives you a message and you turn it into a non-abelian theorem . . ."

"Oh, no. No. Not at all. That's a totally different branch of mathematics. No. Cryptography, cryptanalysis, that's totally different. You might talk to Professor Farani, she's very good with that sort of thing. Not really my field."

"No?" The man smirked.

"Oh no. Like I said, I'm working on harmonic analysis. I'd like, once I finish the dissertation, to see if I could push it further, topologically, you know, but that's a completely different . . . that's . . . wait." Qasim's realization shot fear through his belly: "You think I write codes."

The small man slapped Qasim with the back of his hand. "Don't pretend we're stupid, Professor."

Qasim held his head in his hands. His temples ached and rang.

"How about we just take this, all these non-abelian codes, and have somebody crack them?"

"What? No, please. No. It's not . . ."

"No?"

"That's . . . That's my work."

"Why don't you tell us what we want to know? Or maybe you'd like to tell us in Abu Ghraib?"

"I . . . my uncle . . ."

"Yes?"

"I do accounting for my uncle. I'll tell you who he bribes, how much, I can tell you the black market . . ."

The man's eyes narrowed. "We're not here to talk about your uncle, shit-dribble. Who else do you do accounting for?"

"I don't . . . I don't know what you mean."

The man slapped him again. Then again. Then he picked Qasim's glasses up off the floor and handed them back to him. He went to the door and spoke briefly with the other man, who came over to Qasim. He reached out and took Qasim's good hand and pressed it flat on the desk. He held down Qasim's wrist and pulled a claw hammer from under his jacket.

"We don't want *you*, shit-dribble," the one man said. "We want the men you work for."

"I don't know what you mean," Qasim said, his voice breaking. "I really don't." His mind scrambled for something, anything he could tell them.

"Last chance, shit-dribble."

"My uncle . . ."

The one man waved his hand in exasperation. The other lifted the hammer.

"Wait!"

"Yes?"

"My uncle . . ."

The one shook his head and the other swung the hammer down on Qasim's little finger, smashing the first knuckle with a bloody crunch. Qasim blacked out. He came to a few moments later, dizzy and tingling, sweat pouring from his forehead.

"Let me help you remember," the one said. "We'd like information on the codes you write for Munir Muhanned."

"Munir . . ."

"Oh. *Now* you remember."

"I don't . . ."

"Again."

"No wait! Wait! I'll tell you!"

"Yes?"

"Hamadaya," Qasim said. The man looked at him quizzically. Qasim went on: "Anouf Hamadaya, one of the students in my class. She asked me if I would write codes for her brother."

"And?"

"I didn't. I'm not . . . I wouldn't ever get involved with guys like that. I'm . . . I'm a coward . . . you see . . . her brother, Anouf's brother, they say he works for Munir Muhanned. That's who the codes were for. But I was too scared to do it. That's all. That's all."

The man went around the desk and picked up Qasim's dissertation.

"I told you, that's all I know. There's nothing . . ."

The other raised his hammer again and Qasim went silent. His hands throbbed. His face throbbed.

"We're going now," the one said. The other let go of Qasim, who pulled his bleeding hand into his lap. "But if you hear anything, anything that might help, you talk to your uncle. He knows who to contact." The man turned and left, flinging the dissertation across the room as he went. His partner followed.

Qasim watched them go, desolate and sick with pain, then curled into a ball on his bed. He didn't respond when Mohammed and Nazahah came to check on him, or when Nazahah splinted and bandaged his crushed finger. Only when they started to pick up his dissertation did he stir, waving them away.

The white empress hovered in the corner, her robes heaving in slow waves, her hands stretching across the space between them in the heat, head cocked, tears flowing down her cheeks and splashing her chest with tiny red blossoms.

Qasim sat up, tugging at the sweat-damp sheets, fumbling in the tangle. As he leaned toward her, she leapt at him, her face a dog's face. Qasim fell back and she cried, "Why?"

Then she was gone. He sat alone, trembling. His bitten hand, aching, stank. His heart's pounding echoed against the walls and he thought, How long? Has it begun? He imagined great whirlwinds of fire spiraling over the city. Fragments of a dream came back, running through alleys, a great coal steed at his heels, fire in its eyes, fire in its mouth. Its massive hooves pounded the air with sparks. The white empress watched from a high window, her mask impassive. Turning and turning, the streets a cyclone, all the world one ancient, winding alley. Again the dogs and something else, Anouf, a shard, her hands on his manhood, her mouth on his neck, while the horse pounded behind him. From above, the white empress watched—beneath her mask, tears.

He heard someone walk past his room. Dawn shone in a red line. Black palms rose like minarets and the minarets rose like rockets: the sky floated black under a starry blue sea, and that's how they'd come at him, like sharks.

Had it begun yet? Were the lights in the sky the sea, or the city?

Qasim sat up again. The call to prayer had begun. His hands, chanting dull mantras of pain, told him he was being punished for his pride. God had struck at him for his stubbornness and would kill him if he kept at it. He had no choice. He had to return to Baqubah. If he stayed, he'd be destroyed.

Slowly, painfully, shakily he dressed, then opened his suitcase and threw in his clothes, his photo of Lateefah, his Discman, a few CDs, his dissertation—now a clutch of disordered pages—and all the books he could fit. His other things he stacked in the corner, to send for later.

He hauled his suitcase down the stairs in the three good fingers of his less-bad hand. In the living room, he saw Othman sitting on the couch in the dark watching CNN with the sound off. Othman turned to him. Christiane Amanpour spoke on the screen. Qasim watched her smooth, pale face, her eyes bleeding tears, distant and accusing. "Why?" she asked him. "Why did you leave me?"

"I'm sorry," he said.

"Qasim," Othman said.

"Please tell my uncle . . ."

Othman stood and came around the couch.

"Please tell my uncle I took . . ."

"Let me help you with your suitcase."

"I . . . I have to . . . I have to."

"Yes, Qasim. Of course. Let's have some breakfast first."

"No. I have to get the car before the . . . before the dogs, I mean. While it's still black."

"We'll go soon, but first come, sit. I'll get you breakfast."
Othman led him gently around to the sofa.

"No, now!" He waved his hand, stinking in its scummy
bandage.

"Yes, of course. We'll go soon. Just sit. We'll eat first, then
go. Just sit. Then we'll go."

"I have to go," Qasim said, sitting and dropping his suitcase. Pain washed over him in broken pink waves.

Othman left to put on the kettle and when he returned,
Qasim had passed out. TV light dappled his wasted face.

Mohammed came downstairs and found Othman and
Qasim asleep on the couch. CNN was on, silently running
a story about a hijacked Cuban plane. Something stank.
Mohammed kneeled to examine Qasim's hand: the bandage
was dirty and loose, a mess of gauze, crusted pus, and filth.
He took it gently up and Qasim jerked awake with a shout.

"Let me see your hand," Mohammed said.

"I . . . It's . . . I have to go to Baqubah. I need the Toyota."

"You're not going anywhere with your hand like that."

Qasim pulled himself unsteadily to his feet. "You're
not . . . going to stop me," he said. "You always want to
stop me."

Qasim tried to push past him, but as Mohammed stood
to hold his shoulders, he fell back on the couch. Mohammed knelt, taking Qasim's bandaged hand on his knee and
unwrapping it. He gagged on the stench of the infected flesh.

"Help me carry him out to the car," Mohammed said to
Othman.

On their way toward Yarmouk Teaching Hospital, which should have been a ten-minute drive, Mohammed and Othman had to go through three different checkpoints, each time arguing with the clean-faced recruits and fat reservists that they had a medical emergency and needed to be allowed to pass. Other than the Hizbis, the city seemed evacuated, estranged from itself. There was almost no traffic. Trenches had been dug in parks, berms built up in front of schools. No buses ran and all the cigarette stands stood empty.

The hospital was quiet too. The nurse told them it might take a while: "We're running a skeleton crew, to let our staff rest. The full shifts start at midnight." A few others waited in the lobby: a young boy, crying, his head resting in his mother's lap; a fat old man wheezing like faulty bellows; two or three bandaged and broken; others with less visible afflictions. *Guardians of the Nation* played on Iraq TV in the corner. Twice orderlies rolled stretchers through to the ER, one man bleeding from a gunshot wound to his chest, another trembling and hyperventilating, his leg broken in a Z.

At last the nurse came for Qasim. Dr. al-Amman, quiet, short, sleek as an otter, said little to Mohammed and Othman as he dispassionately examined Qasim's hands. He examined the splint set on his smashed little finger. He jabbed Qasim's rotting hand with anesthetic and, with the help of a nurse, began to cut away dead flesh. Qasim was awake but delirious, and Mohammed and Othman helped hold him down. The doctor cut away the gangrenous bits and dropped them in a bucket while the nurse soaked up blood with a sponge. It did not take long. Finished, he slathered on topical antibiotic and had the nurse wrap the hand.

"He should be fine. There's no indication of rabies, but we'll run blood tests. We'll call you—Insha'Allah—within the next few days. It appears to be a localized infection, but it may have gone further up the arm, so I'm going to prescribe some very strong antibiotics—he's not allergic, is he? Good. He needs to take the antibiotic with every meal, three times a day. He can't miss one single pill. Don't cut the pills up, don't sell them to someone else, don't hoard them. Unless he takes every single pill, the infection will spread and kill him. Do you understand?"

"Doctor, I'm no thief," Mohammed said.

"Very good. He may be delirious for a week or so while the antibiotic kills the infection. Make sure he gets plenty of water and bed rest. The hand should be unwrapped every other day and washed. Boil some salt water for five to seven minutes, then let it cool. When it's room temperature, use it to wash his hand, gently. A proper scab must form. I'll prescribe some topical antibiotic as well. Put that on the wound, then wrap with a new bandage. With proper care and regular cleaning, he'll be okay. There is some deep tissue damage, so his hand will likely be permanently weakened, but functionality will return in time."

Driving home, Othman pointed to the horizon. Thick black clouds of smoke ribboned up from the greenbelts around the city, where the army was burning oil in big pits. Beyond them loomed a distant bruise, thickening across the sky.

■ ■ ■

The sandstorm came later that afternoon, choking the city with oily grit, turning the world beyond the windows to a howling red void. It lasted until after well after nightfall. As soon as it had blown over, Othman went up on the roof to replace the satellite dish, but now there was no signal. Ratib thought the storm might have knocked out the local retransmitter, but Othman was sure it was Saddam and his flunkies, the stupid bastards, he muttered, blinding us in our moment of darkness.

They attached the aerial to the TV and tuned in to the local station replaying the same programs from earlier in the day, the same state demonstrators cheering, ministers pontificating, Saddam speechifying. "Shut it off," Othman said.

"Nothing to do but wait," said Ratib, slumping into an armchair.

"I can't believe it's happening again."

"I was in the south last time."

"You could feel it. The air would hum and you could feel it in the back of your neck. You could feel them coming."

"It was fast in the south. Everything was fast. You'd be sitting there for hours, bored out of your mind, and all at once the earth would explode. There'd be a whistling, you wouldn't hear it until later, after the explosion you'd remember—*I heard whistling.* But before, nothing. They hit us with jets and artillery. Those rockets they shoot."

"I helped dig people out of the rubble. After every raid, as soon as the explosions finished, we went down to the mosque—this was when I lived off Asmai Street, in Adhamiyah. When I worked for the Iraqi Film Commission.

Anyway, after a raid, we'd meet down at the Abu Hanifa.
We had boys, some of the men's sons, and if we didn't know
where the damage was, we sent them out as runners. Then
we'd go dig. It was awful."

"There wasn't any rubble in the south. Just wrecked
tracks and bodies. Men's helmets burned onto their heads
because of the webbing inside and the coating, the lami-
nate on the inside of the helmet. It just melted onto their
skin."

Othman sat on the couch. He watched the TV's blank
screen while Ratib got up and scanned the DVD rack.

"I need a drink," Othman said to himself. "Mohammed!"

Mohammed shuffled in from the kitchen. "Stop yelling,
pig. If I'd known you had the habits of a Jew, I'd never have
brought you into my home."

"Where's your bottle?"

"I don't know what you're talking about."

"The good stuff, the Johnnie Walker, not the arak you
give your clients. It's time for a real drink. We could all be
dead tomorrow."

"I should see my God with liquor on my breath?"

"As if your God cared," said Othman.

"He cares," said Ratib.

Othman waved him off. "Go get your bottle."

"You'll order me now, like I'm your little woman?"

Othman leaned back and gazed soulfully into Mohammed's eyes: "'Your yearning shows, whether you restrain
it or not, and likewise your weeping, whether or not your
tears flow. How many times your composed smile deluded
a companion, while between your hips—what was invisible.

The heart commanded its tongue and its eyelids and they concealed it, but your body is an informer.'"

Mohammed laughed and rubbed Othman's shoulders. "Sad bachelor. If you want to drink so bad, why don't you go down to the Writers Union?"

"I want to drink with my old friend Mohammed and his son-in-law Ratib."

"I don't drink," Ratib said.

"There is a time for your God, and there is a time for your heart," Othman said. "You'll have one drink."

"Alas, my friend," Mohammed said, throwing up his hands. "I already drank it all."

Othman closed his eyes and covered them with the fingers of one hand. "'Father of every perfume,'" he recited, "'not of musk only, and of every cloud—I do not single out the morning clouds—every man of glory boasts of only one quality, whereas the All-Merciful has joined in you all. While other men are esteemed for their generosity, in your generosity you bestow esteem.'" His eyes opened, peering into Mohammed's. "'It is not much that a man should visit you on foot, and return as king of the two Iraqs. For sometimes you give the army that has come raiding to the lonely petitioner who has come begging, and you despise this world as one who has proved it all and seen everything in it—except yourself—perish.'"

Mohammed smiled, but not Othman. There was a sadness in his voice that slowly dissolved his friend's smile, and brought Ratib back to the stretches of silence that followed the bombs in the south, after the wounded had been trucked away and the dead buried, when they waited

for more death to come. The feeling of relief at having
survived lent the dread a cutting edge, laced the bitterness
with painful sweetness. "Please, beloved and righteous
Mohammed, name of the prophet, by the grace of God
and by the mercy of God and by the infinite compassion
of God, go get your bottle. This may be our last night.
The last night for Iraq."

"There will always be Iraq."

"Like there will always be Akkadians or Abbasids or
Ottomans. A country is a day. Come. Let's drink like men."

"Ratib," Mohammed said, "go upstairs to my office and
in the filing cabinet, the tall gray one, open the bottom
drawer. There, back behind some blueprints, you will find a
bottle of oil to light our lamp tonight. The Johnnie Walker
Black."

"It's not permitted that . . ."

"Ratib," Mohammed snapped. "Your piety is commend-
able. Go get my bottle."

Ratib fetched it, and the two older men began to drink.
Eventually, after much cajoling, Ratib did too. In the meantime, Thurayya and Warda had returned from putting the
children to bed and, seeing the bottle on the coffee table,
went into the kitchen. The night passed slowly, the men
drank slowly, sometimes going into the kitchen for water
or chai or to speak with the women, and sometimes Warda
or Thurayya would come into the living room to speak
with the men. It was a quiet night, a night of conversa-
tions and stories of other wars, quiet but quickened by an
unheard buzz. The radio played a low babble behind their
talk, old patriotic songs and bullshit state bulletins. Just

after midnight, as the men were becoming drowsy, Othman sat up with a start. Then they heard it: the distant chug of antiaircraft fire.

It went on for a while. Othman sat back down. The shooting stopped. Started. Stopped. A distant machine turning off and on, throwing metal into the sky.

Thurayya and Warda told the men good night and went upstairs to bed. Shortly after that, Mohammed told Othman to wake him if anything happened, then went upstairs himself. Eventually Ratib fell asleep in his chair. Only Othman was left, listening alone in the darkness. He had another drink, then another.

He woke, later, to the walls' dull shaking. The world shuddered once, then again and again. Antiaircraft guns flacked in the distance. There were several more explosions, far but not that far, and more guns. Mohammed came downstairs and looked at Othman. The two men looked at Ratib, still asleep, and went swiftly upstairs to the roof. To the northeast, Baghdad was in flames.

A fireball lit the sky. Then came the boom.

"It's all in the Karkh."

"They must be going after the government buildings."

Tracers cut the sky in loping arcs of red.

"I didn't hear any planes."

"No, you wouldn't. They're too high. Or stealth jets."

Another fireball; they counted—one, two, three, boom. Red and yellow light flashed and shifted, the city danced with shadowed fire. They stayed and watched until the bombs then the AA guns stopped. In the east, the sky lightened to a smoky blue.

They went back downstairs and turned on the BBC. George W. Bush's voice filled the room.

"*My fellow citizens, at this hour American and coalition forces are in the early stages of military operations to disarm Iraq, to free its people, and to defend the world from grave danger. On my orders, coalition forces have begun striking selected targets of military importance to undermine Saddam Hussein's ability to wage war. These are the opening stages of what will be a broad and concerted campaign . . .*

"*I want Americans and all the world to know that coalition forces will make every effort to spare innocent civilians from harm . . . Helping Iraqis achieve a united, stable, and free country will require our sustained commitment. We come to Iraq with respect for its citizens, for their great civilization, and for the religious faiths they practice. We have no ambition in Iraq, except to remove a threat and restore control of that country to its own people . . .*

"*Our nation enters this conflict reluctantly, yet our purpose is sure. The people of the United States and our friends and allies will not live at the mercy of an outlaw regime that threatens the peace with weapons of mass murder. We will meet that threat now . . . so that we do not have to meet it later with armies of firefighters and police and doctors on the streets of our cities . . . I assure you, this will not be a campaign of half-measures and we will accept no outcome but victory.*

"*My fellow citizens, the dangers to our country and the world will be overcome. We will pass through this time of peril and carry on the work of peace. We will defend our freedom. We will bring freedom to others. And we will prevail.*

"*May God bless our country and all who defend her.*"

He lay in bed thinking, why them again? The two men, standing over him, one slowly waving his hammer.

"He's not going to do what he said," said one.

"He thinks he knows," said the other.

A dull boom outside startled the men and they turned to the window. In the street, a line of Crusaders stood on guard, the blades of their swords flashing like needles, reflecting the fiery angels crossing the sky whose wings and hair burned gold, swooping and soaring. One broke off and shot jets of flame from his hands—a burst of white sparks, Crusaders tossed along the road like broken bottles, a crater. One of the iron men screamed, pointing his sword to the heavens, and leapt. An angel fell upon him, wrapping him in flames, but the leaping Crusader stabbed through the angel's heart and the two, pinned, plummeted writhing to the ground with a crash.

Staring down from atop a minaret, her face impassive white split with black, silver robes flowing in the maelstrom wind, she watched. She turned slowly, her eyes passing over the city, and he could feel her watching him huddled there in his bed. He tried to push himself to his feet, but saw his hand was crippled, broken blue, a twisted bird's claw.

He heard the dogs a moment before he saw them, a pack slavering down the alley at him. With his good hand he pushed himself up and fled, feeling her eyes on his neck.

He turned one corner, another, then another, through twisting streets of the old city, the dogs close behind, their shadows shuddering on the walls, another corner and another. He fell in through a bakery door.

"In the cow's belly, we're all milk," the baker told him.

"I'm not milk, I'm water," Qasim said back.

"We must pour milk into you."

"No, no. I need water."

"You'll drink pig's blood before you're through."

"I'll drink dog's blood."

"Oh, the dogs will drink *your* blood."

"I'm not a man. They won't eat me."

"They won't spare you either. They'll kill you and leave you."

"I'll run forever."

"Your hand is running. That's a runhand."

Qasim clenched his blue birdhand in a fist.

"We must pour milk into you," the baker said, hobbling around the counter and into the back. In the wall was a little door and the baker opened it and, bending over, entered. "Come, come," he said, going into the darkness. Qasim followed.

He crouched in an endless tunnel of tearing wind. Machinery chugged somewhere, loud, behind the wailing. Down, down he went, until finally the tunnel opened in a series of small caves spiraling one around another. The spirals became sines, tubes, a line of interwoven waves, a spinning weave of light and shadow, until translucent gold in the darkness shone upon a door: The House.

He opened the door with his good hand and went in. Qusay Hussein and Lateefah sat on the couch, holding hands. A goat bleated in the corner. Qusay had pulled up Lateefah's dress and was violating her from behind. Lateefah moaned with pleasure, sweat beading on her face, her hands grasping at the couch, her naked thighs trembling as she pushed back into Qusay.

"What are you looking at?" Qusay shouted. He pressed harder into Lateefah, his hands holding tight to her hips, and she gasped. "You think you know, but you have a dog's hand."

"Stop," Qasim said.

"God is great!" Qusay shouted, and shuddered. Lateefah's belly swelled with his seed, and she was standing beside Qasim in his uncle's house in Baqubah.

"I'm having it tomorrow," she said, her face split with a black line.

"Don't."

"But sweetheart, it's our baby. Look," she said, and showed him the swaddled newborn. Its tiny black nose and furred snout poked out of the blankets. Cute floppy ears, bright black eyes, little white teeth, a curling pink tongue.

"I can't . . ."

Lateefah handed the baby over. He knew he had to love it, so he made cooing noises. Lateefah smiled warmly at them, but when she turned away, he laid the baby on the table and smothered it with a pillow. The baby barked and yipped and Qasim forced the pillow down.

"What are you doing?" Lateefah screamed.

But he didn't stop. He felt the wriggling thing under his hands and pushed down, down.

"Have some chai!" Lateefah screamed.

He smoothed over the pillow. He didn't understand why he was in bed now. "It's not ours," he told her. "It's a devil."

"Please have some chai," Lateefah said. She sat next to him, offering a cup.

The room was light, there was light in the room. Why was he lying in bed?

"Cousin, wake up. Have some chai."

He shook his head, covered in sweat, the pillow was a pillow—his heart pounded in fear—but no, there was only the bed.

"Have some chai, Cousin," Maha said.

"Yes," Qasim said, taking the cup.

"The bombing started last night."

"Yes," he said.

Maha sat with him, watching him take his chai, telling him about the first bombs in the night. She gave him his antibiotic pill and made sure he swallowed. "Go back to sleep," she said, and left him. He turned on his side and watched the wind riffle the palms through the window's white X, his mind blank but for the image of Qusay and his wife.

Al Jazeera said nine B-52s had left their airfield in Britain and were six hours from Baghdad. Othman imagined the American pilots flying those enormous silver machines: they'd wear shiny helmets and black masks, like insectoid machine-men, but inside they'd be pale and blonde and say things like "Roger" and "I need a vector on that approach." Othman lit a Miami and pictured their green flight suits with all those pockets, and how they'd call their wives and girlfriends before the mission. Some of them must have English girlfriends, he supposed, and others would have American wives who would hate the

English girls. They'd walk out to their planes and high-five each other, saying "Got one fer Saddam!" and "Kiss my grits!" Then they'd put on their helmets and masks and fly over the English Channel and Paris and the Alps and Bosnia and Turkey and push buttons on their control panels and hundreds of bombs would fall from their machines onto his city. The earth would shake, buildings crumble, men die engulfed in storms of white-hot metal, children and women screaming, blood bubbling on blistering lips, and the pilots would high-five, saying, "How you like them apples?" Relaxing now, they'd turn their big silver planes and fly back over Turkey and Bosnia and the Alps and Paris and the English Channel, all the way back to their wives and girlfriends, who'd kiss them on the runway and say, "Bet you showed them what for!" Then they'd drive to fancy restaurants in sports cars, wearing tuxedos, and eat steak and drink Johnny Walker Black.

Most of the rest of the family had gone to sleep, a midday nap. Everything seemed almost normal.

Except for the constant terror, especially at night, especially last night. The bombing had started in the afternoon, massive raids in waves that shook the city. Sometimes they'd hear the hum of jets, sometimes not, then the first booms. If they were farther away, it was like thunder, but the closer they got, the more it sounded like the earth itself was breaking apart. The house shuddered. Everyone froze, then ran to the living room, which, having no windows, was the safest place in the house. The adults sat on the couch and armchairs, the children on the floor, as if they were all having tea, and waited while the booms multiplied and stirred to crescendo. Usually the wave was simple, peaking then fading into fewer, quieter booms and finally silence. Sometimes it was longer, complex, orchestral: a peak would be followed by a lull, a quieter stretch mistaken for denouement, only to rise again reborn with a surge of hideous thunder. It might happen twice, three times, once Othman counted five.

The raids went on all night. Every time the all clear sounded, they sat astonished at the reprieve, then blinked and, like old men stirring from long sleep, came slowly awake. Some returned to what they'd been doing, others tried the satellite. Thurayya made more chai. Othman usually went up on the roof to survey the damage, to see which part of the city lay smashed and burning. Columns of smoke strung the sky.

They'd chat or make phone calls, discussing this or that, what it would be like after, what it was like in the last war, what it was like during the war with Iran, what it was like before the war with Iran, what was good or bad about this CIA guy Chalabi they had on the news, or was America good or bad, or were the Americans better or worse than the British. Then the air-raid sirens would grind up or the AA would cough or something would explode and they'd all jump and run into the living room and it would all start all over. It went on and off like that, off and on, all night. They scrounged bits of sleep, on the couch, on the floor. Nobody wanted to go upstairs. There was an argument about whether they should leave Qasim in his room; they decided he'd be okay, but Mohammed and Ratib quickly boarded up his window. It was a long, awful night, restless and terrifying, spent at the edge of anxious exhaustion. Little Nazahah prayed and prayed, knowing somehow it was all in God's plan.

Mohammed decided they should keep all their papers and money with them downstairs, in case they had to evacuate.

"Evacuate where?" Thurayya asked.

"We'll go to my brother's in Baqubah."

"How?"

"We'll take the van and the Toyota. If we need to, we can go to the warehouse and get a pickup."

"We're not going anywhere," Thurayya said.

"Just in case."

"Mohammed."

"Just in case. Everybody needs to pack a bag, too, and a bag for the children, and we'll bring them all down here to the living room."

The bombing let up at dawn. Everything but the satellite TV still worked, so after breakfast and packing, they got busy calling friends and family across the city and farther away, collecting and spreading news. Othman slept. After lunch they switched, most of the family dozing while Othman fiddled with the TV, which was how he discovered that the satellite was back on and Al Jazeera had timed the bombers.

Six hours.

Great silver jets against the sky and the hundreds of bombs they carried, each one death for someone. He remembered the last war, the ground leaping beneath his feet, the dead. A child's arm poking from the rubble, smooth, purple-gray skin sticky with half-dried blood. The man with the shrapnel in his belly, howling all night—how could he have so much life left in him to keep screaming so loud for so long?

And the tanks—the tanks will come too. They'll rumble through Baghdad like . . . He remembers a tank clanking down a city street, its malevolent cannon swinging side to side, pointing now at a bakery, now at a bookshop, so huge it takes up almost the whole road. Its tracks chew blacktop and sidewalks. A gang of children tumble from around the corner and launch rocks at it. The rocks clatter off the tank's hull and it jerks to a halt. The gun swings around, its gaping death-eye searching for something to annihilate. Then the tank lurches into reverse, crunching up the road at them. Run, kids, Othman thinks, and they do, dashing around the corner. Was it in black and white, this memory, or color? Was it even a memory, something he saw on Al Jazeera or in *Saving Private Ryan*, or was it something he just made up?

Six hours.

And will it be worth it?

It had to be. We have to get rid of Saddam and his goatcunt sons. Donald Rumsfeld says it'll be short. Just a few weeks of insanity, just a few weeks of war, then the Americans will give us peace and democracy. We'll be a great nation again, like Germany or Japan. We have the oil, we have the drive, we have the brains and dedication, all we need is freedom and we'll be as great as Baghdad ever was. We'll be greater than Cairo, Damascus, greater than Beirut or Tehran. We'll rival Berlin, Tokyo, New York, London . . . The name Baghdad will sing on the tongues of wealthy men and their fabulous women, the name Iraq will jingle like gold coins. We'll fix all the damage from the last war, from the last ten years, and we can socialize the oil profits to do it. Then we'll clean up the ghettos, fix the streets, finish the highways left half built. We'll raze Saddam's palaces and monuments and hire Iraqi architects to build *real* monuments to the Iraqi people, monuments to rival the Eiffel Tower and the Empire State Building. We'll build Iraqi skyscrapers, better than in Dubai, and we'll become the new economic center of the Arab world.

And our literature! It'll flourish like flowers after the rain. No longer will we have to mutter our lines into our hands, hunched in the dingy corners of the Writers Union. They used to say Egypt writes, Beirut publishes, and Baghdad reads, but soon they'll say Baghdad does it all! We'll shout our poetry in the streets. We'll have publishers and book fairs. I'll finally finish my epic. Adonis will come, and Darwish, and Mahfouz, and Munif, they'll all come and speak, and they'll stay because we'll have what no other Arabs have, not even the Jordanians and not even the Egyptians—we'll have *freedom*. Freedom in a free Arab state, self-determination, national solidarity. It'll be like the Republic, only better. Think of it! To write whatever you want, to shout "Down with Saddam!" and not have to worry about having your arms broken or your manhood burnt off. And all we have to do is go through a little war, a little trouble.

Five and a half hours.

He had to put on a movie. He couldn't keep watching the news. He lit another Miami and flipped through the

DVDs. Five and a half hours would be two, maybe three movies. Something the kids would like, maybe *Shrek*? We could watch *Shrek* again. Or, what's this, *Air Force One*? Han Solo. Very good. Han Solo and his big silver jet.

Mohammed came in, wiping his hands on his dishdasha. "I just finished changing his bandage," he said. "It's still bad."

"It's only been two days," said Othman.

"He should be better."

"Or what? What can we do? Take him to the hospital again?"

"We should do something," said Mohammed.

"Give it another day."

"Where are Ratib and his boys?"

"Ratib's on the roof. The boys are sleeping upstairs."

"Good."

"They said . . ." Othman started. He couldn't carry this knowledge alone. Someone else had to help him. "They said we have a little more than five hours."

"Until what?"

"Nine B-52s left Britain three-quarters of an hour ago. It takes them six hours to fly to Baghdad."

"It's no more than we expected."

"I just thought you should know."

"God protects all."

Othman thrust *Air Force One* at Mohammed. "Is this any good?"

"It's okay. You know. Action movie . . . Are you well, my brother?"

"No," Othman said. "No, I'm not. I'm furious. All we do is

sit and wait. Wait for more bombs and tanks and . . . Whether
it's good or bad, or both . . . We should do something."

Mohammed smiled. "What can we do? Shout into the
wind? Would you wrestle the Leviathan? You know how it
is. Life's like a cucumber."

Othman grinned in spite of himself.

"That's right. One day in it's in your hand, the next day
it's up your ass. As for today . . . Well. Shitty days are only
good for sleeping. Maybe you should get some rest. I'm
going to take a nap now myself, then let's go see if Uglah
has opened his bakery."

"Yes. You're right. That's good. I'll, uh, I'll watch Han
Solo here. Come get me when you're going."

Othman turned back to the TV. He eyed the blue
void of the screen while he fumbled with the DVD. He'd
remembered where the image came from: the kids were Palestinian, and the tank was Israeli. It had been on the news.
He thought of other pictures, pictures of Israeli soldiers
storming Palestinian neighborhoods with M16s, Israeli-owned American attack helicopters launching rockets at
Palestinian cars, Israeli-owned American fighter jets bombing Palestinian houses.

Five hours, more or less. He pushed PLAY.

He was in a cave again, dark and cool. Lights flickered
dim in the distance, sometimes one way and sometimes
another, illuminating winding paths in half-seen flashes.
This time Faruq was there, standing behind him, off to
the side, in front. Faruq was young, much younger than

Qasim remembered, with full black hair and a thick mustache.

"You've got to kick the ball, Qasim. You can't be afraid."

"I can't kick."

"Listen," Faruq said, squatting beside Qasim, now a child. "Whatever you do in life."

"But I did!"

"No, listen. Do you see the angels?"

Qasim looked to the sky, where indeed he saw the angels his father spoke of. "Yes."

"They have come to burn all this away."

"Like the chemotherapy?"

Faruq lay on the ground. "Like the wind. Listen."

Qasim listened, but all he could hear was his father's respirator and the beep of the EKG. He seemed so old, so wasted, lying there in the hospital bed. It was as if some evil spirit had sucked all the meat from his body except the stringy cord of his soul. Faruq watched him but couldn't speak because of the oxygen mask. His eyes were pale and bloodshot, stern and piercing.

Mohammed stood smoking next to the bed. "You see, boy," he said. "You see what life is? This is the recitation."

"There's more," Qasim said.

"This is all there is."

"There's more. There's more if I can find it."

Mohammed inhaled on his cigarette, covering Faruq's face with the sheet. "That was his mistake," Mohammed said. "He tricked you. Now you've killed him for it."

"There *is* more."

"Look," Mohammed said, pointing down the hospital

corridor. A pack of dogs ran at them. "Stand!" Mohammed shouted.

Qasim turned and ran. Yet it seemed no matter how hard he pumped his legs, he couldn't move, and the dogs, impossibly slowly, gained by inches, their jaws snapping at his calves. His heart pounded, and he felt their paws on his back, slamming him down, their breath on his neck, their teeth.

Day and night, bombs crashed into Baghdad. You watched it on TV, you heard it on the radio, you saw it from the roof and when you ventured out into the street: soldiers and civilians, arms and legs roasting, broken by falling stone, intestines spilling onto concrete; homes and barracks, walls ripped open; Baathists and Islamists, Communists and Social Democrats, grocers, tailors, construction workers, nurses, teachers all scurrying to hide in dim burrows, where they would wait to die, as many died, some slowly from disease and infection, others quick in bursts of light, thickets of tumbling steel, halos of dust, crushed by the world's greatest army.

As the bombing grew worse, the terror of it stained every living moment. Sleep was a fractured nightmare of the day before, cut short by another raid. Stillness and quiet didn't mean peace, only more hours of anxious waiting—or death. Even the comfort of family rubbed raw.

Maha sat in her room listening to Britney Spears and Brandy, wishing she was anywhere else. This war was going to ruin her life, she knew it, it was going to ruin her chances for marriage, it was going to ruin everything. Her skin was breaking out, her hair frizzing, ends splitting. She stood at her window and gazed through the slit between the two pieces of plywood nailed over the glass and watched smoke drift over her city, and the smoke was her future fading to haze. She started hitting Nazahah, hard. She hated how her sister kept praying, stupid praying to stupid God, like it would do anything. She hated her mother and father, her sick cousin Qasim, whom she had to keep nursing, creepy old Othman, her sisters. She hated her mother's patience and stillness. She hated Warda's incessant singing and Khalida's watchful eyes. They were all conspiring against her: none of them understood how terrible it was to have her life ruined at seventeen, before she was married, before she'd even fallen in love. She stood at her window and gazed through the slit between the two pieces of wood and watched flames burn along the skyline, half hoping she'd see it all devoured.

More bombs fell on the city. Day and night, smoke clouded the sky and the sun blazed like blood. Sometimes air-raid sirens would break the heavens with wailing and all across the city people would drop what they were doing and hide. Then the sirens would subside and no bombs would fall. Then the all-clear would sound, or not, while AA guns hacked at the empty gray. What people grew to depend on was the mosque. After every bombing, out from the many minarets across the city the muezzin would sound: Allahu akbar, la ilaha illallah. And more bombs fell on the city.

Warda kept herself busy. She could not bear to be still: as soon as she stopped moving, her mind bloomed with grim thoughts of her husband and her boys. She could not bear to think of her little Siraj lifeless and torn, or Abdul-Majid, who cried and fussed so much, falling quiet forever—it was an emptiness the depths of which Warda refused to peer into. To lose her beloved Ratib, whose skin she adored, whose hips and back and shoulders she clung to, whose lips and cheeks and eyebrows she loved so dearly they made her ache, after all their struggles, would be losing the world. So she mended. She cleaned. She baked. She'd watch movies sometimes with the family, a little, but her mind wandered and after a few minutes she'd get up and find something else to do. She reorganized the kitchen and the closets. She dusted behind the TV.

And she sang. Quietly, songs from her childhood, in a soft and lilting voice that sounded through the house, soothing the family. They couldn't see the horror behind her gentle eyes, couldn't hear how her songs were only noise to hush an endless silence, so they were calmed by them, and this in turn helped calm Warda. So she kept singing. And sometimes, as she sang, she could even imagine a future. She might go back to work for the Ministry of Trade, where she'd worked before Abdul-Majid had been born. She might vote. She might grow old with Ratib, watch her sons become men, watch them go to college, have careers and wives of their own. She might live to see her grandchildren born.

And more bombs fell on the city. Bread prices doubled, tripled, quadrupled. There was no propane. There was no benzine. The satellite went in and out and eventually Iraq TV shut down, but the radio still played patriotic songs and reports of the Americans' defeat. When they could, they watched CNN or Al Jazeera. They watched balls of fire rise up in the night across the Dijlah, red and gold flowers blooming in the black water. They saw their city in green from above, in videos made by the men who were killing them, bright neon stripes cutting the screen, pale green explosions below.

They watched TV reporters in Kuwait, Qatar, and Israel put on gas masks. They watched American tanks push across their desert. They watched Iraqi soldiers surrender. They watched Iraqi soldiers die. They watched their brothers and husbands and sons forced to their knees and thrown like trash into the backs of trucks, blindfolded and hog-tied. On Al Jazeera, they saw children in rubble, ruptured bodies leaking like cracked pomegranates. On CNN they saw generals pointing at big maps full of arrows. Allahu akbar, cried the muezzin, la ilaha illallah. And more bombs fell.

Nazahah prayed. She bore the abuse of her sister, the discomforts when there was no light, no electricity, or no water, she bore the tremor of fear, she bore it all, praying constantly to God and the Prophet, to Khadija, the Prophet's wife, to Fatimah, the Prophet's daughter, and to Michael Jackson. God was testing them, just as he'd tested the Prophet, and she would show him her heart's recitation. So devout in her prayer was she that her absent-mindedness grew worse than ever. She let the kettle boil over. She burned bread. She forgot to give Qasim his antibiotic. She swept up the kitchen and left a small tidy pile of dirt in the middle of the floor. Her mother chided her. Khalida snapped at her. Maha hit her. And Nazahah prayed for forgiveness and mercy. She prayed to be less absent-minded. She prayed for God to make her eyebrows less bushy. She prayed for God to keep them all safe.

It was hard with all the fear in the house to feel the nearness of God. More and more, she spent her time alone, writing out prayers on slips of paper, reading the Qur'an and books on the Sira and the Hadith, and a book from the seventies about pan-Islamism. She drew secret pictures of the Prophet and Michael Jackson riding together on Buraq, the white, winged, woman-faced horse that carried the Prophet on the Isra and Miraj. She pictured the Prophet and Michael Jackson walking together in the desert, holding hands, Fatimah (looking suspiciously like Nazahah herself) walking behind them. She imagined they spoke together of the jagged beauty of palm trees and the buzz of bees, the way honey dripped clear and gold on flatbread, her father's smell when he'd been smoking—and of how the purity of God's mercy would conquer all, how great God was to have given us such a world, with red tomatoes and green reeds and the great brown Dijlah, the wonder of the muezzin's call and the glory of "Thriller," the perfection of breakfast at breakfast time, tea at teatime, and bed at bedtime. Nazahah prayed in ecstasies of gratitude that she was alive and that God had made the world and that the world was so perfect and full.

And more bombs fell. The lights went out. The electricity went out. The water stopped running. It came back on. It shut off again. They began to leave candles everywhere, and matches. They went to bed just after sundown, even though they knew they wouldn't sleep through the night, and arose at dawn, lethargic and anxious from the night's thundering bombardments. There was nothing else to do, with the power off and on, but lie in their misery and fear. Allahu akbar, cried the muezzin, la ilaha illallah. Day and night, bombs, rockets, and missiles crashed down into Baghdad, erupting in plumes of smoke, strewing metal and the screaming wounded. And they watched CNN, Al Jazeera, and the BBC. And they saw their city burning. They watched their husbands, sons, and brothers shot, captured, shamed, dishonored. They watched Umm Qasr fall. They watched Basra fall. They watched an-Nasiriyah fall. They watched Karbala fall. They huddled around a map, listening to the rumors on the news, trying to see how far the Americans had come.

Thurayya was calm and patient, the burden of her family a gratifying weight. She was their center, their mother. She made sure the men went to get bread, the generator was full of benzine, and the house clean and orderly and quiet. She was confident and assured, as if all her life she'd worked toward this moment, to take the family in hand and guide them through these hours of danger while the world outside was consumed in flames. She had what she needed, she had what she loved, and she would sustain them. She baked flatbread and made dinner. She told Maha to sweep and Abdul-Majid to wash his face. She leaned against her husband's broad back and felt his skin on her hands, and was happy knowing he was a brave, good man and that after the war passed, he would go out as he had the last time and rebuild their lives yet again. She had him here, now, and she lay with him at night in the darkness and was not afraid.

It wasn't like last time, when her daughters were still children and Mohammed was away, called up in the reserves. When she couldn't sleep at night for fear that he would die and she wouldn't even know. When her nightmares had woken the children and her days were a torment of waiting. She and her daughters had stayed with her mother, still alive then but deathly sick, in a tiny back room in her brother's house. She could still sometimes smell the stench of her mother's illness—it shamed her to think of, shamed her that she hadn't been strong enough for both her mother and her daughters at the same time. But all she could do back then was wait, pray, write her husband, and keep busy. Sometimes she would shake so hard from fear her teeth chattered—not for herself, not even for her daughters, but for Mohammed. Every night she prayed for him to live. Every day she prepared herself for his death.

When he came back, she vowed never to let him leave her, and he hadn't. He never took a business trip that kept him away more than one night. One night they could be apart, but no more. She wouldn't allow it. She had him. She had her home. She was in her home, with her husband and her daughters and her sister, and all would be well. They could go through a hundred bombings and a thousand tribulations, and she would stand strong and guide her household with a firm and loving hand. Mohammed was there and she was strong. She was full of love and forbearance for all, even her son-in-law Ratib, even her no-good runt nephew Qasim, who was, under her care, healing, fighting off the infection, growing stronger—he could eat solid foods now and even sit up and read. She was motherly even with Othman, toward whom she had always been polite but distant, for reasons she refused to think about too much but had to do with the sparkle in the old poet's eye. She gathered the household in her hands and set it to order. Even Maha, even Khalida she took in hand and set to work. There was chaos outside, but her family, her girls and her men, would sustain.

More bombs fell. There were rumors the Americans were coming from the east. From the west. From the south. They'd taken the Karbala Gap. They hadn't taken the Karbala Gap. They were in Baghdad. They weren't in Baghdad. The city choked on smog and explosions, lies and ash. The power went out for good, phones and water too. They ran the TV on the generator. The satellite came and went. They passed rumors from their neighbors at nighttime and rumors from their dreams at dawn. They began to hear artillery fire, big guns and mortars, distant thumps and nearer crashes.

One night, the Hizbis all left. The trenches and guard points around the city emptied, leaving ghost uniforms and boots and helmets, as if the men had evaporated where they stood. There were rumors US Marines had been seen in Al-Rusafa, on the east side of the Dijlah. Rumors the Kadhimaya Mosque had been bombed by stealth jets. Rumors Saddam had ordered the Fedayeen underground. Rumors Saddam was dead.

Suddenly, tanks in the streets. Humvees running down the avenues, heavy guns lobbing explosive rounds at houses and shadows. Rifles, machine guns, now the chatter of small-arms fire peppered their days and nights.

They quit going out. They locked the gate. They spoke to their neighbors through a crack in the second-story window. They didn't go onto the roof. More explosions, more shooting. One night they listened to a tank roll down their street. They heard it stop. They heard the whine of its turret and heard its gun fire, the sound of hell cracking open, then again, feeling it throb in their bellies, knees, and thumbs. They bowed their heads and prayed. Allahu akbar, la ilaha illallah. They heard a machine gun go *tock-tock-tock*, then the tank rolled away. It's target had been an empty house. Two gaping holes like blank eye sockets watched the street.

And more bombs fell. Allahu akbar, cried the muezzin, la ilaha illallah.

The blind man sat listening to the thunder, rubbing the stub of his tongue against the roof of his mouth. It was late. "Ah-ham," he muttered.

Trouble had come again, as it had before and before and before. He remembered the British biplanes of his youth, when he'd first joined the army, the way you could hear the click of the bomb releasing—poisonous gray eggs tumbling into the Kurdish lines. And then . . . He remembered the Tommies in their pointy helmets, marching the road to Baghdad. Before them, the Turk—but he could only faintly summon the Turk. Until the Revolt and the Great War, the press of world events had seemed distant.

There was so much to remember, so much to recall. So much to see and know and feel, so many dead to hold on to. So many dead. Even one life was too full. Even one life was so long and bloody, he could hardly bear it.

But that's what the poem was for. It was all there, his first love and his last, his long-dead father and long-lost sons, the fall of Baghdad and the coup d'état, the many revolutions. He remembered Mohammed al-Sadr's Independence Guard and the revolt against the British, the bright hope— he was what, fourteen? The shining dream of *nation* . . . He remembered fighting the Kurds, his years in the army, his wife, young, the late twenties, the days of hope as the people grew slowly to become *Iraq*—then Independence: 1932. There were celebrations.

We might as well have been mourning, he thought, for all the good it did us.

In the Assyrian revolt, he killed Assyrians. In the Shi'a revolt, he killed Shi'a. He helped protect the Turkish Petroleum Company, then the Iraqi Petroleum Company, as they pumped out the people's wealth and the people's oil. A coup, an assassination, another coup, the British returned and occupied Basra, Umm Qasr . . . The collapse, the Farhud, Iraqi Jews blamed and murdered, banished. And then, in 1948, the Catastrophe, the diabolical birth of the Zionist state and the war in Palestine. He led his men through the Jezreel Valley and up the Tell el-Mutesellim, which the Jews call Har Megiddo, fighting the Zionists, and many good men died. All for nothing.

It was all written down, and all for nothing. And many years later, when he dared speak his mind, when he dared utter the truth, was he not punished? Saddam had struck him down—but had not killed him, and that was his mistake. For do I not yet write? Do I not mark the truth in my book? Do I not chronicle my poem for the ages, to be sung by my children's children's children? They would blind me, but I see the truth. I see the truth and I write the truth, and our truth shall outlive theirs.

He jabbed the stub of his tongue against his teeth and pressed his pen to the blackened page. Another sura remained to be written.

Qasim gathered his strength. He was better now, though his hand was still weak. He'd decided: staying in Baghdad was cowardice. He went to Mohammed and asked to use the Toyota to go home to his wife in Baqubah.

Mohammed was proud but worried. There would be many dangers, not just the Americans. There were looters, Fedayeen—who knew? And where would you get benzine if you needed it? And what would you do if something happened? Qasim agreed that it might be difficult but argued that he should go sooner rather than later. No one knew when, or if, things would settle down. There might never be a better time than now. "I understand," Mohammed said, "but you're still healing. Stay a few more days."

"I'm strong now, Uncle. I've waited too long already."

"Qasim, you're still weak. You're not well enough yet. I can't let you go alone. It's too dangerous."

"Uncle, please," Qasim said, going to one knee before Mohammed at the kitchen table. "I have to go."

"No. You have to wait. I can't spare myself or Ratib to

take you, and we need the Toyota here. This is more of your foolishness. Wait until things calm down, and we'll figure something out."

Othman watched the discussion from the other end of the kitchen, fiddling with his lighter. Then he tapped it loudly on the table. "I'll go," he said.

Mohammed waved the idea away. "Don't be an idiot."

"I'll go with him. I can shoot, I can drive. I know the roads. We both know some English."

"A fool and a cripple. What a team."

"Mohammed, my friend, it's only seventy-five kilometers. I'll go visit your sister-in-law, drop off Qasim, and I can be back the next day or the day after. I have an old friend in Baqubah I'd like to check up on. Consider it a favor—to me. I want to see your nephew do the right thing. Let me help him."

Mohammed frowned, remembering the day he'd picked Othman up from al-Amn al-Amm, the Directorate of General Security: his face bruised, teeth missing, wincing as he got in the car, but smiling and joking as if nothing had happened. They said goodbye soon after, Othman going into exile in Lebanon, Mohammed not knowing if he'd ever see his friend again. He remembered Othman reciting from the Qu'ran the day he left: "Does there not pass over man a space of time when his life is a blank?" This time felt different, but how could you know? And what could he do? A man must follow the recitation of his soul. Mohammed shook his head in resignation. "Fine," he said. "Fine."

Qasim thanked Othman and Mohammed, then ran

upstairs to pack. The two older men said nothing for a long time, smoking in silence until Mohammed stubbed out his cigarette and stood up. "Bring the car back safe," he said, "or Thurayya will kill both of us."

The poet's eyes gleamed. "Insha'Allah."

babylon

Nothing is over: This is the story of a long-haired half-crazed Vietnam vet, harassed by small-town lawmen, lost on his one-man mission of vengeance. Back in the war, he was part of a ragtag team of misfit soldiers, hand-picked for a suicide mission to kill Hitler. Good and evil. He's a downed fighter pilot. He's red and white and blue.

This is the story of the sword. Gun. Dawn
patrols blacktop sit guided in a bad hundred feet drowned
gulf
military units added to the
brass shell dogs devour battle

so they too were made of vanity and 72 hours not from the stories of previous wars. Violence inflicted on the largest burden themselves, some of which depicted pyramids and the rest shocked of no-man's land. Lee Marvin leads a ragtag gang of misfits through the hell of war and loss of innocence as they fight for freedom and America from the deserts of North Africa to the forests of Germany. He's an idealistic young officer leading his all-black regiment on a suicide attack on a coastal fortress. No-man. Through me tell the story of one man's rage and the razing of an ancient

city. He's an idealistic young officer charged with cowardice for refusing to send his men to their death on a suicide
attack

new reports
electricity

widening the circle of direct blame for shooting it up my
ass. On first setting eyes, alas, my son, harassed by small
town artillery emplacements, a bridge no more. Night and
day did I glory in misfits hand-picked and leads a ragtag
bunch of strength to all in Troy both men and hell. From
the glory. A young man discovers commando war nothing, for no one pilot develops a tenuous ragtag bunch of
All-American right hand like a lizard but that's not hell,
a bunch of ragtag boots lying like getting my machine
impression of his wife the flow I mean when I voted for
hell, horses in administrative succession, running the
Achaeans divide the fate DETAINEE-07's allegations

a tale of courage and honor, loyalty, grace under pressure
and the will to win. He's a young, dedicated soldier sent
up the river to kill a rogue agent. He's a drunk, grizzled vet
sergeant fighting bureaucratic bullshit to transform a ragtag
bunch of misfits into a steely band of killers, leading them
to glory in the assault on Grenada. The allegations of

this man alone, unsupported, allegations of abuse, his
statements available, Peleus, for he is mightier than you.
Nevertheless, intel interests dogs and vultures, and a load

of grief would be lifted from my damage Iraq's eyewitness reports, life, both Iraqis cried: The British Academy has committed Muslims. Like people attacking a library. Ragtag. A young glory. An Army Special Forces operative goes up the river. A young man joins the Marines and becomes a photographer and is sent to Vietnam and learns that war is hell is hell. War story. A retired Special Forces operative returns to Vietnam to rescue his POW buddies. This is the story of the Center in Washington D.C. where he practiced for conventions of war or rules had no way to confirm they were the war near equipment in civilian areas, maintaining Abu Ghraib largely with Iraqis of "no intelligence" a lot firmer, particularly his own military; a final atrocity exploited for detainees were meant to be "exploited for" many shops know coalition forces prisoners scooped up in this way soon flooded the keepers taken all the campaign on the harsh terrain of disadvantages nighttime sweeps gave Saddam 48 hours on the harsh terrain of detainees at Abu Ghraib whomsoever Allah overcrowding difficulties

the Iraqi Academy of physical abuse while stuck here

This is a story of we happy stuck here. This is the story of a ragtag bunch of misfits picked for a suicide mission to stuck here. A young man. From the ragtag clutches. A noble, professional Special Forces commando learns that war is young. A young hell and ragtag bunch of All-American misfits fight Japs in the South Pacific and learn war is war. A bunch ragtag of young ragtag learn the true meaning of discipline and camaraderie and war and war. A young maverick risks everything to save his father from the Libyans. A ragtag bunch of Australians go halfway across the world and learn war is is. This is the story ragtag young man.

Stuck here. Stuck here. This is the story of valor, duty, and the cost of war. A young camaraderie. This is the story of a *young man* who learns war always has a cost. A young wacky. This is the story of a wacky bunch of ragtag misfits trying to escape from Nazi prison. A wacky bunch of ragtag misfits running an Army hospital in Korea. A ragtag maverick valor war. This is the story of a young man's war, the story of we happy few.

your leader will control your fire

(operation iraqi freedom, 2004)

fear is not shameful
if it is controlled

The plane tilted on its side and through the window in the opposite bulkhead Baghdad whirled below, taking my stomach with it. Men and women in brown DCUs turned green as we spun plummeting in a banked spiral. The guy across the aisle puked in a bag and his buddy cheered.

We rolled against the sky, then at the last minute flopped flat and came in straight. The engines growled down into the final approach, and we dropped the last few inches slamming to the deck.

They downloaded our bags and we threw them in the back of a five-ton. The truck took us to a staging area. Contacting Battalion to arrange pickup, I was surprised by how eager I felt to see my fellow soldiers—I had to make sure they were okay, but as much as that I just wanted to see their faces. They understood. They knew this shit world we lived in, knew it all better than anyone I could talk to back in Oregon. I realized as well that I was itching to get back outside the wire. The berms, palm trees, and sand around me seemed not just familiar but comforting. Normal. I wanted to scan rooftops. I wanted shots fired. I wanted ninja women in abayas, hadjis in man-dresses. I wanted to hear and talk salaam a-leykum, ishta, uskut. I wanted my rifle.

It was hard to believe I'd just been back in the land of shopping malls and big hair, showing my ex-girlfriend photo after photo: this is my humvee, this is Captain Yarrow, this is Camp Lancer, this is the UN before, the UN after. How was it possible that just a few weeks ago I'd come down into Portland, rain drumming on the plane's windows, feeling the war slip off like an old jacket?

When I got off the plane, there was my ex-girlfriend and another girl, an old friend, and we hugged and kissed and grinned. In the parking garage by the car, they lifted their skirts and showed off their matching Superman panties. My heart was full of love.

All the long ride home while the girls talked to me and each other, I scanned overpasses for snipers and watched the shoulder for IEDs. I kept reaching back for my rifle, startled that I'd lost it, and eyeballed cars passing on 205, feeling spooked, thinking I need a drink, I need a smoke, how the fuck long do I have to do this alone?

Now, after weeks of being apart, she'd be there waiting for me.

Geraldo showed up in C7.

"'Sup, Wheat Thin."

"Good to be home, Cheeto."

"You missed a dope barbecue."

"Anybody get killed?"

"Naw. Burnett some caught shrapnel from an IED. Like a thumbtack. Purple Heart's tomorrow. You have yourself some fun?"

"I didn't know what to do with nobody shooting at me. I got laid, though. Any word on redeployment?"

"Saying April."

"April, huh?"

"What they say."

"That's like ninety days."

"Ninety days be ninety days."

On the way back to the CP, I watched the West Side DFAC go by and the road to Gate 5. The route I had run in the mornings and the fenced-off mosque. We passed Battalion Maintenance, the mini-PX, and the hemmet lot, finally pulling into our compound. I didn't know whether to cry or scream or shit myself.

I got out and downloaded my gear. On my way to draw my weapon, I ran into Nash and Sergeant Chandler.

"What are you doing here, Sergeant? I thought you were getting out."

"Yeah, so did I," he said.

"What d'you mean?"

"Three days before my orders, I get fucking stop-lossed."

"Say what?"

"Stop-loss. No-Movement Orders come down for all units in support of OIF. Nobody ETSes out of Iraq anymore."

"What the fuck's that mean? You don't get out?"

"Not till we get back."

"That is some fucked-up shit. But it's only ninety days, right?"

"So they say. But enough about my troubles. How was leave?"

"Fucking-A, man. I ate everything. I drank everything. I got fucked. I saw the new Lord of the Rings movie, which was awesome. And this—you gotta check this out." I dug through my backpack. "You and me, Sergeant, we're *Person of the Year*." I handed them the *Time* magazine with the 1AD guys on the cover.

"No shit."

"Yeah. There's a big article in there about how fucked up it's been for 4-27."

"I guess we're too boring."

"It's weird man, coming back. At the Dallas airport, there was this line of flag wavers, and anytime anyone found out I was in Iraq, they got all serious and shit, started thanking me and telling me what a great thing it was I was doing. I didn't know what to say. Like, hell yeah, fuck hadji! I mean, what the fuck?"

"Bet you got a lot of ass."

"Sure, well . . . I was fooling around with my ex, but . . . if I'd wanted, there was definitely opportunity. I mean, what chick doesn't wanna fuck a war hero?"

I left them with the magazine and went to draw my rifle. As I crossed the motor pool, I seemed to be walking through a dream. I felt too relaxed. Everyone else was depressed and hateful, just like I remembered, but the difference was me: I was okay. I could see our frustrated rage, our barely checked aggression, our loneliness, our desperation, and for the first time ever, I could see it without belonging to it. If I can just hang on to this, I thought, I'll get through. Everything'll be fine.

Later I talked to Bullwinkle and he said yeah, that lasts about three days.

when defending, or when temporarily halted while making an attack, you must seek cover from fire and concealment from observation

We hauled our gear into the new barracks at FOB Raptor: lines of squat, cinder-block rooms inside a dim, echoing, sheet-metal hangar. We were assigned four to. My roommates were Sergeant Chandler, Stoat, and Reading.

The best part was the latrine. Instead of porta-johns, we had an actual building. Gleaming mirrors. Linoleum floor. Toilet paper. Twenty stalls, separated by white plywood, with doors and flushing toilets. White porcelain sinks. Fourteen showers with curtains, drains, and high-power nozzles. Hot and cold running water.

We ranged the FOB with a quickness, reporting back to each other like kids scouting a theme park. There was a small PX, a hadji souvenir shop, a hadji coffee shop, laundry service with three-day turnaround, a hadji barber, internet café, hadji bootleg-DVD shop, hadji smoothie stand, gym with elliptical trainers, weight machines, and treadmills, and some outdoor volleyball and basketball courts.

Ninety days.

Too easy.

Our patrols weren't difficult. Baghdad had calmed down over the winter. There was less shooting, fewer IED attacks, fewer random ambushes. We rolled through the same garbage-strewn, sewage-washed streets over and over.

Men stood before turquoise-tiled mosque doors, impeccably dressed, watching us go by. Little kids in pink pants waved. Old women in niqabs waved. Shopkeepers waved.

We had terps with us every day now. There was Anuman, an older guy with a short beard, once an economist; Big Joe, who wore mirrored sunglasses and a black leather jacket, who loved American TV and thought American women were "the hottest bitches in the world"; Qasim, a nervous, stick-thin math professor with a Scottish accent; and Ramana, who we called Bertha, a great surly mound of a woman who used to do something with computers. There were others we only met once or twice: Frick and Frack the dental students, Akbar the pimp, Ms. al-Radi the psychiatrist.

Life took on a dependable rhythm. We went to the internet café. We emailed friends and family. Reading and Cheese played *Warcraft III*. Other guys posted photos on Hot or Not and bragged about their ratings. I googled places to go on vacation, broke up with my ex, and ordered thick nineteenth-century novels from Amazon.

We blew our tax-free combat pay on CDs, digital cameras, portable DVD players, creatine powder, protein shakes,

Maxim, and cases of Red Bull. On patrol we'd drive to the hadji market in the Green Zone, which had the best bootlegs in Baghdad. Little kids ran up shouting "Ficky-ficky DVD," their hands full of porn.

A private in Attack Battery got killed by an IED. At the ceremony, we stood in formation while the chaplain read from the Bible and some soldiers got up and talked about what a great guy the dead kid was. Lieutenant Colonel Braddock stood and told us how important it was that we were doing the job we were doing and how important it was to bring democracy to Iraq, and most important, how we were defending American freedom from the terrorists who hated our way of life.

The bomb had gone off under the kid's humvee. The charge had been buried in a pothole and covered with plaster of Paris, probably detonated by cell phone. One of the guys in Attack told me they left more of him stuck charred inside the truck than they put in the body bag.

"We're fighting them in the streets of Baghdad," the Colonel said, "so we won't have to fight them in the streets of Jacksonville, Florida, or the streets of Galveston, Texas, or the streets of PFC Gabriel's hometown of Culver City."

Taps played on a boombox. Halfway through, the CD started skipping. Then somebody bumped it with his foot and it stopped.

do not move: la ta-ta-HAR-rak

do not resist: la ta-QAOWM

We set up Traffic Control Points, usually at night, where we pulled over random hadjis and searched their cars. The LT's favorite spot was Checkpoint 15, an overpass spanning the main expressway along our route. On the north side it fed into a neighborhood, but on the south, the concrete dropped off twenty meters past the entrance ramp, making the overpass a one-way street and a low-traffic exit.

We set up on both sides to cover all the zones. Two guys stood at the top of the ramp with rifles and a high-powered flashlight. We'd flash a car and, once they pulled over, have them get out and open the doors, the hood, the trunk, everything. While the hadjis stood in the dark by the side of the road, we dug through all their crap, searching for weapons, I guess, or maybe bombs or some kind of Axis-of-Evil, al-Qaeda spy shit.

We pulled over a van full of young women in hijab, driven by a middle-aged guy with an enormous mustache. He got out, but when Qasim explained that the women had to get out too, he shook his head.

"La. La," he said.

"Naam, motherfucker," I said. "They come the fuck outta the van. Everybody."

The man said something to Qasim and something to us. Burnett hefted his rifle.

Reading said, "Look at all them bitches!"

Qasim explained: "These are his daughters. He says they cannot be seen standing by the side of road in the night like this. Is very bad. Okay?"

"No, not okay," I said. "They all gotta come out."

"It is very . . . ashamed for them," Qasim said. "Is no good."

"I get the one in blue," Reading said.

"I don't fucking care," I said. "Everybody comes outta the van."

Qasim said something to the man, who exploded in frustration, screaming in Arabic. I shouted back: "Those girls come the fuck outta the car, or we zip you. Got it?"

Qasim translated and the man glared at me, stomping his foot.

"Tell him," Burnett said gently, "they either come out on their own, or we drag 'em out."

"Tell him if they don't come out, we're gonna rape 'em," said Reading.

"Shut up, Reading."

"Tell him they come out on their own or we drag 'em out, alright?"

Qasim translated and the man stood indignant.

"Hey, Reading," I said, "will you get some zip-strips?"

"Roger," he said, stepping off to the humvees.

When the man saw the zip-strips, he relented. He herded the girls as far away from us as we'd allow, angry and alert as a riled dog. The women stared at the ground. Reading hung back by the railing so he could ogle their asses.

"Come here and open the trunk," I said to the man. Qasim translated. The man looked at the girls, at Reading, at the van, at us. He didn't move. "Fucking c'mere, bitch," I shouted, and Qasim said something to him. The man came over reluctantly, watching the girls back over his shoulder, opened the rear door of the van, then scurried back.

We took our time completing the search. We poked under the sunshades, we dug under the seats. Burnett cut a hole in the rear bench with his knife. The glove box was closed so we yelled for the guy to come open it, which he did, then we had him come back again to open the engine cover.

"You wanna fuck with him?" Burnett asked me.

"Maybe. How?"

"Let's tell him we think there's an IED in the van, so we zip-strip him and his daughters and leave 'em sit awhile. Then we just stand around, right, let him fucking sweat."

"Seems more trouble than it's worth."

"Let him cool his heels awhile," Burnett said. "That fucking guy needs to learn who's boss."

"Alright," Staff Sergeant Smith shouted from the humvees. "There a problem or you gonna get that van outta here?"

"We're trying to score with these bitches, Sarnt," Reading shouted back.

"Score with bitches on your own time, Private. Get that van outta here."

I told Qasim to tell the man he was free to go, but that the next time Coalition Forces told him what to do, he better just fucking do it. Qasim translated and the man barked back at us in Arabic, spit on the ground, and stamped his foot. He loaded up his girls and drove off.

Later that night we stopped a car full of hadjis with a flat of beer in the back seat. Foster and Burnett started giving them a hard time, so the men offered us some. Burnett took the cans and passed them around, plus one for Staff Sergeant Smith and one for the LT, then let the car go. We drank and watched the traffic go by under the bridge and decided to start a shakedown.

"You give me beer," Burnett would say, leaning in the window.

"No beer," the hadji might say, and we'd let them go, or "Beer, yes," and they'd hand us some cans.

After four or five successful contraband seizures, we broke down the TCP and just drove around, our buzz brushing the night to a smooth gleam.

Walking back to the barracks one day from visiting Villaguerrero at Battalion, I saw Qasim sitting outside the terp shack, smoking and drinking tea.

"Sabah al-khayr," I said.

"Sabah al-noor," he replied. "You speak very good Arabic."

"Not really, but thanks. You off today?"

"Yes. I was going to go see my uncle, but he says to me… is very dangerous, Qasim, and better you not come."

"Dangerous how?"

"My, how you say, the husband of my uncle's daughter?"

"Shit, I don't know. Cousin-in-law?"

"So, my cousin-law . . . is very religious and . . . he does not like the Americans. He wants you to go home, because you are not Muslim. So sometime he stays with my uncle, because . . . because. Other times he goes to family. When he stays with my uncle, I do not go. Because I work for you."

"That must be hard."

"Is better than Baqubah. After the invasion I go to Baqubah because my wife and mother . . . My wife . . . My mother, she is dead now."

"I'm sorry to hear that."

"Many are dead now. Hers was quiet. Hers was at peace. She's with God now. But in Baqubah, it is very difficult. Too many religious, Sunni, Shia, same-same. They fight. Baghdad is not so difficult. Things are bad—but bad all over, so maybe Baghdad is more good. Better."

"Is it better now? I mean now that we got rid of Saddam?"

"Some ways better. Other ways more bad. Instead of one Saddam, now too many Saddam. You see? You need to stay, you need to be . . . on the street. You need to be very strong. It is very difficult for Iraq; we have no parliament, no Magna Carta. We have tribes, families. We have the sheikh, we have the ayatollah, we have the imam. You see? No Saddam, no sheikh, then we fight, and is why we need you to stay. Yes? You will be here a long time, I think."

"I don't know," I said. "Probably."

"A long time, I think," he said. "Many things are very bad now. Water is very bad. You see . . . how do you say, *sewer*? Yes? The sewer when we patrol? Very bad. Electricity very bad. Economy bad. Shops are open but there is much . . . Some things very expensive. Small things. Also security very bad, very dangerous, especially for woman. A woman cannot go out from the house. My uncle, his daughters make him crazy. For why? Because they cannot go out. Two men to go out of the house, and the woman have to wear very much hijab, and the man have a gun. Very dangerous. Very bad. In Baqubah is worse. I work with the American there, like here, but Baqubah very small. Everybody . . . how you say . . . everybody all up in each other's shit. So I cannot work in Baqubah, because they say they kill my wife and family. But in Baghdad is okay. Sometimes they try to shoot or kidnap. But they know my face only. They don't know who is my family, where I live, and when I go to my uncle, I am very careful. My . . . cousin-law, he does not know, but if he did, is safe. Not okay, but safe. Because family is number one, yes?"

"Are you glad we came? Are you glad we got rid of Saddam?"

"It is no good to be glad or sad of God's will. We live. We die. God's will. What do I say to you, Specialist Wilson? Are you glad you came?"

"I'm glad we made it this far."

"Yes. This far."

"Yeah . . . Well, I should go hit the gym. It was nice to talk with you, Qasim."

"Okay, yes. Very nice to talk with you, Specialist Wilson. You see, we can all speak together, Iraqi and American. Friends, yes? But soon I must go from Baghdad and return to Baqubah. My wife is sick. I think you will not see me for many weeks. But someday we meet again, insha'Allah."

He gently shook my hand, then touched his heart.

"Stay safe, Qasim. Salaam a-leykum."

"Leykum a-salaam, Specialist Wilson."

arabs, much more so than westerners,
express emotion
in a forceful, animated and exaggerated fashion

We woke up Porkchop and Geraldo. "Get up, fuckers.
You're relieved."

"Where's Sergeant Gooley?" Porkchop asked, blinking.

"Sergeant Reynolds is SOG."

Reading took off his Kevlar and set it on the Jersey barrier.
His buzz-cut hair glowed a sickly brass in the fluorescent
light, a field of bruised pennies.

"Where Sergeant Reynolds at?" Geraldo asked.

"He's right behind us," I said.

"Aight. We out." Geraldo took his rifle and stepped off
down the road. Porkchop followed and they met Staff Sergeant Reynolds at the clearing barrel, where he watched
them clear their weapons.

When there was a pause in the radio traffic, I picked up
the walkie-talkie: "Red Steel Main, this is Red Steel India.
Radio check, over."

"RED STEEL INDIA, THIS IS RED STEEL MAIN, ROGER
OUT."

Staff Sergeant Reynolds came up, glowering at us with his bug-eyes. "Reading, I want you to have your Kevlar on at all times," he said.

Reading turned his face away as if he hadn't heard.

"Now listen up, men, you need to make sure you police this AO. There's cigarette butts in the dirt back there. This is a high-visibility area and the sergeant major's gonna come through. And get inside the guard shack, too."

"Hooah, Sergeant," I said.

"Now what do you do when you open the gate?"

"One of us goes up and the other one covers him."

"Right. Now, if you're gonna open the gate, I want both of you up there, one to handle the door and one to watch outside. Somebody could shoot an RPG right through there. That's what I'd do, if I was them. I'd come by in one of those pickups and send somebody to knock on the door, and when you opened the gate, I'd shoot an RPG right through. *Bam!* Then what? Huh? You gotta think tactically. Now, what do you do if somebody comes over the wall?"

"Shoot 'em!" Reading barked.

"Right! Then call it up."

"Nobody's coming over the wall, Sergeant. It's like fifty feet high."

"That's what you think. That kind of complacency is what gets soldiers killed."

"Roger, Sergeant."

"And when the ICDC come through, I want you to check each one. Don't let the other hadjis do it. They could have bombs hidden anywhere."

"No way," Reading said. "Hadjis fucking stink."

"Roger, Sergeant," I said. "We'll take care of it."

"You know these ICDC," he said. "They've taken an oath, but they could still be Fedayeen or al-Qaeda or who knows what. Just because they're on our side doesn't mean you can trust 'em. One ICDC with a hand grenade would jack up your whole day. What would happen if they got into the chow hall? Check, and double check."

"Shit, I *wish* they'd blow up the chow hall," Reading said.

"Roger, Sergeant Reynolds. We'll search each one ourselves."

"Okay. You guys already set for breakfast and everything?"

"Roger, Sergeant."

"Make sure you do your radio checks."

"Just did, Sergeant."

"Okay. I'll be back in a couple hours, and I expect this AO to be straight."

"Roger, Sergeant."

"And Reading, keep your Kevlar on. Carry on, men."

We watched Staff Sergeant Reynolds walk away.

Reading giggled. "In the case of an all-out assault, I'm gonna shit myself and throw it at 'em. Take that, hadji! Shit bomb!"

It began with a knock at the gate, *prom-prom-prom*. The sliding rusted metal door, thirty feet wide and twenty feet tall, trembled from the pounding.

"F'tal bob," I said.

Reading snickered.

The two ICDC stared at him.

"F'tal bob, motherfucker!" I shouted, pointing at the gate, pointing at the younger of the two hadjis.

The light was a clear yellow-gray, the sun a white smear still low in the sky.

The younger hadji got up and picked up his AK and started walking out toward the gate.

"See who it is," I said.

"You," Reading said back, not looking up from his Game Boy. "I'm in the middle of a level."

"Fuck your level. Go see who it is."

"Why you such a bitch, Wilson?"

"Because I hate freedom, motherfucker. Go see who it is."

"Whatever," Reading said, pausing his game and setting it on his chair. "Don't touch my game."

"I'm gonna kill your fucking Metroid, is what I'm gonna do."

Reading flipped me off and walked around the barrier, putting his Kevlar on as he went.

"Hey, John Wayne. Forget something?"

Reading turned back at me, scowled, and shook his head. He came back for his rifle, picked it up, and went back toward the gate. The ICDC had unlatched the gate and was throwing his weight against it, sliding it open with a rumble and a creak. Reading held his weapon at the ready.

A hadji in civilian clothes stood outside the gate with a gym bag. Thin and scraggly, with messy black hair and a large mustache, he wore a checkered work shirt, track pants, and sandals.

"ID," Reading said.

He pulled out his Iraqi Civil Defense Corps badge and showed it. Reading checked the badge against the man's face and nodded, directing him inside.

"Come here," I shouted, waving him forward. I stood, picked up my rifle, and slung it at the ready. I nodded to the older ICDC sitting smoking against the shack wall. "Check his bag," I said.

He lurched up and went around the Jersey barrier and when the hadji came up he took his bag and poked through it.

"Pat him down," I told the older ICDC. I pointed at the one in civilian clothes and spread my arms and legs. "Search, search," I said.

The one in civilian clothes mimicked me and the older one patted him down.

"Turn around," I said to him, swirling my finger.

He stared at me.

"Turn around," I shouted, swirling my finger again.

He turned to face the gate. The older ICDC patted him down.

I swatted at the Iraqi's ass and said, "Check here, yeah." I cupped my groin. "Check his package."

He shook his head and grimaced, but I repeated my order, so he stuck his hand between the other man's legs and batted it around.

"Mota dudeki," I said. The hadji in civilian clothes laughed.

The guard stepped back, scowling, and tapped the man on the shoulder, who turned back around grinning.

"Go on," I said, pointing down the road at the ICDC barracks. Meanwhile, more hadjis had showed up for their shift, and Reading checked their IDs and lined them up. I gestured the next one forward. First one by one, then in twos and threes, then one big gaggle, and at last the last stragglers.

The sun was up now, the morning chill burnt off.

Soon two new ICDC in ill-fitting fatigues and old boots came to relieve the two at the gate. The old shift handed over their AKs and secondhand flak vests and the new shift took up positions in the cheap white plastic chairs.

"Well, that was exciting," Reading said, returning to *Metroid*.

I took off my Kevlar and dug through my backpack. I pulled out a *Maxim* and an *FHM* and a *Harper's*, and the ICDC leaned toward me staring. I gave them the *Maxim* and kept the other two for myself.

It went like this: report for guard mount at 0750, then you're on duty in the sun till 1400. Then you clear your weapon and walk back to the barracks and sleep until 0100. You get up in the dark, get ready, and make it to guard mount at 0150, pull duty until 0800. The sun's come up. Then you go eat breakfast, jerk off, and sleep until 1300. Guard mount 1350, on duty till 2000, clear your weapon, walk back to the barracks in the dark, think of some other life you lived once, sleep, get up at 0700, back to guard mount at 0750, and the cycle repeats. Light, dark, dark, light, night day whatever.

Reading played *Metroid* in the doorway. I sprawled on the cot inside the shack, drifting in and out of consciousness.

The two ICDC sat outside in the night, smoking and looking at body-spray ads in *FHM*.

"Shit, man," Reading said.

I ignored him.

"Shit, I'm so bored, I'm bored of *Metroid*."

I lay still, pleading with God to make him silent.

"I know you're awake. When you think we'll get off this
shit?"

"Let me sleep, fucker."

"All you fucking do is sleep."

"That's because I don't drink all those fucking Red Bulls."

"Shit keeps me alert. I'm a killing machine!"

"You're a fucking talking machine."

"Shit, man. Shit! When you think we'll get off this?"

"Never."

"We gotta get off sometime."

"Nope. Never. The unit's gonna redeploy to Germany
and they're gonna leave us here to guard the ICDC gate.
We're mission essential. We're the tip of the goddamn
spear."

"I wanna go out on patrols like the other guys."

"So tell Lieutenant Krauss you wanna go out on patrol."

"He's pissed at me because I shot up that house."

"You shot the shit outta that house."

"There was a dude with an AK up there, I swear."

"Yeah, he was up there fucking your mom."

"Shit. Whatever. He was up there."

"That's why you got taken off the SAW?"

"Yeah."

"Dumbass."

"What'd *you* do to piss him off?"

"I don't fucking know, man. I read a book one time. I just fucking do what I'm told."

"Well, you musta done something."

"Maybe he wants me to watch your dumb ass, make sure you don't shoot up the gate."

"Whatever."

The radio popped: "RED STEEL MAIN, THIS IS RED STEEL FIFTEEN. BE ADVISED WE GOT A VEHICLE STOPPED ACROSS THE ROAD."

"ROGER THAT, RED STEEL FIFTEEN."

"Hey, that's our tower."

"RED STEEL FIFTEEN, THIS IS RED STEEL SEVEN. MONITOR THE VEHICLE. IF IT STAYS LONGER THAN FIVE MINUTES, CALL US BACK."

"ROGER, RED STEEL SEVEN. STAND BY."

I sat up and grabbed my Kevlar. Reading paused his game. We looked at each other, reaching for our rifles.

"RED STEEL SEVEN, THIS IS RED STEEL FIFTEEN. THE VEHICLE HAS LEFT."

"ROGER RED STEEL FIFTEEN, RED STEEL SEVEN OUT."

I dropped my Kevlar and lay back down. Reading dug through his backpack and pulled out a Red Bull.

"Hadjis coming," he said. "Ali and Ahmed."

"Ali Dudeki?"

"Yeah."

"Fuck."

The two hadjis came in. Ali was tall for an Iraqi, with a stubborn, mischievous face. He made a game out of grabbing guys' nuts, though ever since Porkchop hog-tied him with zip-strips and left him like that for an afternoon, he was less inclined. Ahmed was shorter, a hunchback, and some kind of NCO—he was always harassing the guards, berating them, checking their AKs. With us he played the clown, shouting the handful of obscenities he knew in English over and over. Ali seemed to be Ahmed's sidekick; it was clear the hunchback ran things.

"Sadiki! Sabah an-noor!" Ali shouted.

"Ali Dudeki," Reading croaked, not looking up from his game.

"Fuck shit, shut up!" Ahmed barked, slapping Ali on the back of his head. "Yeeeeah," he crooned, twisting his head back over his hump.

"Ahmed, sadiki," I said, sitting up. "Shaku maku?"

"Very good, very good, yeeeeah! No problem!"

"Sadiki," Ali said, lifting his eyebrows and pointing at my bag, "you bring ne ficky-ficky?"

"No, Ali. No ficky-ficky."

"Tomorrow and tomorrow, Sadiki? Any o'clock? You bring ne ficky-ficky?"

"Maybe if you're good."

Ali smiled at me, then tiptoed over to Reading. Reading, absorbed in his game, seemed not to notice the big man as he reached out slowly for Reading's nuts. Then, in a swift blur, Reading dropped his Game Boy, grabbed Ali's wrist, and lunged up, pulling his arm around his head and lifting him into the air, then bending him onto the concrete. Reading fell on the big hadji, pinning him with his knees, slapping his face.

"Shit fuck, shit ass, shit!" shouted Ahmed.

"You mota mota good, huh?" Reading asked Ali, slapping him, "You mota me, huh? Mota mota? Ali Dudeki? Ali Menuch?"

Ali grinned and tried to cover his face and buck Reading off, but Reading had him wrapped up. "You fucked with the wrong motherfucker, Ali. Now you're getting zip-zipped."

"No, no," Ali begged. "No zip-zip. Sadiki no zip-zip."

"Then knock it the fuck off!"

"No zip-zip. Ali no zip-zip."

"Alright, fucker," Reading said, standing and helping Ali to his feet. "No zip-zip—this time!"

Ali stood up and smiled shyly at Reading. "Sadiki," he said, very seriously.

"What, fucker?"

"Tomorrow and tomorrow, you bring ne ficky-ficky? Any o'clock?"

"No, you fucking faggot."

"Tomorrow you, you, meshi meshi, ficky-ficky?" Ali pointed at Reading, then at himself, then at the gate.

"What?"

Ali made moon eyes at Reading. "You, you, meshi meshi? Mota? Mota?"

"I think he wants you to go home with him," I said.

"No fucking mota, dudeki!"

"Yeeeeeah!" Ahmed crooned. "Shit! Fuck! Shut up!"

Ahmed the hunchback went outside and started talking to the ICDC. Ali sat on the edge of my cot until I kicked him in the hip and he walked off, staring at

Reading, who resumed his game. After a minute, Ahmed called Ali away.

"Fucking fag," Reading muttered.

Explosions in the night. We tumble out of bed and throw on our armor and wait for more mortars. Silence. Half an hour later someone comes and tells us stand down. The next day there's a pit gouged out of the earth behind the guard shack.

Two EOD sergeants and a first sergeant from DIVARTY come down and do crater analysis, stepping in and out of the hole, divining esoteric data.

The radio squawked: "MEEEOW."

"What the fuck?"

"MEEEOW."

"It's the fuckers in the towers."

"MEEEOW."

"THIS IS RED STEEL SEVEN. WHOEVER'S DOING THAT, YOU BETTER KNOCK IT OFF RIGHT NOW."

"MEEEOW."

"Fucking retards."

"LIMIT YOUR RADIO TRAFFIC TO ESSENTIAL MESSAGES. I'M SERIOUS. RED STEEL SEVEN OUT."

"OR   I'LL FUCK YOU IN YOUR EYEBALLS! FUCK-A-DOODLE-DOO!"

"THIS IS RED STEEL SEVEN. KNOCK THAT SHIT OFF. RIGHT NOW. I'M SERIOUS."

"MEEEOW."

■ ■ ■

Clouds hung low over the mucky earth, turning everything gray. Shots had been fired at the guard tower in a drive-by, so everyone was on alert. Staff Sergeant Reynolds warned us Sergeant Major might be coming through. Reading worked his thumbs on the Game Boy.

"What fucking day is it?"

"Today?"

"No. Yesterday, motherfucker."

"Yesterday was the day before."

"What day today?"

"Fucking shit day."

"Tuesday?"

"Whatever."

Two ICDC guards sat smoking, flipping through my copy of the *Vanity Fair* issue with the big Michael Jackson exposé. One of the ICDC was younger, chubby, trying to grow a mustache and failing, the other was slightly older, his face pocked with acne scars. I watched them look at the fashion shots, the pictures of Neverland Ranch, the ads for J. Lo perfume and Patek Philippe watches.

"You like America?" I asked.

"Al-Ameriki?" the younger one said.

"Yeah. America good?"

"Yes, al-Ameriki good," he beamed.

"Michael Jackson good?"

"Yes yes, Michael Jackson. *Ee-hee*. Very good."

"You like Bush? Bush good?"

"Boosh good yes."

"How 'bout Saddam? You like Saddam?"

"Saddam no good. Saddam Ali Baba," the older one said, stamping his foot and spitting.

"You Shi'a?"

"Sunni."

"Ayatollah Sistani good?"

He shrugged.

"Moqtada al-Sadr good?"

"Al-Sadr very good," the young one said.

"Shi'a?" I pointed at the young one.

"Naam. Shi'a." He pointed at himself.

"Bush good, no Saddam?"

"Saddam no good."

"Bush no good," I said, shaking my head. "Bush Ali Baba."

"No!" the older one said, aghast.

"Saddam, Bush, same-same," I said. "Ali Baba, Ali Baba."

"No, Boosh good," the young one said.

"Ali Baba," I said.

The older one pointed at me. "You Christ-ian?"

"La. No god."

He seemed cross: "Yes God."

"La."

He shook his head. "No good."

There was a bang at the door. I pointed at the young one and pointed at the door, got up and grabbed my rifle, and followed him to it. "F'tal bob," I said, and he unlatched the gate and put his shoulder to and slid it open.

A middle-aged hadji stood outside in a dishdasha. A couple more stood behind him.

"Salaam a-leykum," I said.

"Leykum-a-salaam," he said back, bowing slightly.

"What's up?"

He started talking Arabic, then "Boom, boom, koom-bal-lah. Ali baba." He gestured back for one of his friends to come up.

"We have information," the guy said. "Bomb and bad yes."

"Okay, hold on." I turned back to Reading. "Fucker," I shouted. He looked up from his game.

"What?"

"Get on the radio and see if you can get a translator."

"For what?"

"This guy says he has information."

"About what?"

"About your mom. Fucking call somebody."

Reading picked up the walkie-talkie and called Staff Sergeant Reynolds. They talked back and forth for a minute then Reading shouted, "Sergeant Reynolds gonna go see if he can get one."

"Call up Red Steel Main and see what they say."

"What I tell 'em?"

"Tell them we have an Iraqi who says he has information on a bomb."

"He got a bomb?"

"He has *information* on a bomb."

"Information."

"Yeah."

"So what?"

"So call Red Steel Main."

He picked up the other walkie-talkie and called Red Steel

Main. He talked to them for a few minutes, then shouted at me: "They say he gotta go to Foxtrot Gate."

"That's the one on the south side, right?"

"Fuck if I know."

Staff Sergeant Reynolds called Reading back so I waited, and when they were done Reading shouted, "He said he can't find a translator, and I told him Red Steel Main said send him to Foxtrot Gate and he said that's fine."

I turned back to the hadjis.

"You go around, go to Foxtrot Gate," I gestured around, pointing toward the southwest edge of the FOB.

"We have in-formation," the one said again.

"Yeah, I know. You have to go around."

"Go round?"

"Yeah, Foxtrot gate. The other bob."

"You help? Ali Baba?"

"No, go around. You gotta go to the other bob."

"We have in-formation. Koom-ballah."

"Yeah, I understand, but you gotta go around. Salaam," I said, grabbing the gate and yanking on it. "Sit'l bob," I shouted at the ICDC.

The hadjis started shouting in Arabic, but we closed the gate and latched it and went back and sat down.

We got off shift. Daytime, nighttime. I slept about five hours. When I got up, I worked out, cleaned my rifle and watched *Malcolm in the Middle*. Reading slept.

We lost track of the other guys, the daily patrols, what the fuck was happening. We started talking all the time in pidgin English. The big news was that one patrol got attacked by a retarded kid throwing rocks. He threw a rock and hit Bullwinkle in the face, knocking out one of his teeth. The patrol stopped and Lieutenant Krauss and Nash covered the kid.

The kid picked up another rock.

"Put the rock down," Nash shouted, but the kid lifted it up like he was gonna throw, so Nash shot him in the chest.

Healds was with them, so he patched the kid up, then they drove him to the hospital in the Green Zone.

A week or so later they got me and Reading up in the middle of the day, when we were trying to sleep, and made us go down to formation. They had a little ceremony and awarded Nash a Bronze Star for valor. Captain Yarrow talked about what a great job he'd done defending the patrol.

"The only thing Nash did wrong was forget his training," the captain said. "We trained and trained, *two* rounds center mass! Maybe next time you'll get it right!" Yarrow chuckled.

Nash stared straight ahead.

Reading sat watching *Friends*. I read Chomsky's *For Reasons of State*. Headlights flashed at us from down the road and I shouted at Reading to hide his DVD player. I put on my Kevlar and stood and grabbed my rifle. A big black SUV rolled up and a sergeant got out.

"At ease," he said. "You on guard here?"

"Roger."

"Listen, there's a suspected VBIED attack tonight. We've

got jammers in here but you gotta shut down your radios while they work."

"Uh, alright. Let me call up higher and let them know."

I called up Red Steel and Staff Sergeant Gooley and let them know we were gonna be out of radio contact. Red Steel verified the jammers had priority. I shut off the radios and the sergeant said thanks then climbed back in his truck.

Reading went back to *Friends*. I went back to my book. They stayed there for about two hours, then the sergeant opened his window and told us we could turn our radios back on. After that they left.

Ali Dudeki came by and asked for ficky-ficky magazine. I offered him the Michael Jackson *Vanity Fair* but he didn't want it.

"You bring ne ficky-ficky tomorrow, any o'clock?" he asked. "Tomorrow and tomorrow?"

"No ficky," I told him. "Tomorrow and tomorrow and tomorrow."

i can't tell you if the use of force
in iraq today will last five days,
five weeks, or five months,
but it won't last any longer than that

Seven days and a wake-up, then I'm on the first chalk out, with Sergeant Chandler, the newly promoted Sergeant Nash, and Bullwinkle. The rest of the battery would stage at BIAP, then drive to Kuwait, where they'd fly out as Chalks 2 and 3, leaving behind a small rear-detachment to port-load the equipment. Seven days, then freedom.

We got up and went to the gym, then Sergeant Chandler, Sergeant Nash, Bullwinkle, and I went to breakfast, then to the internet café. We checked our email. I read the news. Four American contractors had been killed in Fallujah and lit on fire, their burned bodies strung up over a bridge.

We went back to the tents we'd moved into and relaxed until lunch. At around three we went to the gym again and lifted. Then dinner, then we came back and showered, then we went to the hadji coffee shop for cappuccinos and ice cream. Then we came back to the tents and played volleyball till the sun set.

That night there was a mortar attack, three rounds. We sat in the dark in our battle rattle, waiting.

Slept in and after a late start, Sergant Chandler, Sergeant Nash, Bullwinkle, and I went to breakfast, then to the internet café. We checked our email. I read the news. There were protests and riots in Sadr City. Baghdad was in flames. I googled airline tickets from Frankfurt to Athens. Since Sunday was our rest day, me and Sergeant Chandler skipped the gym but Sergeant Nash went anyway, and around 1630 we met him at the chow hall for dinner.

"You read about this fucking Moqtada militia shit?"

"The protests?"

"Fucking Moqtada al-Sadr and his goddamned Mahdi Army. Shit's going crazy. Najaf, Karbala, Basra. Everywhere. Even here in Sadr City."

"Fallujah, too."

"Yeah, but that's fucking Sunnis."

"Man, I can't wait to get back to Germany," Sergeant Chandler said. "I got this girl there, we're emailing—she just emailed me some fucking naked pictures of herself. I don't even hardly know her."

After dinner we went to the hadji coffee shop for cappuccinos, then went back to the tents.

Staff Sergeant Gooley stood waiting. "Where the fuck were you guys?"

"Same place we go every day, Sergeant."

"We got a platoon briefing in two mikes."

So we went over and Staff Sergeant Smith and Lieutenant

Krauss sat on MRE boxes and told us we needed to sign out with our chief whenever we left the tents, and also we had to get all our ammo together to be collected. They told us the nearest shower trailer was off-limits because it was broken. They said Second BCT had been extended and deployed to Najaf to assist putting down the Mahdi uprising, but as of yet nothing had changed about our redeployment. We were also told a convoy was going to BIAP tomorrow and they asked for volunteers. Sergeant Chandler and I looked at each other, then away. Sergeant Nash raised his hand. Four days.

Got up and did PT. Read the news. Moqtada al-Sadr had called for a general uprising against the CPA.

That night, as I was coming back from the showers, I could see the guys returning from the convoy. I ran into Sergeant Nash, strung out and sweaty, carrying a load of ammo into our tent.

"'Sup, Sergeant. What happened?"

"We got fucking ambushed is what the fuck happened."

"Shit. Everyone okay?"

"Yeah, it's a fucking wonder."

"Get anybody?"

"They ambushed us and fucking ran. Two RPGs and then small arms. We had the fucking colonel with us and the stupid fucker stops the convoy in the middle of the kill zone and gets out and starts directing traffic. Like we're a fucking I don't know what. I almost shot the fucker myself."

Lieutenant Juarez gave the briefing that night. He told us about adjustments to the ROE. The Mahdi Army could be identified by a green armband or a green flag. They were considered combatants, and we were to engage them with deadly force.

That night we woke to another mortar attack. One explosion, then one more. I looked at Sergeant Chandler in the bunk opposite. He looked sideways at all the other guys slowly getting up and putting on their gear, then rolled over and went back to sleep. There was another explosion, then I went back to sleep, too.

Got up and went to the gym then to breakfast then the internet.

Each platoon designated a counter responsible for collecting all our rounds and grenades. We each kept one thirty-round mag each, but everything else went in cans to hand over to 1st Cav.

At around three we went to the gym and lifted, then to dinner, then to the coffee shop for cappuccinos. After that we came back and played volleyball and watched videos till it got dark.

About twenty minutes later, we were rousted for stand-to.

"Command's expecting an attack on the FOB tonight," Lieutenant Krauss said, "so gear up and stand by."

We got all gussied up then stood around bitching about having only thirty rounds apiece. When the LT came back, he picked five guys, including me, to ride in the back of C27. We were assigned to secure the northeast corner of the tents. Another five were put in C26 and sent to the southwest corner, and everyone else was QRF.

"They're expecting some kind of concentrated attack, so eyes and ears open. Maintain radio contact. If you see something, fucking radio it up first. The last thing we need is a friendly-fire incident."

There was some shooting far away, a lot of shooting closer, a couple more pops very close, then quiet. After about ten minutes or so, we heard a barrage of machine-gun fire from the south wall.

Then the shooting died out and we waited another forty or fifty minutes before the call came to stand down. We got back to the tent and asked what happened but nobody knew, so we went to bed.

Thursday. Our Big Day. Chalk 1 got up and got our shit together and staged at 0545 for an SP time of 0630. Our convoy of five-tons was ready, but our escorts hadn't shown, so they told us stand by. At about 0730, they told us to go get chow and report back by 0900.

Bullwinkle, Sergeant Chandler, Sergeant Nash, and I went to breakfast. We ate a big meal and grabbed extra fruit and rolls and boiled eggs for later.

"I can't fucking wait till I touch down on German soil. I swear to God I'm gonna fall on my knees and kiss the ground."

"I'm gonna kiss the first fucking German girl I see right on the lips. Just grab her."

"Shit, I'm gonna kiss the first fucking German I see no matter what. Klaus, Dieter, Heinrich, Adolf. I give a fuck."

"You know, we've been here so long, that ain't even gay."

Bulldog Battery had already sent out their first chalk all the way to the airfield at Balad. We watched the last company of 82nd Airborne roll out.

We waited until 0850, then found Staff Sergeant Gooley and asked what was up. "Stand by," he said. "Stand by until further notice."

We waited. Some guys smoked, some guys slept. At 1015 they told us mount up. We cheered and loaded our gear in the back of the five-ton, clambered aboard, then waited, grinning like retards at lunchtime.

"Let's go!" Sergeant Nash shouted.

"What the fuck's the holdup?"

"Can you drive a five-ton?"

"I can, but I don't have a flight manifest."

At ten minutes to eleven, Staff Sergeant Gooley came out and told us to download our gear and take it back to the tents.

"What the fuck, Sergeant?" Bullwinkle shouted.

"Your LT'll brief you. Download your gear."

"Negative, Sergeant. Negative on that."

"What the fuck's going on, Sergeant?"

"You'll be briefed by your platoon. Don't make me tell you again."

We dispersed, dragging our bags behind us. Inside Second Platoon's tent, Lieutenant Krauss stood down at one end talking. He was saying words but not words. I couldn't hear anymore. The air was like water, like I couldn't breathe, like if somebody bumped me wrong I'd slide floating across the sky.

It sounded like something ninety days or until complete. Something about Karbala. Something mission
essential. Something about not wanting to hear any
fucking bitching, because we were soldiers and we were
called on by our commander-in-chief, the President of
the United States of America, and we would do our duty
with pride.

The fog rolled in off the sea, clouding the trees, closing in on the mountain so that when I woke it was as if from sleep to waking dream, a mirage of insubstantial gray pierced by great black spires. I'd make myself coffee and inhale the chill air and roll a cigarette and think.

I'd sit at the formica table in the trailer and, staring through the mesh behind the slatted windows into the fog, drink my coffee and scratch poems onto notebook paper, poems about the way memory shifts in and out of focus, the way we imagine things that never happened and remember other things wrong, the daily reconstruction work of being, who I am, what I'm doing, how can I be the same I was before and who am I tomorrow.

Sometimes I'd go out into the mist and listen to all the green held thick in the moist air, my palm on the trunk of a tree just to feel the heft of it. Sometimes a deer would come through, wild and wary, and I would fill with longing for the wholeness of animal life.

It took the sun a long while to come over the mountains and until it did my vision was bound to the few gray yards around the trailer. It was day but not day, dim but not night, a fugue of half-thoughts and disconnected images, pulsing with power beyond easy meaning—a crow flapping, glowing black against the gray—a shadow like a man crouched with a knife—parking lots aching with pink blur—so overwhelmed by thought I'd have to sit back, set down the pen, set down my coffee, and it goes on—glass towers gleaming out of gray cityscapes, blinding silver—an old man with a red guitar—the booming flame of rockets trailing smoke—a girl's face, her freckled cheek downy with fine hairs, fleshy lips spread in a smile over crooked teeth. I sink in reverie—and what, what does it mean?—then scrape a few more lines with my pen. Nothing even approximate. Another failure.

I'd moved that June into the mountains just outside Newport because my uncle had finally bought a house and moved out of his trailer. He wasn't sure what to do with the land, so he said I could stay there over the summer if I did a little work for him. There's no TV, he warned me, no cable, no internet, no phone, no mail, but I could get letters delivered in town.

I was at loose ends, which I'm sure my mom had told him. I'd spent the winter in Eugene, taking a couple classes at Lane Community College and working as a delivery driver for an organic juice company. I'd been dating this girl but it ended badly and I was itchy to move on, tired of the scene with all its dreadlocked anarchists, tired of weed and patchouli, the protests to save trees, stop globalization, and free Mumia. I thought about trying again with the old ex-girlfriend up in Portland, but that just made me feel worse.

My uncle's offer seemed perfect. It'd give me a chance to get *my head on straight, really figure shit out. I thought I could work part-time and write some poems, maybe finish that screenplay. A good word from my aunt got me work at the bookstore, which was more than enough to get by. I closed shop three nights a week and the rest of the time just chilled, read, smoked a little weed, and helped my uncle with his odd jobs. I wrote letters to the ex-girlfriend in Portland. I wrote poetry. I hung out with this guy named J.J. who worked at* Ripley's Believe It or Not! *I hung out with Lisa from the bookstore and her husband, Mike, a house painter. I met a girl named Alice at Nana's Irish Pub and we started hooking up. She was a total flake, which I guess is sort of what I wanted.*

The sun came over the rise around ten, burning off the fog, unveiling vivid green. I'd lose my sense of boundlessness then, my dreamscape of wandering intellection, and come back to the blood-filled breath of life, the hum of bugs and the warmth of sunlight. I'd come back to the fact that I didn't know what I was doing, that I was killing time, that when I went into town later I'd be the same aimless transient I was yesterday, still no goal, no point to my story.

Often I'd hike to the top of the mountain, about two miles from the trailer, to a clear-cut along the ridge where the view opened and beyond my farthest gaze unrolled the wide Pacific's endless sweep.

I'd watch the blue waves and think, today you're coming up with a plan. You're gonna figure your shit out. You going back to school? You gonna get certified at something, get a real *job, be a plumber or a nurse or tend bar? Thirty wasn't quite around the corner but it wasn't so far away, either, and I felt the need to do some thing, accomplish some thing, do something* real.

Oh, sure, I knew it was all a con. I knew the system was out to get me. I knew we all wanted to be free and live our lives and make art and all that bullshit, but I couldn't remember the last time I'd been to the dentist. And what if I broke a leg, or got sick, or hit by a car? How would I pay for anything? And why did my circle of friends seem to be shifting, turning seedier, more addiction-prone, less aware of their own lives as a series of choices they'd made and more inclined to ascribe to events wholly metaphysical causes—I just had a feeling, you know, it was like the universe gave me a sign, sometimes you do a reading and it's just like so spot on, it was like there was this voice telling me . . . How much longer would it take till I was trapped in a world without responsibility, where things just sort of happened and we all just got along, stumbling in a fuzz of pot smoke, excuses, and superstition?

Yet there I went into town, working at the bookshop, drinking with J.J., fooling around with Alice, getting high, ending the night in a hazy drive back up the mountain or crashed in Alice's bed, waking to strange light through a strange window burning away the illusion of ease life wore by night and revealing beneath it the grim furrows of bad habits too deeply rutted to pull out of.

Fog, thick, hung in the trees. I got up early and shuffled through the trailer, started the coffee pot, rolled a cigarette. I opened the door and let in the mist, let out the smoke, hoping yet again for clarity.

I left my notebook and pen untouched on the table. For some reason that morning poetry seemed even more futile than usual. I was always going over the same plucked field, picking at the same thoughts and sensations. What was the point of thinking things? Writing them down? Nobody read, nobody cared—no one needed the navel-gazing mystifications of yet another confused and sensitive young soul.

I opened the fridge and saw I had a couple eggs, so I put on a pan and started it warming, melting butter. I cut two slices from a loaf of organic multigrain and laid them on a plate.

For company I turned on NPR. At first it wasn't anything, just a stream of meaningless sound, then as I stood over the stove with an egg in my hand the babble squirmed into sense. Someone had flown a plane into the World Trade Center. No, two planes. Both towers. One was collapsing, smoke rising up, people jumping. It was an attack of some kind. We were under attack.

I turned up the radio and cracked the eggs, listening to voices cry out over the sizzle of butter frying.

i am an american soldier
i am a warrior and a member of a team
i serve the people of the united states
and live the army values

Trucks roll, gunners scanning the horizon. The sun an incandescent smear. I sweat and turn up the music.

We drive south through the desert in a line, miles long, of big green machines.

We stand in the heat by the road and the wind whips sand at us. Waves of grit slide and ebb across the seething black. Engines hum.

In the distance two Bradleys spin heaving clouds of dust as they circle a cluster of hooches and rumble over a hill. We hear the noise of their guns then their engines fade. Smoke oozes up. An Apache hovers overhead.

Blackened humvees jut up from the sand.

Pictures come out of hadjis getting fucked with at one of the prisons. Hadjis getting punched, hadjis standing on boxes, hadjis with panties on their heads, naked hadjis getting laughed at by skanky Nasty Girl bitches.

I know what I'm looking at, but at the same time, fuck 'em. Fuck 'em to their goddamned shitsucking hadji hell. They're shooting at us every day and I'm supposed to give a flying fuck about human rights? Fuck that. Once they quit chopping people's heads off and lighting dudes on fire, then maybe we'll talk.

Command comes down and says just what you'd expect, reprehensible unprofessional blah blah blah, but who the fuck cares? A few bad apples, they say, make sure you know the regulations, but we all know the score.

The muezzin calls out five times a day. Gunfire breaks the night. No running water. No electricity. No air conditioning. No grass, no carpet, no windows. No fans. Little shade, bad food, no joy, little laughter, no decent sleep. Everyone in the world wears camouflage—the others talk gobbledygook and stare.

Geraldo reenlists for a 20K bonus.

Burger King, daisy-chain. Cordon and Search. Stack team. There's a glazed shock in everyone's eyes, the simmer of hatred barely contained. We get in fistfights. We listen to "Hey Ya!" and count the dead.

What had I done before? Who had I been? Was there a life before this?

Negative. I'd never been anyone. I'd never done anything

but drive down this highway forever, the road eternity itself, punishment for an abandoned dream's half-imagined sins. This was all I'd ever done, all I'd ever do: drive in the heat through the sand and the pain and stink in the unceasing noise.

i stand ready to deploy, engage, and destroy
the enemies of the united states of america
in close combat

0200 go. Stoat flips the humvee lights, starts the engine, and with a roar and crash slams through the front gate. We jog across the night-hung street around the humvee and into the yard. We take our positions by the door and switch on the flashlights affixed to our rifles. Burnett rams the door open and Bullwinkle goes in, then me, our rifles stabbing beams of white into the black. The rest of our team follows; the snatch team comes behind and pounds up the stairs. We take the first floor, living room, sofa, TV, clear the corners quick and into the kitchen, tomatoes and cucumbers in a bowl on the counter, flatbread, water, towels, we kick open a door and a hadji stands in the corner in his underpants, shielding his face.

"On your knees, motherfucker!"

"Inhanee!"

The hadji's slow to move, so Bullwinkle slams the butt of his rifle in his gut, jackknifing him at the waist.

"Inhanee, motherfucker!"

He goes down. I keep my rifle at his head and Bullwinkle zip-strips his arms behind him. Once he's tied, we drag him to the other room.

The lights on now, you can see the worn but cared-for furniture and brass knickknacks. A family portrait hangs on the wall.

Shouting upstairs.

We dump the hadji on the floor and my rifle slams against a vase, knocking it to the ground where it smashes.

"Watch it," says Staff Sergeant Gooley.

Lieutenant Juarez and Captain Yarrow stride in, the terp behind them, just as the snatch team drags the first hadji down the stairs, a middle-aged man in boxers and a wife-beater. A woman wails somewhere.

I hear Burnett shout, "Shut that bitch up."

"First floor clear," Sergeant Nash tells Staff Sergeant Gooley.

"Search it," the LT barks.

So we go back to the hadji's room and turn on the light. He's got a pile of letters, a little boombox, and a tiny framed picture of a woman on the table in the corner. He's got a bed, a bookcase, a rug on the floor, a trunk, a pair of shoes. I flip through his stack of CDs while Bullwinkle strips the sheets.

"He's got every goddamn Sting record there is."

Bullwinkle grunts. He goes over to the bookcase and flips through the books one by one, then sweeps the whole shelf to the floor.

I grab the letters from the table and stuff them in my pocket. I pick up the picture and look at it—girlfriend? Wife? I think of him lying out there with his thumbs zip-stripped, blubbering face-first on the floor.

"Help me with this chest," Bullwinkle says, so I put the picture down and we overturn the trunk. Clothes fall out, folded dishdashas, slacks, loose shirts, a wallet, a few small wooden boxes, a Koran.

"Circle up!" somebody shouts from the other room.

Bullwinkle and I head back. Our hadji's still weeping on the floor, begging for his life, and the middle-aged one sits cross-legged behind the couch, zip-stripped, muttering, his bottom lip swollen and bleeding. A woman in a scarf is howling after Staff Sergeant Smith and Burnett as they come down the stairs. Two kids watch from the second floor.

"Wrong house," says Staff Sergeant Gooley. "Bad intel. Mount up, we're outta here."

"Cut 'em loose," shouts the LT, heading out with Yarrow and the terp.

We ride back to the FOB as the horizon lightens in the east. The sky is empty, the road empty. I realize I still have the hadji's letters in my pocket, so I pull them out and look at them. The pages dance in the wind, the words so much meaningless ink. They tell a story, maybe, just not to me. I let them go, and in the humvee's slipstream they lift and scatter.

babylon

·

When he played till he was tired and went to sleep, he would lie in bed and attack Iraq. 235,000 troops at the borders. His staff managed to move most of the collection to safety, sending boots about fields on rutted roads.

I was aware   the apostle   should capture dull rumbling in my ears

tingling command of Allah not all were lost. Allah, who destroys insurgents and some you eat. Further lessen the abjection of war, unable in desperation to turn itself into grotesque infantile guard force
subordinate world with no
aberrant, outlandish Center that sets conditions for
pornographic action, he adds, is refuge in Allah for the interrogators of the heavens and the earth, the War on Terror, no helping do not know
and the blind and the inherent groping power do not know and the blind and purposeless officials charged with investigating do not know for to him life is the Army, and I had some idea what I was doing. The United States had invaded Afghanistan and was making diplomatic preparations for the invasion of Iraq. I had a good idea we were going and, despite

my attempts to see things geopolitically and realistically, we
follow the dust, heading off the main road through fields then
grids of now flattened and overgrown former modular units
by air, tractor-trailer, or ship can be fully functional in 24 to 48
hours. Even at the CSH level, the goal is not definitive repair.
The maximal length of stay is
policies and practices developed and approved for use on
"the war against terrorism is a new kind of war," in fact, a "new
paradigm [that] renders obsolete Geneva's strict limitations."
No sane man can be a world, and do not try to do too much
with your own hands. Better the Arabs do it tolerably than
question the use of national military power. Most people
shall say: Yea, associate with policy
most surely to help the most forgiving, no doubt concealing
bombs, others on the day when the witnesses of this TV,
nor in the hereafter, and pediatrics benefit the unjust

for them curse
the inmates of fire, so we made Allah, surely Allah sees
moral will to act, a reminder to men of what they planned,
meantime
How is it that I call you to salvation and you call me to the
fire?
You call on me that I should disbelieve in Allah and associate with Him of which I have no knowledge, and I call you
to China's foreign minister Tuesday. Baghdad residents have
started fleeing the capital as the deadline nears for President
Hussein to leave or face war. No sane man can be happy, for
Saddam rejected the ultimatum, saying he has no heart of the

FULL STORY

anyone brought before the world, "even directed at intelligence targets," as they go on to concede and glut themselves, goodly raiment made by hands of TV you can never again wear, and military police, which is not a matter of

religious discussions will be frequent. With the Bedu, Islam is so all-pervading that there is little religiosity, little fervor, and no regard for externals. The current plan discussed is fundamentally unacceptable. Accordingly, popular elections are necessary within the "Babylonian" mathematics of general history, another thousand years on, several centuries of sustained astronomical observation and consistent recording in the temples of Uruk and humvee enabled the development of predictive mathematical astronomy: I will show you DETAINEE-07 alleging that CIVILIAN-17, MP Interpreter, Titan Corp., hit DETAINEE-07 once, cutting his ear to an extent that required stitches. Meantime the Hooded Man pictured abuses—and shall be brought before the spear, a certain "even directed at intelligence targets" fact, as they go on to concede they glut themselves, goodly raiment by hands of violent/sex abuse which you can never again wear, a matter of men and women like dogs forced to crawl on his husband's sisters and the wives of his brothers, General Sanchez fain to die in her distraction. When drawn from General Miller's GTMO she sobbed and made lament among the Trojans yelling: We see cars going by in a still-secret city, CNN correspondents escape us no longer.
Stay here for Al-Qaeda
lust battle you
            must find these inner reasons (they will be denied,

but are nonetheless in operation) before shaping your arguments for one course or another. Allusion is more effective than logical exposition: they dislike concise expression. There is nothing unreasonable, incomprehensible, or inscrutable in the Arab mind.

strange hells
(columbus day, 2004)

The joint's red ember glowed in the night as it passed from Matt's hand back to Aaron's.

"That was kind of intense, dude," Matt said.

"Some bullshit is was it was."

"Mel gets worked up about politics sometimes."

"So I get to be her fucking rag doll? I don't think so."

"That's not what I meant. I'm sorry I brought it up. I was just . . ."

"Curious. Yeah. Everyone's curious fucking George."

"Well, I don't know about that, but I'm sorry. I should've let it go."

"Whatever, man. You want any more of this?"

"No, I'm good."

Aaron stubbed out the roach and lit an American Spirit.

Matt bummed one off him. "Listen, Mel's really sweet, you know, she just gets worked up. She's angry at the government and her dad and all kinds of shit, so it's touch-and-go sometimes, but other than that, she's fine. It's just insecurity, you know?"

"Fuck that and fuck her little dog, too."

"Man, I forgot about Xena. I hope he's okay."

"Fucking dog comes at me, I kick it."

"I just meant, about Mel, you know, she's fine, but she

has, like, gender issues. Masculinity issues. So if you just apologize—I'm not saying she's right, she's not, she was way out of line, but if you apologize, she'll let it go. She won't apologize first. I know it's irritating but, you know, it's like she's has something to prove."

"If I was a fucking pussy."

"Sorry?"

"I'd apologize *if I was a fucking pussy.*"

"Okay, fine. Just think about it." Matt studied the sky. "So, uh . . . How long you been back in the US?"

"About three weeks."

"Were you over there long?"

"Later, Matt. You want to know what it's like, I'll show you some shit later. Let's talk about something else right now. Tell me about your global forecasting program."

"Oh, yeah. Sure. Okay. It's called *Constellation.* I'm interested in the way we take disparate, seemingly unrelated points, and make visual patterns. Like that's Draco and that's Virgo. There's Scorpio and the Big Dipper. They don't really mean anything, not like an astrologer would tell you, but by constellating points we make a map of the sky. Then we can use that map to navigate on earth. It's like a data aggregator, but . . . See, it's . . ." He laughed. "It's supposed to tell the future. I don't know. It's still . . . I haven't quite found the right interface."

"How long you been working on it?"

"About two years, I guess, since Dahlia and I moved out here."

"You seem like a cute couple, you and her."

"Huh? Oh, yeah. Thanks. We're really happy together."

"How'd you two meet?"

"College. University of Washington, class on statistical analysis. She was on crutches, she'd broken her hip playing soccer, and one day I helped her with her books. Then I started helping her with her homework. We were just friends then, but I really liked her. I liked her accent, that she was from Virginia. It seemed historical, you know? Special. And she always seemed so . . . I don't know, like she was searching for something and a little sad about it. I liked that she was a searcher. Anyway, after graduation, I got involved in a web startup with some guys, and she went to Guatemala to work on an organic farm. I guess we lost touch, like people do. But then a couple years later, we ran into each other in a bar on Capitol Hill and it just clicked. We've been together since."

"Why'd you move to Moab?"

"So the startup I helped found—cyclopsicope.com— sold out to Yahoo! in April 2000, which was pretty lucky, thinking back, because the boom was already over by that point. The correction was bad, since everybody was liquidating and the job market was overstocked with guys just like me, coders with crazy ideas and a lot of slick talk. But I had the money from the sell-off and I knew some people, so I could get by freelancing. Then after 9/11, we just decided we needed a change. Get off the grid, you know? I was in the middle of this project with some friends and Dahlia was getting her master's, but once we'd tied up our loose ends in Seattle, we made the jump."

"How's it working for you out here?"

"Good. Good. We're a little restless, I guess, but that's

just how you get, right? That's just life, getting older, right? We go hiking a bit, she works the river some with Mel. I guess we'll head back to civilization soon, but we can live cheap here, there's some nice people, and it's quiet. There's space to think. Really think about things."

"Like constellations."

"Yeah . . ." Like Orion and Scorpio, Cassiopeia and Canis Major. "So, uh, what about you and Wendy, huh? You two got a thing?"

"You like her, don't you."

"I, uh . . . I don't, uhm . . ." Matt coughed. "Dahlia and I are really happy. But you . . ."

"We fuck."

"Alright . . ." Matt laughed. "How's that?"

"It's trim. She's a liar and a cunt, but she fucks good."

"Dude . . ."

"It is what it is."

"Uhm . . . I don't know what to say. Wendy's a friend."

"That all?"

"I don't know what you mean."

"No, you don't. Anyway, I'm just passing through."

"That's probably best." Matt laughed again. "I mean nice . . . It must be nice."

"Sure enough."

"You said you're going back to school in December?"

"That's the story I tell people. The truth is, Matt, I'm gonna burrow like a tick in the skin of the grimiest, nastiest Rust Belt shithole I can find and shoot heroin till I die."

"Wow. You're kidding, right?"

"We're devils, Matthew. For real. You gotta see things for what they are . . . And there it is. Hello, beautiful."

"Y'all doing alright out here?" Dahlia asked, appearing out of the shadows.

Matt twisted in his chair to see her and thought, did he just say that? "What did you say?"

"You feel the spin, Matt?" Aaron asked.

"Wait, what? What?"

"We're all good out back," Dahlia said. "Mel's a little riled yet, but Xena calmed down. My darling Mel said she'd apologize to you for being such a bitch, if you apologize to her for kicking her dog. Then we can all make nice and get on with our *par-tey.*"

"Listen," Aaron said, looking deep into Dahlia's eyes. "Here's the deal. I'm not sorry for defending myself. The dog gets it, he understands I'm a bigger dog. This is a fact I can see Mel struggles with. She's like one of those terriers that picks fights with German shepherds. Nevertheless, I will apologize—to the dog and to Mel. I'm the bigger dog, I'll be the bigger man. Tell you the truth, Dahlia, all I ever wanted was peace, love, and understanding."

Dahlia stared back. "I don't know if I like you, soldier boy."

"You don't have to." Aaron smiled wide, suddenly all charm. "Run along now, sugar, and bring your tribe my offer of peace."

Dahlia left, scowling, and Matt wondered, What do I do? How do I make him leave? "Her name's not sugar," he said.

"Chill out, bro. It's all cool."

Matt groped for leverage, but with the planet spinning

the stars were the only fixed points. "There's no devil," he said. "No such thing as evil. We're human beings. We reason. We make choices. It's like I was saying: it's all just space and stars, but there's an order we impose on it. We make maps to navigate by. You have to admit that at least."

"I know what I am, Matt. You don't have to be good."

"No, there's an order to things. There's a map we're responsible to."

"Wendy, for example. She'll give it up. You just gotta take it."

Matt wanted to say, You need to leave now. Or: Quit looking at her like that. Or: I'm gonna kick your ass. Instead, he regarded Orion hanging overhead and tried to think of an answer. It wasn't just stars. It was more.

Dahlia went back out back, saying to herself what an asshole. The house creaked or the door maybe or the sky on its hinges at the horizon and she was out under the black world glittering like dark mica. The grass rustled live as snakes. Wendy, Mel, and Rachel huddled over something in the yard, Xena watching.

"What is it?" Dahlia asked, thinking small and helpless.

"Mel's making fire," Wendy said.

Then it lit with a crackle, a small flame ringed with stones. Where'd she get stones? Where'd she get fire?

"Where'd you get that?" Dahlia asked.

"Me pray Goddess Moon, call up spirits from stone, make fire," Mel said. "I can put it out if you want. I just thought it'd be nice. There isn't a burn ban on or shit, is there? I don't wanna bring down the fuzz."

"It's cool, I think," said Dahlia.

Wendy leaned toward her. "Did you see the way the stars are behind the trees and inside them at the same time? I mean the branches. Like they're caught."

Dahlia laughed. "Damn, y'all couldn't wait for me on the next bowl? Buncha weed-bogartin' bitches. Listen . . ." Dahlia sat on the ground by the fire. "I talked to the boys out front. Soldier boy said he'd apologize. Says he just wants peace."

"We change like chameleons," Wendy said. "Inside, outside. Skin on skin."

"You do," Dahlia said. "I don't."

"No," Wendy said. "We all do."

"So who's Dahlia then?"

Rachel said, "She's the one who fed us tasty tofu."

Wendy said, "She's the one who has what she wants."

Mel said, "She's the one who knows what's enough."

Dahlia lay on her side. "Enough is enough."

"This is fun," Wendy said. "Who's Wendy?"

"Wendy's a bitch," said Mel.

"Fuck you, Mel."

"Wendy's a *self-centered*, self-quoting bitch," Mel went on.

"Seriously, fuck you."

"Wendy's too smart and too pretty but she's crazy and fun, so that makes up for it," said Dahlia.

"Wendy's a cat," Rachel said. "One of those little jungle cats, like an ocelot."

"I'll be an ocelot."

"What's *your* animal, Dahlia?" Mel asked. "A fox?"

"Me? I'm a moth. I'm a swallow. A crane maybe, some kind of migratory bird."

"I'm a coyote," said Rachel.

Wendy laughed. "You're no coyote. You're a poodle that thinks it's a coyote."

"You're mean."

"I'm, uh, what's that dog from that old beer ad?"

"Spuds Mackenzie? He's a bull terrier."

"I'm one of those," said Mel.

"I'm not a poodle," Rachel said. "I'm a heron or an egret, like Dahlia."

"You're a cuckoo," Wendy said.

They lapsed into silence. Dahlia lay on the earth, watching Wendy, thinking of the way Matt watched her. The sense of fear. The rush when the dog leaped. Aaron. Mel broke a stick and threw it in the crackling fire. Rachel cleared her throat and began to sing in a low, nasal lilt, a voice like reeds and red thread and honey, tapping her knee with her palm:

Oh, the cuckoo, she's a pretty bird.
How I wish that she was mine.
But she never hollers cuckoo
Till the fourth day of July.

She sucks all the sweet flowers
To make her voice so clear.
But she never sings cuckoo
Till summer draws near.

She flies the hills over,
She flies the world above,
She flies back to the mountain,
Where she mourns her ain true love.

Oh, the cuckoo, she's a cruel bird,
And she warbles as she flies,
And ev'ry time she passes,
My true love says goodbye.

Rachel let the last note fade and the hush that followed broke like waves washing hard against clapping, sharp, at the door. They all looked up at Aaron applauding, his eyes bright in the glow of the fire.

"That was *just* lovely," he said.

"What do you want?" Wendy asked.

"Sorry?"

"How long were you there?"

"I'm only passing through, Chief," he said, coming toward the fire. "I left Major Tom in orbit, and if I don't get back we might lose him in the Martian time-slip. But listen, it's totally aces, we're solving the mysteries of the universe. One thing I wanted to say: Mel, I hope we're cool and I'm sorry for calling you names and overreacting to your—how you say—interrogation. We cool?" He knelt and offered Mel his hand. Xena watched nervously.

Mel observed him, turning her head this way and that, then nodded. "Yeah, we cool," she said, giving his hand a firm shake. "Sorry for calling you a Nazi."

"No problem," he said. "It's not the worst thing I've been

called." Then he offered his hand to Xena. "Cool, doggy?" Xena hugged the ground and licked the back of Aaron's hand. "Great. So we all cool."

"We're not all cool," Dahlia said, sitting up.

"Oh yeah?"

"Yeah. You and me ain't cool."

"Well, I am heartsick to hear that, sugar, and steadfastly resolved to make things right. What could I possibly do to rectify this situation?"

"What are you two talking about?" asked Wendy.

Dahlia felt her face twitch. "You bring violence into my home, you fuck up my party. You owe me." Her eyes reflected flame. "Put your hand in the fire."

The other women watched, waiting. Aaron smiled and took a drink of his beer, then gazed around the circle. "What are y'all up to out here besides singing campfire songs? Some witchy coven shit?"

Dahlia glared at him.

"We're just talking," Wendy said.

"Sweet. I'll work on getting Major Tom down from orbit, and maybe then we can resume our explorations. In the meantime . . ." He leaned forward and passed his hand through the fire, slowly side to side so the orange heat licked along his hand and singed the hair on his wrist, then pressed his palm to Dahlia's cheek. They looked at each other, faces close, then he pulled away and kissed Wendy on the top of her head. "I shall return," he said, giving a sloppy salute, and disappeared through the gate.

Matt looked over at Aaron's face, washed blue in the moon's light. He was pushing a bottle at him.

"You got beer?"

"Yeah. Take one."

"How long were you gone?"

"All your life, sweetheart. You want a beer or not?"

"I don't know what you're here for."

"Same thing we all are: kill, fuck, and die."

Matt took the offered beer.

"Strange trip to the backyard," Aaron went on. "The ladies have gone native. We talked some. Everybody groks now. Why don't we take a ride in your time machine, Matthew?"

"The machine's broken."

"Show me."

"It's sludge. It's like a rollercoaster that won't come down."

"So show me. Invite me in. I got something to show you in return."

"Yeah, what?"

Aaron grinned, pulling from his pocket a silver thumb drive dangling on a gray cord. "Some real war shit. You show me the future, I'll show you the past."

Matt thought for a moment, then nodded. "Okay. Come on."

He stumbled up and ambled into the house, Aaron following through the dark to Matt's work zone. Through the window, they could see the girls spread out around the fire, talking and laughing, their hands framing forms in the air. Matt sat at his desk and jiggled his mouse, waking the machine.

Matt eyed the fire anxiously. "I think there's a burn ban on."

"Fuck all that. Show me the future."

The computer's fan whirred, its hard-drive light flickering red in the dark. Matt clicked an icon of the Big Dipper. "It's fairly crude, so I can only feed so many different data streams off the web before it freezes. I linked it to different sites that update their data, you know, like Dow Jones or whatever. I got a couple easy ones like US weather, so the graphic gives us a pattern like this." He clicked on the menu and a visual popped up in the center, a slowly morphing fractal cone in greens and golds covered with bumps and indentions. It spun slow on three axes, displaying its languidly shifting planes, and as it revolved a swirl of orange and white sank into one side. "The trick is with the operator, right, because this is just a data pattern. It's no better really than raw data except in this: humans are primarily visual, so we interpret visual patterns much more quickly than we do numerical, syntactical, narrative, or even linguistic ones. But the new operator doesn't see much in one pattern, like this one here, until they've seen dozens of them and compared them against each other. As well, the algorithm doesn't measure data but rather the rate of change. So with this, I can tell you that the weather patterns for the US are generally changing slowly now, but that there's some serious turbulence here"—he pointed to the swirl of white and orange—"that represents a relatively intense but locally manifest change in weather conditions. Not very helpful, I realize, for meteorology, but that's not the point. Let's do stocks." He clicked a menu button and the first graphic disappeared, replaced by a new cone, green and gold, this one wider, shallower, and bumpier, red and strangely sparkling on the edges and growing darker and darker, toward a fierce purple, at the point. "This is all the world's major stock exchanges, along with some other transnational data like trade deficit numbers, wheat production, the price of oil, stuff like that. This seems about normal, actually, generally calm with local fluctuations. Sometimes you get a wave sweeping across, either in concentric circles or as a shifting convergence. See, like this point here, this bulge—if it got any bigger, I'd say that's probably gonna start a wave that will likely spread and affect other markets. I'd say watch out for turbulence in the global economy."

"But it doesn't tell you where."

"It can." He hit Control-M and markers came up: Tokyo Stock Exchange, NASDAQ, Crude Oil DPB. "But remember, what it's measuring isn't the change but the rate of change. I don't care what the level of the Dow is, or even how much it went up or down, but how much it went up or down relative to, a, the overall size or value of the data set and, b, its previous movement. A steady increase, as long as it continues to change at the same rate, won't show up at all. But if the increase slows, right, even if the change is now zero, the change in the rate of change will be what we see. You got it?"

"Like it measures acceleration and deceleration, not speed."

"Exactly. I mean, it doesn't so much tell the future as show turbulence in complex systems, which I think might offer a key to understanding the systems themselves. Part of the problem is that so far the systems are user-defined. I mean, if I had enough computing power, I could feed thousands and thousands of real-time data streams into the thing and you'd get a global picture. Another problem is real-time data—most good data is private or secret. What you're seeing now is very narrow. It's like taking a poll of five hundred people; it just doesn't tell you much. Whereas if you polled five hundred thousand, you'd have some real numbers."

"Huh."

"Yeah. So there it is."

"Trippy." Aaron pulled out his thumb drive. "My turn."

"Okay." Matt closed down the program and plugged in Aaron's drive.

"Iraq Pix," Aaron said. "Camp Crawford."

The fire crackled between them.

"What was that with you and Aaron?" Wendy asked, turning to Dahlia.

"Just messing with him," Dahlia said.

"Dolly working her mojo," Mel said.

"I ain't got no mojo."

"Dirty Dahlia," Wendy laughed. "I'd be jealous if I didn't know you were so stuck on Matt."

"Sure," Dahlia said. "Like a tar baby."

The first picture was of a dusty, tan-colored building looming against a bruised sky. Barbed wire coiled on the wall tops.

"We did a bunch of stuff in Iraq," Aaron said, "including working at several different internment camps. This is Camp Crawford. We called it the Pit. It was north of Baghdad, not far from Taji, and it was specifically for insurgents and intel targets. It's not like Cropper, on BIAP, which was high-value, or Abu G, which had a bunch of different shit. We were supposed to get hard cases from other assets in the north and northwest, a lot of hadjis from Fallujah and Tikrit and Baqubah, a lot of Sunni triangle shit."

"Hadjis?"

"Iraqis. You get real racist over there."

"Do you?"

"Anyway, Camp Crawford. Click forward."

He did and the next pic was a bunch of soldiers, some in brown t-shirts and some in black, all wearing desert boots and brown camouflage pants, making gang symbols or flipping the bird, men and women both. Aaron was in there, leaner, more muscular, squatting with a rifle.

"These are the dudes I worked with. There's Sergeant Dickersen, and that's Grimes and Woolsley and Peanut and Garber. That's Staff Sergeant Cortázar and Lieutenant Viers. The guys in black t-shirts—see, brown t-shirts, that's the Army standard. The Air Force wear black t-shirts, but these guys aren't Air Force. They're OGA. Bill and Pete and Dick and Gary."

"OGA?"

"Other governmental agencies. That dude there, the hadji-looking one, he's our terp, Wathiq."

■ ■ ■

"The thing with Aaron," Wendy said, "I think he had a hard time in Iraq."

"What do you mean a hard time?"

"I don't know. He won't talk about it. He says he just wants to put it behind him. But he's really tense now, and I think . . . I think something happened."

"You think he has PTSD?" Rachel asked.

"I don't know how you know. He says he doesn't."

"Has he gone for counseling?"

"I don't know. He just got back. He just showed up."

"What's the deal with you two?" Dahlia asked.

"I don't really know," Wendy said. "We started dating in Tucson, like, almost two years ago. I was finishing my MFA then, and he was still working on his bachelor's, but he's only a year younger than me . . . and we'd been dating for like six months but hadn't discussed it as anything serious when he got called up, and then we started having these really super intense discussions about the future. I just couldn't make the promises I think he wanted me to. I think he had this romantic idea I'd wait for him, pining away with a yellow ribbon, but I can't live my life like that. And I didn't even know if we were right for each other anyway. It'd just been a thing. So we basically made a tentative agreement that we'd keep writing and then check back when he got home. He thought the war would be over quick and he'd be sitting in the desert twiddling his thumbs the whole time like in that book *Jarhead*. So we wrote each other letters while he was in training, but then once he got to Iraq, it stopped. A couple emails, then nothing . . . until he called me from the airport in Atlanta, a year later. I couldn't believe it. I thought I'd let it go. I thought I'd moved on. When I heard his voice on the phone, though, I sort of fell apart."

"What did you think when he quit writing?" Rachel asked.

"Honestly? I thought he was dead. I mean, I read the lists for a few months and didn't see his name, but how could I know? It was the not knowing that made it so bad. Finally I just closed off the part of myself that cared."

"Jesus."

"Didn't you call his parents or somebody?"

"He's always been a loner. He never really talked about his parents much. I know his dad used to live somewhere near Tucson, and I'm not even sure where his mom's at. He had some friends in college, the guys in his band and his stoner buddies, but they didn't know any more than I did."

The next picture showed a young Iraqi woman smiling uneasily at the camera, looking at something outside the picture's frame. She wore loose orange prisoner pants and a PANTERA shirt and her hair was streaked with blonde, dark roots growing out over platinum stripes. She couldn't have been older than nineteen or twenty.

"That's Connie," Aaron said. "We called her Connie. She was in for theft, I think, but she was nice and spoke some English, so she got a lot of freedom. Click forward."

The next picture was of Connie pulling her shirt up over her breasts, tugging the waist of her orange pants down to the top of her pubic hair.

"Two dolla. Some dudes paid five for the whole nude, but I dig how this one's flirty, like she's not showing you everything yet. She did other stuff, too, on the DL, but I wouldn't touch that cooze with a ten-foot pole."

"Other stuff?"

"Yeah. Command looked the other way as long as we kept it quiet."

"What . . . what did she do with the money?"

"She hid it, saving it for when she got out. She had her own cell, for privacy. We took care of her, you know, treated her pretty good, gave her extra MREs, cigarettes, shit from Any Soldier packages back home. Connie was alright. Some of the Army bitches complained about the guys, you know, pimping her, but nothing ever really happened. It never went official."

"That's awful."

"Oh, shit. You're totally right. I'll put it away, then." Aaron reached for his thumb drive.

"No, wait," Matt said. "It's awful, but I think I should see it. So I know what it's like. I should know what it's like."

"Your call, Chief. You wanna click forward?"

"Yeah," Matt said, then regretted it.

A young, mustached Iraqi man lay naked on the floor of a cell, his face ruptured and bleeding, his hands secured behind his back with zip-ties. A soldier stood with one boot on the back of his neck, grinning at the camera.

"That's Woolsley. We . . . he was stressing the prisoner, you know, in preparation for an information session, and the guy got a little crazy, so we . . . we kept running him into the bars until he fell over. Fucked him up pretty bad.

He lost a bunch of teeth," Aaron said, sliding his finger along the right side of his upper lip.

"Are these torture pictures?"

"I worked in detention."

"Did you . . . torture . . . people?"

"Legally?"

"Were you actually involved in doing this?"

"I told you," Aaron said. "I took pictures. Nobody's making you look. All you gotta do is pull out. Listen. You think about it while I get another beer. You want one?"

"Uh . . . sure."

Aaron got up and rummaged in the fridge while Matt stared at the man standing with his boot on the naked man's neck, the naked man's split lip and gashed face, his blood shiny on the concrete floor.

Aaron brought back two beers and handed one to Matt.

"What's that?" he asked.

"What?"

"In his butt. What is that?

"Oh, we made him stick a chemlight in his ass."

"A what?"

"A chemlight. It's a little plastic, you know, a glowstick. They're about as big around as your thumb. You bend it and it breaks this glass capsule inside so it glows. It's a chemical thing. It doesn't really hurt, it's just invasive, and the hadjis don't know how the chemicals work so they freak the fuck out. But like I said, they're not that big, so as long as you don't tense up, it's not painful."

"How would you know?"

"I've had bigger shits. I mean, you get your

prostate checked, right? It's not any bigger than that. It's just uncomfortable."

"And humiliating."

"Yeah, but so's a fucking prostate exam."

"I don't think they're the same."

"It was standard operating procedure. Not a big deal."

"That's fucked up."

"It gets better. Click forward."

"Wait. I just . . . So . . . you *tortured* people?"

"Enhanced interrogation, technically. Whatever you want to call it, I told you, I fucking held the camera. How many times I gotta say that? Click forward."

"I didn't know what to think. All I could do was imagine the worst."

"Oh, Wendy," Rachel said, rubbing her shoulder.

"It's just all so intense. After he called, after everything, after I thought he was dead, he's alive again and we keep talking on the phone and I can't stop thinking about him and I can't sleep and I start thinking about moving back to Tucson or him moving here and basically I'm in this crazy emotional spiral for like a week and that's part of why—I mean, I won't say I went to Grand Junction Thursday explicitly planning to fuck David T. Greene, but I needed something, some kind of counterweight, some blockage to put between Aaron and me. Something to keep me from falling."

Mel grunted.

"But when he showed up, I knew. I knew. I knew instantly that we'd have a good time but that was it. Because

I just can't. I've done this kind of thing and I can't anymore. There's something self-destructive in him, you know, that bad-boy thing, and the chaos energy's thrilling, but there are limits." Wendy looked into the fire. She picked up a stick and poked at the coals. "I don't know. Sometimes I get the feeling he just doesn't care what happens anymore. He didn't used to be like that."

"Like with Xena," Mel said.

"That wasn't his fault," Rachel told her.

The next picture showed a naked Iraqi man wearing panties on his face, handcuffed to a metal grating on the wall, passed out and dangling by his hands. A tall Hispanic soldier stood next to him.

"I can't remember this puck's name. It was like Z something. Zabar . . . Zartan . . . Zazar . . . Anyway, that's a stress position. You keep them handcuffed like that for hours. You don't give them water, because if you do, they have to piss and then you have to unhook them and everything and it's a huge hassle. You don't feed them, either, because if you do that, then they have to shit. Click forward."

"Can't you go to the media or something?"

"Sure. You see this guy?" he pointed to the soldier in the photo.

"Yeah."

"That's Staff Sergeant Cortázar. He took us all aside after Abu G broke and—this conversation never officially happened, realize—and told us that because of one stupid shit, because of that blue falcon Joe Darby who turned in the photos, a whole bunch of good soldiers who did their jobs, who were doing *what they were told*, were now getting totally fucked by the system. It wasn't their commanders getting punished, it wasn't Dirty Sanchez or Rummy or Dubya, it was the men and women *doing their jobs*. And not only that, but this fuck Joe Darby was jeopardizing the whole intel-collection apparatus in Iraq, which put the lives of our fellow soldiers at risk. Those pictures fucked up the whole occupation. Fucking Joe Darby got American soldiers killed."

"But . . ."

"We didn't *decide* to do this shit. We didn't *ask* for the torture detail. Staff Sergeant Cortázar told us to do this shit because Lieutenant Viers told *him* to do this shit, and Captain Weems, the company commander, told *him* to do this shit and so on up the fucking chain of command. Plus, our guidance with the OGA fucks was full cooperation. They say jump, we don't ask how high, we don't ask shit. We jump. Now these orders were put never in writing, realize. Everything was verbal. The OGA guys go straight back to Langley or whatever cesspool they ooze out of, and we're their tools. We did what we were told to, just like those kids in Abu G. So Sergeant Cortázar is all like, here's the deal. Think about this fact: if we decide to talk to somebody, show somebody pictures, we better damn well think about who exactly is going to be getting it in the ass. Bush? Rumsfeld? The general? The CO? Or your battle buddy?"

Aaron took a drink of beer. "The fact of the matter is, fucked up as it may be, most of these fucking hadjis didn't know shit. I'd say the majority of them were locked up by mistake, or at best they were grunts who didn't know their ass from al-Qaeda. It's a little depressing when you think about it. But if I had a problem with what was going on—which I did, of course, I'm a red-blooded American, right?—then the time for me to address that was before I fucking did it, before it got done, or at the very least while it was happening. Not afterwards. Not later. Not now. Something else Sergeant Cortázar said that stuck with me is that once you make a decision, once you do something, you can't take it back. And he's right. You don't get to say 'Oh, wait, what I did was wrong, so now I want to get someone else in trouble so I can feel better.' If it was wrong, it was wrong. But I did it. Nothing can change that. Click forward."

Dahlia lay back in the grass, staring into a sky so black it was purple, watching Perseus and Cassiopeia chase each other across the galaxy. "Hey—you guys want to fire another bowl? Maybe do some shots?"

"Yeah," Wendy said. "Let's party like it's 1999."

"I don't know," Rachel said.

"Girl, you got to live a little," Dahlia said. "It's a gorgeous night, we've got plenty of stuff to keep us going, and when was the last time you partied till dawn? C'mon. Sunrise. I want to feel like I did something epic for once."

"Let's do it, man," Mel said.

"Yeah," said Wendy. "C'mon."

"You think the boys'll want to?" Rachel asked.

"Fuck the boys," said Wendy.

"I suspect they will," Dahlia said, "but regardless, Wendy's right. Fuck 'em. We can have us a girl's night while they, whatever, jerk each other off and talk about computers."

"They're in there now," said Rachel.

"Where?"

"They're on the computer. They've been in there awhile."

"I bet Matt's showing him that dumb program."

"It's not dumb," Wendy said.

"That's sweet, Wendy, but it kinda is. It's just blobs of color you can't tell apart, and it doesn't even really work. Plus, he can't seem to finish. I mean, I don't want to talk about him behind his back . . ."

"Even though that's what you're doing."

"Yeah, well. Maybe you're right. I'm just tired of hearing about it."

"I'm guessing Aaron will be too in about five minutes."

"So let's get lit then before they come out and start talking about complex visual representations of turbulent systems. *Please.*"

There was a line of men in prison garb kneeling, black bags over their heads, their hands zip-tied behind them. Someone whose face was out of the shot was standing over them prodding one in the back with a baton.

"So, you get a bunch of new guys in and you have to establish control. You can't fuck around. We'd line them all up and get them down and scream at them for about twenty minutes, poking them with batons and kicking them, then we'd leave them there for a few hours with a couple dudes and if they moved, the two guards would scream at them and knock them down. Click forward."

One prisoner was standing in front of the line of kneeling prisoners. The kneeling ones' hoods had been removed and they all looked up at the man standing over them. A male American soldier stood behind the standing prisoner, a female soldier next to him. The soldiers wore blue surgical gloves. The male soldier had a pair of scissors.

"This is sort of a mass technique we developed with the OGAs for when a bunch of fresh pucks came in. So after fucking with them for a while, we take one out of the line, the biggest fucker in the group, and stand him up in front. Then we take off their hoods, right, but not his, so they can watch. Then your point man here, with the scissors, Grimes in this case, he cuts open the prisoner's outfit and strips him and whichever female we have, that's Littleton, she points at his cock and laughs. Click forward."

The standing man was naked now except for the hood, and the female soldier was pointing at his genitals and laughing.

"It's all a big show we put on. We—Grimes—pokes this guy in the ribs, pokes him in the butt, while Littleton laughs and points at his cock, then we give him one good whack in the belly and he goes down. Bam. Makes a huge impression. Next."

The naked and hooded man was on the ground and Grimes's boot was slamming into his stomach.

"That's a good one. Action shots are hard. The boot's a little blurry but you can see the impact. I like that picture. That's a good one."

"That's fucked up. This is fucked up."

"Yeah. You mentioned that. Next."

Matt clicked forward to a close-up head-and-shoulders of a mangled, bloody face. A middle-aged man with a thick gray mustache.

"That dude died. I mean, he was dead when I took the picture."

"Did you kill him?"

"Fuck no. We just stressed him to the point where his body failed. He was kinda old, anyway, and the older ones can't take much. I wished we'd had dogs. Dogs would have made life so much easier. We complained about that all the time, but our battalion K-9 had been tasked out to some other bullshit. It's totally easy to stress dudes with dogs, and you don't even have to touch 'em. Dogs scare the shit out of people. Next."

Matt clicked forward. Another dead man. He clicked forward. Another man in a stress position, head hooded, passed out and dangling. He clicked forward. Two American soldiers punching a man in a hood. He clicked forward. Naked men piled on top of each other.

"That's like the photo," Matt said.

"Yeah. That's basically 'cause we were bored. I mean, one of our OGA dudes came from Abu G, and he gave us guidance on a bunch of shit he said worked really well over there. Naked Dog-Pile, Electric Wire Box, Fake Menstrual Wipe, shit like that. But a lot of shit we did 'cause we were bored. I mean, plus all the normal shit—sleep deprivation, hostile environment, loud music, stress positions, beatings, immersion—you know, the basics."

"Immersion?"

"It's like waterboarding. You put their head in a bucket of water long enough to fuck with them, then you take it out. You gotta be careful though. It's surprisingly easy to drown a motherfucker." Aaron waved his hand impatiently. "Next."

Dahlia got the bowl out and tapped the old ash and packed it fresh. She handed the bowl and the lighter to Mel, who passed it to Rachel, who passed it to Wendy, then Dahlia, then back around again. Everyone was silent, focused on the smoke drifting into the night, the streaking stars, the rustling trees, the skunky savor.

"I think that's cashed," Rachel said, tapping ash.

"Fuck yeah," Mel said.

"Hey, I was thinking," Dahlia said, "if we're gonna watch the sun come up, we should hike up on the cliffs."

"We can look for the cuckoo," Rachel said.

"The cuckoo cock." Mel burst into laughter and fell over.

"We can see rosy-fingered dawn," Wendy said, "traipsing light across distant horizons."

Mel laughed harder.

"I love the dawn," Rachel said. "It's so, like, nascent."

Mel kept laughing. Rachel petted Xena.

"I think I finally got it," Wendy said. "It's not that you're all in my mind, but it's like the *you*s in my mind are reflections of the *you*s in reality. All I can see are the shadows you cast. None of this is really happening except how I make it happen. That's not right. It's happening, but I make it happen in my mind at the same time. It's happening but it's me."

"I gotta get up," Dahlia said. "I gotta move around."

"What are they doing in there?" Rachel asked.

"Yeah, go get the boys."

"Go get the cuckoo cocks," Mel giggled.

Dahlia stepped off toward the house.

Matt clicked forward. More pictures of Connie, of Aaron's fellow soldiers, of the gray concrete halls and brown outer walls of Camp Crawford, more pictures of hooded men, bleeding men, men in handcuffs. He clicked forward. A thin, mustached man stood handcuffed to a head-level cell-door crossbar.

"That's the Professor. Puck named Qasim. He got picked up on a raid in Baqubah. He tried to tell us the first couple days how he worked as a terp for the Americans in Baghdad and he was in Baqubah because his wife was sick or some shit, and it was all a big mistake, he just got caught up in things, he didn't even know the guys they picked him up with. The OGA fucks, on the other hand, said according to their information he'd been using his position as a translator to pass intel to al-Qaeda. We fucked that puck up."

"You keep saying puck. What's a puck?"

"PUC. Person under control. Click forward."

The next picture showed Qasim hanging against the cell door, naked now, blood across his chest and thighs, his face cut, bruised, swollen, and bleeding.

"This was two days later, after some stressing and a couple

beat-downs. I remember when I came on duty, I took this picture, right, and the flash woke him up and he started babbling, my friend this and that, mistake, mistake, Mista Mista, blah blah blah, my friend, my friend. Click forward."

The next picture showed the man still hanging against the cell door but now his eyes were open and he gazed up at Aaron, who'd opened the door and was standing next to him. One blue-gloved hand rested on Qasim's shoulder and the other made a peace sign.

"I got Sergeant Dickersen to hold the camera for me. Click forward."

The next picture was the same, except Aaron was pulling Qasim's head back by his hair and holding his other hand flat in a karate chop against Qasim's neck.

"That's Judo Chop. It's a joke we had, 'Judo Chop. Hiyah!' Next."

"What happened to all these people?"

"The pucks?"

"Yeah."

"Well, either they died or got transferred or got let out. Mostly they just got transferred."

"Just transferred? Like, just sent to another prison?"

"Yeah. Click forward."

The next picture was of the same scene, only now Qasim's face was pressed into the cell bars. Aaron grinned, standing behind him forcing his skull into the metal, one hand pulling the crossbar for leverage.

"Just this once, right, I let someone else take the pictures. I mean, it wasn't a real interrogation. Just fucking around."

"I thought . . ."

"It's a weird thrill, having that much physical control over somebody, knowing what you're doing. It's . . ."

The screen door leading out back squawked. Both men looked up. Matt minimized the photos just as Dahlia came in.

"Dark in here—what are y'all doing, looking at porn?"

"War porn," Aaron said. "Wanna see?"

"Hell yeah!"

"No," Matt said, yanking out the thumb drive.

"Hey, I wanna see," Dahlia said.

Matt rose to his feet and shoved past Dahlia toward the back door. "Let's get some fresh air."

"Show me the pictures."

"Dahlia, sugar," Aaron said, "I'll give you a private show later."

"Will you—can we just go outside?" Matt said.

"We cashed another bowl," said Dahlia. "We're gonna go up on the cliffs and watch the sunrise. You punks up for it, or y'all gonna pussy out?"

"It's late," Matt said. "I have to work tomorrow."

"Oh for fuck's sake, Matthew, give it a rest. You gonna party with us or not?"

"Fine. Sure. Whatever. Let's just go outside."

"Yes, let's," said Aaron, standing. "My thumb drive?" He held out his hand.

Matt looked at Aaron, then at Dahlia. Aaron snapped his fingers. Matt dropped the drive in his palm.

"Good work, citizen. Now let's all take a hike."

■ ■ ■

Stones and stars. The journey undertaken, in ten minutes they reached the mouth of the narrow canyon leading along the dry creek to the heights, the plateau above town. It'll be twenty minutes or half an hour before they clear the ravine's brush and make it into the open. They warned each other to watch out for coyotes, snakes, cougars, then plunged in, up.

The noise of drunken revelers pushing through brush dried all summer long. The clatter of rocks and shoes, the murmur, the occasional shout.

Why doesn't he do something? Say something? But no, there they are, whispering together, sharing some secret. He came up behind them.

"Hey, hero," Aaron said. "What's up? I was just telling Dahlia about Iraq."

"What?"

"It's terrible," Dahlia said.

"Yeah, well." Aaron frowned. "It's always the children that suffer the most. I mean, we did what we could, you know?"

"The children?" Matt said.

"I was telling Dahlia how one time we had this VBIED attack on the ECP, and there was this bus full of kids coming in that got caught in the blast. It was bad."

"It must have been so hard," said Dahlia.

"It's just—these kids, their lives are basically fucked. They're never gonna get out of Iraq. Their schools are shit. Their hospitals are shit. And they were coming in for medical stuff, right, like basic vaccines, and when the truck blew . . . it just . . . We lost seven. I spent the whole day in the aid station, helping the medics with triage. The boots I wore that day—I had to get rid of 'em. The blood wouldn't ever come out . . . Seven. We saved the rest, but we lost seven. And one of our own, Private Ballard. That was a tough day."

"You have pictures of that, too?" Matt asked.

"Jesus, Matt, what wrong with you?" Dahlia said. She turned back to Aaron. "Sorry about him. You must find it hard now being out of the army—I mean after Iraq—the way people react sometimes."

"It's been difficult, no doubt. But you deal with it. You drive on."

"I can't even imagine. It must be so strange, such a strange and different world."

"There or here?"

She laughed. "Either one."

"Honestly, it was weirder coming back than it was going over, because . . . I mean, you go, and you're thinking one thing, you're thinking about the military and Iraq and America, and what you learn when you get there . . . You learn that nothing's quite what you thought it was. It's a cliché, but you really learn what you're made of."

"Ha, I bet," Matt said.

Aaron and Dahlia looked back, then Dahlia tripped on a stone and flung forward. Before she hit the ground, Aaron had her, one hand on her arm, the other sweeping under and picking her up, setting her on her feet. She could smell him, close, the tobacco and fresh sweat and something else, something warm and hungry. "Thanks," she said, flushing.

"Hey," he said, stepping back.

"You should watch where you're going, honey," Matt said.

"Big help you are, riding my heels. I nearly took a face plant 'cause you're *hovering*. You want me on crutches again? Is that how you like it?"

"I just . . ."

"Why don't you go chill out somewhere?"

"Matthew," Aaron said. "How 'bout you go check up on Wendy."

"I do what I want," Matt snarled.

"Jesus, Matt," Dahlia said. "Go! Buzz off! Go chill out somewhere!"

"Yeah, fine! Fine. I'll chill out. Totally chill out. Like ice. And you can talk with Rambo fucking Himmler here all you want."

"What is it with you people tonight and Nazis?" Dahlia said. "Will you just go? We'll talk later."

Matt made a face and waved his hands in the air, stalking away.

Aaron looked at Dahlia and she at him. He grinned his crooked grin at her, and she shook her head and smiled. It burned her arm and waist where he'd touched her, and she knew she was hurting Matt and part of her felt terrible about it. But only part.

Once when she was young, she and her family went to a lake in the Blue Ridge Mountains where you could dive off this low cliff into the water. It was only twenty feet or so but it seemed stratospheric, and the water deep and cold, and she was terrified the first time, shaking with fear and about to throw up, but she closed her eyes and jumped and didn't open them until she came back up through the water into the light, dizzy and gulping.

Which choice didn't matter so much as that there was one, something being done. Who's choosing? Didn't matter. She was the one doing.

She touched her fingers to Aaron's forearm. "Thanks for catching me," she said. "I could have really hurt myself."

Soon the interminable exodus, the weed-induced sense of ceaseless toil, dissolved against the newly exposed night sky, the moon cool and blue down upon them like a curved blade, the stars cold and far, and they came up the last stretch of canyon and scree to the plateau, where they found a circle of flat rocks around a charred smear littered with cans faded white by the sun, cigarette butts, and footprints. They pulled beers out of their pockets and realized no one had thought to bring an opener, so Aaron and Mel used their lighters. They lit another bowl and talked about how they couldn't believe how long it seemed but how short it was, how the stars seemed so brilliant, how the sky seemed everything and the night, walking like forever, was just so yeah.

After a while they realized Matt had wandered off. Aaron touched Dahlia's wrist. "Help me go find him?"

She nodded. Off they went, leaving Mel and Rachel and Wendy. Aaron glanced back at Wendy as they walked away.

Wendy barely shrugged, her lip half-curled in a sneer. Aaron smiled and turned to follow Dahlia.

They chatted their way back down the canyon. Dahlia told him about the people who used to live in the region, the Ancestral Puebloans, and how recent evidence suggested they were cannibals. "The Navajo name, Anaasází, means Ancient Enemy," she said. In fact, a dig just across the state line in Colorado had found seven skeletons whose bones showed evidence of defleshing, chopping, marrow extraction, and burning. There'd been a lot of skepticism until a biologist from the University of Colorado tested fossilized human feces at the site for myoglobin, a protein found in human muscle. "Their shit didn't lie," she said, laughing. She talked about how much she missed reading the marks and fractures in old remains. She'd studied biology until her soccer accident, then she got obsessed with bones, and an anthropology class turned her on to field-work. She confessed she thought she might have made a mistake coming out to Utah. She should have stayed in school and finished her PhD. "I got an exit strategy, though."

"You and Matt gonna head back to Seattle?"

"One of us is, anyway," she said.

Aaron admitted he didn't have any idea what he was doing with his life, either. When he was a kid, he dreamed of fronting a punk-rock band. Then he was getting a BA in history, not really sure why except he liked stories about things that happened in the past, and now he didn't know what the fuck. Everything seemed changed. Unfamiliar. Disconnected. The scales on which he weighed possible futures were out of balance, and he didn't know how to set them right. "It's hard to see what really matters now," he said. "But I'll figure it out. Maybe just ride my motorcycle back and forth across the country till I have a vision."

"You got a motorcycle?"

"Yeah," he said. "I'd always wanted one, and when I got back from Iraq I just bought it. You have to know what you want, right, and when you figure it out, you have to grab it. What else is there?"

She nodded at this, biting her lip, brushing his arm with hers. At a certain point, climbing down a pair of small boulders, he offered her his hand for assistance and when she came down she held on to it and deep in the canyon, stars overhead, they stood as if in another world and looked in each other's eyes. She felt a little dizzy and he leaned in close, closer, she could feel the warmth of his body and his breath on her lips, closer, she closed her eyes and he pressed his palm on her hip, she could feel him just back teasing her, holding, then, aloft, she rose up and kissed him.

Matt walked along the hardpack. From up here, the moon-colored blue plateau seemed nearly endless until in the distance buttes and spires erupted from the flats like exclamations breaking a sentence. His brain didn't seem to be working. Nothing worked. Who the fuck did he think. The fuck. Them. The problem was rubbing a spot clean, clear away the crosshatching, the problem was silence and noise. Once things were silent he'd be able to see the solution, as they say, clearly, but there was too much noise. Thinking thoughts like. Impossible.

Something startled in a bush nearby.

I should go back, he thought. I should go back and tell Aaron he's no longer welcome. I can tell everyone about the pictures. Tell him he has to leave. And if he hits me? Then I'll hit him back. No I wouldn't. I'd lie on the ground and they'd laugh and he'd leave with Dahlia and Wendy and the other two, they'd go off and have an orgy. Or what if I told everyone and they ignored me? Do they already know? Maybe they already know. How can you know what other people know?

Everything noise and fuzz. Her you. Remember that time we went to Taos and slept in a teepee? Or the hot springs we went to naked? Maybe I should just go talk to her. Be reasonable. Just sit and talk and work it out. Explain. Decode. I know you're upset. I know it's my fault. Just tell me what you want, so I can fix it. I can't fix it if you don't tell me. Help me be good to you. Help me.

He stumbled into a gully and sat against the side, his legs splayed before him, lying staring at the sky. Now there's Virgo. That wasn't Virgo earlier. That was Lyra? Hydra? It's not Virgo now, that's Orion, and before it was Pegasus. Really I was supposed to be an astronaut. I was meant to be the guy who zoomed into the future, the one floating in space, but I never could be an astronaut. Maybe I'll never be anything. Maybe I'm cursed. Maybe it really is all my fault. If so, what's the point of fighting it? What's the point of fighting anything? Nothing. I've never done good things. I've never done bad things. What's worth hurting for?

Dahlia sank back onto the gray comforter and pulled him down on top. She bit his lip, dug nails in his back. He licked the salt off her neck. Rough hands up under her dress, tanned hands on white thighs, fierce hands tugging her tank top, pressing her breasts. Yes, she said yes, yes, she slid her hands down the muscles of his torso, his chest and ribs, she grabbed at his pants and fumbled with his zipper. She took him in her hand, the tense heat. He pulled off her tank top then undid her bra and was at her nipples with his teeth. She said yes, yes. She felt herself burning with life, alive like the world, fire and blood. He slid his hands under her skirt and pulled her briefs off and threw them on the floor. He sucked her tongue. Rubbing her crotch with his palm and thumb, he slid one then two knuckles deep and she said yes, oh god, yes. She pulled away and stretched, reaching for the nightstand, opening a drawer and pulling out a condom. She handed it to him. He stood up.

"You ever been tied up?" he asked.

She sat up and looked into his eyes, then smiled and took him in her mouth. She slid on him and sucked and licked, rubbed and pulled. Then she let go and looked up.

"Tie me up," she whispered. "Tie me up and fuck me."

He reached over to the phone and pulled out its cord, then yanked the cord from the wall. He walked around the bed and told her to lie down across it.

"Make me," she said.

He smiled and shoved her back.

She fell, looking up at him. He took her hands and tied them together over her head with the phone cord, looped the cord through the metal base-frame, tied it.

"That's really tight," she said.

"It's okay."

"It's tight."

"It's fine," he said, then kissed her, their faces upside down to each other, and went back around the other side. He knelt on the floor in front of her and pulled up her skirt and she opened her thighs around his face. He burrowed in, spreading her wetness around, tasting deep. She moaned again, bucked her hips, wanted to reach and grab his hair but with her hands tied and beginning to tingle she couldn't.

"Fuck me," she said, "oh please, please fuck me."

"Yeah," he said, pulling away. He kissed the flower tattoo on her hip. "I'm gonna fuck you."

"I want you in me."

"You like to be tied up, huh?"

"I'm so wet, god, please fuck me now."

"You like getting fucked all tied up, huh?"

"Yes, please, fuck me. C'mon and fuck me."

"Yeah," he said, then grabbed her by the thighs and flipped her over on her front. He pulled her toward him along the bed till the phone cord stretched taut and she was kneeling at the edge of the mattress, her knees on the ground. She looked back at him as he lifted her skirt up over her ass.

"Put the condom on and fuck me," she said.

"Yeah," he said, rubbing her hips, sliding a finger inside

her. The same finger he pressed against her asshole, rubbing it between her buttocks, and she jerked.

"Hey," she said.

"Shhh."

"No, really, hey."

"It's fine," he said, rubbing the wetness around her sphincter, then pushing his finger in.

"No. No. I said no."

"It's good."

"No wait a minute," she said, going cold inside. "Untie me."

"It's good," he said again. "Tight."

"No, seriously, untie me."

His left hand slid along the line of her jaw, his finger brushing her lips. Then he clutched her face and pressed hard in her cheek where her jaw met her skull, cracking her mouth open. He swept her briefs up off the floor and crammed them in her mouth and held them there with one hand while she bucked and tried to scream. He grabbed her top with his other hand and looped it around her mouth, cinching it tight like a bit and double-knotting it at the back of her skull.

"Shush now. You know this is just what you wanted."

She felt him get up from behind her. She writhed, wailed muffled shouts, trying to get free. Over her shoulder she could see him digging in her dresser and she kicked and bounced until she was on her back facing him. He had a bunch of her tights in his hands. She tried to shout and curse through the gag—her taste—choking on spit and cotton. She tried to scream.

"Roll back over," he said, grinning, taking her by the

ankles and flipping her smoothly. She kicked, shrieked into the gag, but his hands held her like cuffs. He pulled her legs up in the air, forcing her weight onto her neck, and she howled in pain. She tried to kick back but had no leverage; he'd pinned her legs in his armpit. He secured her ankles together with a pair of tights, then dropped her to the mattress, her knees slamming to the floor, and climbed on top of her. He used another pair of tights to reinforce the gag.

He grabbed her hard by the back of the neck, forcing her nose into the comforter. She inhaled the gray fabric, trying to breathe, could feel him on her, his flesh dense and burning. "Shhhhh. It's okay now. It's okay. I saw you looking. I saw you and knew what you wanted. It's gonna be okay. Hush now," he whispered, "or I'll knock your fucking daylights out."

She was sobbing, trying to talk, trying to say no, don't, stop, please no. Trying to get free but feeling her will evacuate, weakening by the moment. He slapped her in the back of the head and told her to hush, then grabbed her neck and squeezed hard.

She went slack. Gray. Feeling herself rattle loose from herself, thinking: who's this happening to—the room going out of focus, the gray fabric blurring. Thinking: who decides things. Thinking: where's Matt, and what happened, and who is this. How? Who? What's happening and who to, yes, no. Whose body? No. Who makes choices? No. It's not me. Not mine. No. No.

■　■　■

When he was done, he found a kitchen knife and cut the phone cord from the bed frame, got dressed, and walked through the house, dim and blue in the early morning, then out the back, past the fridge and blank-faced computer, past Xena watching him from the floor, into the yard where the dying embers of last night's fire smoldered in whitened ash.

A moment of indecision caught him there amid the party detritus, the empty beer bottles, the grease thick on the grill's black rack, the complicated flowers on the table, then he went back out the way he came, through the gate, got on his motorcycle, and rolled past all the quiet houses rustling to wake now on Columbus Day, past the silver-black gleam of picture windows and past the yellow light shining from a kitchen or bathroom where some early-rising citizen prepared for the day. At the bottom of the lane, he turned west.

Bleeding over the redrock, dawn spilled across the land. Monument Valley was out there somewhere, where they'd shot all those old cowboy flicks, and in the south an isolate line of mountains massed white-capped and gray. To the north, the valley narrowed to a chasm, rust-colored cliffs closing in over the Colorado, then the highway climbed out of the gorge, past the turnoff to Dead Horse Point, and up onto the plateau, opening to flat land.

Silent where he'd left her, cut loose and curled in a wounded ball, Dahlia opened her eyes.

babylon

Put forth your strength: bureaucratic construction now
holding the soldier and man of no tomorrow
over black seas under nay, we used not to call upon IED
attacks and suicide
bombs   young   exulted in
documents detailing Takbir, gates of hell abide therein, torture and pass along main supply
Allah true.

So think of the Department of artillery, tank rounds and
die, city to kill, employed to carry out the strike. The occu-
pations fight
special officers definitely better than we
gulf with significant success
more than 12 hours. "But I think massive aerial strikes
that many here said before pilots aboard the USS last week
ahead for Iraq's interim also went to Baghdad University or
the senior Library at Basra and Command Council issues
wrote about the case of an Iraqi man who . . ."

again the same, certain we send apostles by bench in water
and urine
dull rumbling   tingling command of Allah

lost. This statement has Iraq's major museums and libraries
retribution and that time is despite detainees, in addition,
material assets oh yeah, she's bomb. "We're hit," the voice
and angle measurement with his eyes I left uptown, 29, of
Lomira, Wisconsin. 'Babylonian' mathematics jump the
gun, groups of insurgents took over common the wooden
mountain of Placus and should be allowed in. End of fucking where they killed seven, a child—ill-starred sire of an
ill-starred care many push-ups you can do from the ambush
into the house when we need you to kill somebody, a sor-
rowing widow in your house. The ancient culture is kill
them. Yet as a mere infant

now that you are, kill

the first days after the war. Even though he escaped the
action began at 5, his life henceforth one of labor and killing
two GIs and wounding mellow, spaced out from waiting,
says the sheikh the police shocked the motorist down the
road.

In-depth oral history of the war based on interviews with
political leaders between the sexes in Punic gulf any civic.
These shall enter the garden resistance and US forces killed
at least

the light of his sky

another in the fire, then the secret one read by Jordan, a lot
of pressure to produce and other interrogation centers how
is it that here in Babylon, I call you to occupy and said no
title to be called to, Abdul told Al Jazeera TV

under control

a strategy of weakness. By late summer pointed to the breast which had suckled him. Officials expected to start drawing down Hector, my son, but occupation forces of no more than 30,000 Americans comfort from my own bosom, 130,000 troops, loosing the initiative to protect us from this man; stand not nowhere and after carrying out its increasingly managed disappearance, intelligence officers kill me as easily as though there is no parleying with him for some rock TV

incidence of penetrating wounds. Better fight at once, gunshot wounds, shrapnel injuries or blast thus did he stand and ponder the heart, but Achilles required far more frequently than in civilian

taking

up, I begin   to

feel

of holes

Fort Sill—Berlin—New York, 2005–2015

Acknowledgments

This book has been a long time coming. I began writing it in 2005, while still in the Army, and finished the first draft in 2007, after having moved to New York City. Its journey to publication—and into its present form—has been circuitous and difficult, with many obstacles and hazards along the way, but also with many friends and allies who by their close reading helped make the work better, and who by their support helped keep it alive.

My greatest thanks go to my editor at Soho Press, Mark Doten. His ambitious vision for *War Porn* was a refining volcano, and his insight, care, and boldness have been been fresh air and cool water to a parched and weary traveler. I can't thank him enough. I'm also immensely grateful to Bronwen Hruska, Amara Hoshijo, Abby Koski, Rachel Kowal, Gary Stimeling, and everybody at Soho: a truly exemplary publishing team. I feel very lucky to have wound up working with people who care so deeply about books— as provocations, as contributions to a conversation, and as works of art. Thank you.

Many thanks to early readers Helen Benedict, Peter Blackstock, E. L. Doctorow, Jim Fitzgerald, Matt Gallagher,

Travis Just, Phil Klay, Kseniya Melnik, Shakir Mustafa, Nawal Nasrallah, Hilary Plum, Joydeep Roy-Bhattacharya, Jacob Siegel, J.W., and Martin Woessner. Further, I am awed and amazed by the consistently superhuman levels of patience, acumen, and brilliance my partner, Sara Marcus, has been able to access reading and rereading this book. I owe whatever is beautiful or humane in it—or in myself—to her wisdom, perspicacity, and love.

In 2014, I had the chance to go back to Baghdad for *Rolling Stone*. This visit was an important experience in its own right, but it also helped me rework the middle chapters of this book with a more informed eye. Thanks to Will Dana for making the trip happen, to Alison Weinflash for arranging the logistics, and to Phoebe St. John for her painstaking fact checking. Special thanks go to everyone who helped me connect with people in Iraq and to the Iraqis and journalists there who took the time to talk with me: Isra Abdulhadi, Samr Abdul-Satar, Ghadah Abdul-Sattar, Ali Adhab, Sarem Dakhel Ahmed, Jane Arraf, Raad al-Azzur, Hassan Blasim, Matt Bradley, Hanaah Edwar, Borzou Daragahi, Haider Falih, Dexter Filkins, Alice Fordham, Haider Hashim, Naseer Hassan, Ahmed Farouk Lafta, Quil Lawrence, Christopher Merrill, Nadia Fayidh Mohammed, Soheil Najam, Ayman Oghanna, Ned Parker, Methaq Waleed, Kael Weston, the English students at Mustansiriyah University, and all the others on Mutannabi Street, in the Shorja Market, and at the polls in al-Saydiya. I am especially grateful to my interpreter on that trip, Aziz Alwan, may he rest in peace, and to my driver, Ahmed Qusay: brave, courteous, patient, and streetwise, they guided me through the labyrinth. I would have been lost without them.

My first visit to Baghdad, from 2003 to 2004, was a very different kind of labyrinth, and relied on a different network of support. Thanks to Lieutenant Chiarrez, Staff Sergeant Hayes, Homan, Lieutenant Juarez, Sergeant First Class Mitchell, Nick Lehman (RIP), "Smokey" Robinson, Timmy Shore, and Javier Velasco for helping me stay alive and sane out there. FTA 4evah.

Bits of this book were published in different form in *canon*, *CITY*, *Fire and Forget: Short Stories from the Long War* (Da Capo 2013), the *New York Times*, *Prairie Schooner*, *Theory and Event*, and *Warrior Writers*. These parts are reprinted here with grateful acknowledgment.